SIMONE

SIMONE

A Novel by

LION FEUCHTWANGER

Translated by G. A. Hermann

New York

THE VIKING PRESS

1944

c. 7

HR

Contents

v

vi   *Contents*

I have come to comfort the poor and humble.

(Je suis venue pour la consolation des petites gens.)

JEANNE D'ARC

PART ONE

READINESS

1: The Refugees

SIMONE had only a few more steps; then the narrow path would make a sudden turn and reveal the highway. With heart beating in her throat, she expectantly took these few steps. Yesterday she had first caught sight of the procession of refugees on the arterial highway. By today it would perhaps have reached the narrow side road.

For three weeks there had been talk of the refugees. In the beginning there were only the Dutch and Belgians, but now the people from the north of France also fled southward before the advancing enemy; more and more came, and for the past week the whole of Burgundy had been flooded. Yesterday, when Simone had gone to town to do her daily household shopping, she had hardly been able to pass through the crowds, and today she had even left her bicycle at home.

When Simone Planchard, with her lively imagination, had first heard about refugees, she pictured them as hurrying and frightened people, always hurrying and always frightened. What she had seen in these last few days was less complicated but more dreadful; it held her fast and kept stirring her up; there was no sleep for her at night. As often as she went to the city she had a fear of this pitiful display, but with every day she longed to see it with a sorrowful and turbulent eagerness.

Now she reached the bend and could see a stretch of the road. It was a narrow, neglected road, almost always white and lonely, leading nowhere, leading only to the mountain village, Noiret, with its six houses. But today it was as she had feared—there were people. The huge stream had spattered drops even to this point.

Simone stood still and looked round. A tall, lanky fifteen-year-old, she had on her modest light green striped dress which she always wore for her shopping; a large, closed wicker basket was pressed against her body; her slender arms and naked legs protruded from the dress. Her bony, tanned face framed with dark blond hair was tense; her dark, deep-set eyes under a low but broad and well-shaped forehead eagerly absorbed all that moved before her in the dust. It was the familiar sight: people and vehicles dragging along hopelessly, carriages foolishly piled high with household goods, mattresses on top of automobiles to protect against machine-gunning from low-flying enemy planes, exhausted human beings and animals crawling along without a goal.

There stood Simone Planchard at the bend of the road, her narrow, well-formed lips tightly pressed, gazing. She could scarcely be called beautiful, but her intelligent, thoughtful, some-what stubborn face with its strong chin and its prominent Bur-gundian nose was good to look at. For a full minute, and for another, she stood in the dust and heat of the early afternoon, peering at the fugitives.

But then she tore herself away. She had much to do; Madame had given her many errands. To be sure, the Villa Monrepos, the home of the Planchard family, was well stocked, but it seemed certain that in another or two or three days it would be impossible to make further purchases. And so the list that Simone had received from Madame was lengthy and it would not be easy to dispose of these many errands in the midst of the general excitement and confusion. She did not linger over the scene but walked quickly and directly towards the city.

Soon she had reached the lowest point of her narrow side road where it turned into Route 6 which led in a semicircle around the hilly centre of Saint-Martin. The sight that greeted her here was more pitiful than any of the experiences of the past days. Crosswise to the street stood automobiles that had tried to turn off, other cars had wedged them in; the whole, endless procession of horse-drawn and motor vehicles, bicycles, donkeys, pedes-trians stood in a hopeless jumble. No one even cursed, no one made an effort to disentangle the throng. Resigned, in awkward discomfort, they all squatted in the sultry heat where they had stopped, old and young, men and women, soldiers and civilians, wounded and whole, in sweating, hopeless stupor.

With open, earnest eyes that made her face older than her years, Simone stared at the dust-covered, stalled procession which stood before her strangely silent, like a picture. But she had become quite sensible in the course of her fifteen years; she thought of her errands and, concealing her emotions, sought only to cross the thronged street. The big basket firmly pressed to her side, she climbed over dented fenders, over the rear end of a cart, politely asking pardon of the occupants who scarcely noticed her as they dozed in the heat.

Finally she had crossed the street and mounted the old, crumbling, stepping-stone path that a stranger would scarcely have found. It led steeply up the mountain in capricious serpentines, revealing ever-changing vistas of the ruined fortifications that surrounded the ancient city. At every turn new perspectives of the valley of the winding Cerein River came into view. The landscape was gay and attractive; the wide, bright valley was covered with vineyards, olive and chestnut groves. Every hill-top bore an ancient settlement and in the east towered the forest-covered mountains. In better times countless strangers had come to enjoy this view, and Simone, no matter how well she knew this landscape, had always absorbed it with knowing, understanding eyes. But today she had no feeling for it. Today she only strove to forget what she had seen in the highway, and she was glad that the difficult path claimed her full attention. At some places she actually had to climb, and that was hard because of the big basket. Next time when she came to town she would wear slacks. Some people, to be sure, think it improper for girls to wear slacks in war-time; Madame herself disapproves.

Now Simone had reached the top and entered the city through the Porte Saint-Lazare. She crossed the square in front of the church. At other times this little plaza lay empty and peaceful; quiet, old people sat on the benches under the elms. Now and then tourists stood there and looked at the famous statue over the church portal.

Today the square was crowded. Many of the refugees had

come up. But they had no eyes for the saint; they were looking for gasoline or food or other essentials. They exchanged experiences which they had had here or on the road. They were bitter experiences. Almost every one lacked everything and nothing was to be had here in Saint-Martin. Almost all of them had had narrow escapes from death. There they stood and sat, and the townspeople, including Simone, stood round them and listened to their tales.

The German aeroplanes had shot at the stalled fugitive processions; the refugees had been constantly exposed to their attacks; at the jammed cross-roads, at the bridges, at closed railroad crossings there had been no cover. "We regret that we fled," most of them grimly reported. "It is dreadful to sit inactively at home and wait for the bombs and the Germans, but to be on the road is ten times worse. Everything in this flight is ghastly."

Simone listened, but she had heard it all before. She went on, past the Hall of Justice, a beautiful old building. Through the door she looked into the hall. Straw had been spread and there lay refugees, closely crowded, pitiful. Simone turned her eyes away; with an uncertain feeling of guilt she walked towards the Rue de Sauvigny, keeping close to the houses along the way.

The Rue de Sauvigny, a narrow, winding street with fine old houses, was the main business street of the old part of town. Refugees wandered from store to store but found only signs: "No bread," "No meat," "No gasoline," "No tobacco." Most shops were closed and where the shutters over the show windows were not down one could see an incongruous advertising sign or some useless object, perhaps an intricate piece of pottery intended as a salt shaker or a large storm lantern for which no candles were available. In the window of M. Armand's barber shop, sneering and lonely, stood a huge empty perfume bottle.

If the stores were closed, however, Simone knew the rear entries and she also knew the signals to which the shopkeepers reacted. If to no one else, they were at home to Madame Planchard and to Simone, her messenger; there was always something left for the Planchard family.

Simone collected whatever might be useful additions to the

hoarded supplies in the Villa Monrepos in anticipation of weeks of drought. Here was the store, "L'Agréable et L'Utile." The shop was quite empty. Even Monsieur Carpentier, known as Monsieur L'Utile, had left; only Monsieur Laflèche, known as Monsieur L'Agréable, was present. For Simone he still had a hose and garden sprinkler. And in Monsieur Armand's closed barber shop there was still some shaving soap for Monsieur Planchard. Simone even succeeded in getting into the only department store in the town, the well-barricaded Galeries Bourgignonnes. Only three employees remained in the big store, but Mademoiselle Joséphine, the head of the millinery department, had some ribbons and materials that had been laid aside for Madame Planchard. While she delivered the wares to Simone she whispered to her excitedly that Monsieur Amiot, the owner of the Galeries Bourgignonnes, had also left the city. She named others who had fled: there was Monsieur Raimu, the grocer, Monsieur Laroche of the Crédit Lyonnais, and many other business men, lawyers, and doctors.

Simone had completed only the smaller part of her errands when she left the ancient inner city, passed through the Porte de l'Horloge, and began to make the rounds of the shops in the new section, mostly along the Avenue de la Gare.

Her way led across the Place du Général Gramont, the largest square in town. The annual fair took place here, and on July Fourteenth it was illuminated with flares and coloured lights for a public dance. Today there were more cars and wagons parked than for any fair; many refugees had obviously given up hope of further progress and were prepared to spend the coming days and nights here in their vehicles. General Gramont's monument was scarcely visible amid the cars. Someone had stretched ropes from the General's head and extended arm to some of the automobiles and had hung laundry on them to dry.

It was a wild, confusing scene. There were two ambulances which had somehow found their way here. Simone looked through the open door of one, but quickly turned away; the head which she saw there amid rags and bandages was no longer a human head. The Medical Corps men sat dozing on the running board. There stood a heavily loaded farm wagon, horses still hitched to it. On the driver's seat sat a pregnant woman; perched dangerously on top of the load crouched an unspeakably dirty little child, weeping, a cat in its arms. Soldiers sat or lay between the vehicles; many had replaced parts of their uniforms with civilian clothes, overcoats, hats, scarves; many had taken off their shoes, exposing their bloody feet injured by long marches. There were push carts and baby carriages loaded with strange objects. Simone noticed a perambulator at which a girl was absently but diligently scratching away the crusted mud with which it was covered; wherever the dirt fell away, screaming blue lacquer appeared. Very many of the fugitives looked sick and miserable; all were ragged and obviously in need of the simplest essentials. But the clothes which now hung in rags and tatters were quite apparently not the most suitable; they were Sunday clothes. And the objects which had been brought along were generally not of practical value but often quite casual things which at the moment of departure had seemed particularly desirable—a dignified brocade arm-chair or an oversized phonograph.

In her light green striped dress, the big basket on her arm, Simone stood and stared at the ghastly throng of cars and people. The uncanny spectacle fascinated her. In her clean, neat dress, well fed and well housed, she felt a gap between herself and these people, but at the same time she suffered all the more from that feeling of guilt which had come over her earlier.

Slowly she went her way down the Avenue de la Gare. But here in the new section of town all the stores were closed and into many of them not even Simone found admission. Evidently the owners had fled. Nevertheless the contents of her basket grew, although some things, especially foodstuffs, were still missing. As a last resort she decided to return to the Hôtel de la Poste in the old town. The hotel would still be supplied and she would be able to get something, for the Planchard family had business connexions there and the hotel was under obligations to the Planchards.

The papier mâché cook that used to stand invitingly before

the door of the famous Restaurant de la Poste had been knocked over and lay awkwardly on the pavement, and Monsieur Berthier, the owner of the hotel, was arguing with some refugees who wanted food or lodging. The Hôtel de la Poste had a great reputation. On the way back from Elba Napoleon had stopped here, and the room in which the Emperor had slept was still maintained in the same state. Monsieur Berthier was a direct descendant of the Berthier who had then owned the hotel, and he sometimes rented the imperial room to strangers whom he particularly liked or who had plenty of money. Monsieur Berthier was a man of great dignity, president of the Hotelkeepers' Association of Burgundy, and used to dealing with people. But just now he was out of his depth; he was perspiring, excited, desperate. Yet still more desperate were the others who could not believe that there was nothing to be had and continued to ask if there were no chance.

Simone squeezed past the excited group and went around the block to the other entrance. It lay in the Rue Malherbe behind the little, walled garden of the hotel. It was an inconspicuous gate and, of course, locked. But Simone knew what to do; she picked up a stone and knocked sharply several times at short intervals.

Two people were sitting on the garden wall, one a boy of perhaps fourteen, the other a man of middle years. Both were watching her, the man absently, but the boy attentively. Simone knew that a window would soon open in the caretaker's house, someone would furtively look out and nod his head, and the boy, with his bright eyes, would see it. And so it happened. The boy saw the window, looked from the window to Simone, saw the basket and saw the door opening. Simone did not want to look at the boy, but as she passed through the gate she could not resist turning her head towards him. She saw that the boy's bright, strong eyes were still directed towards her, and she swallowed hard.

In the hotel kitchen it developed that Simone could actually have some of the items on her list. They gave her a jar of their special meat paste, a piece of wonderful smoked ham, and many other things. Her basket was full and Simone had to carry a piece of Roblechon cheese, wrapped in paper, in her hand. She stepped out of the garden gate, the heavy basket on her arm and the little package in her hand. The two refugees were still sitting on the wall, watching her attentively. Suddenly, with a timid motion, Simone put the package of Roblechon cheese into the boy's hand. He looked at her angrily and did not thank her; hastily she went on, as though she had done wrong.

It seemed to her as if the two were looking after her with hostile eyes until she turned the corner. She was a little frightened. If the fugitives knew what was in her basket they would take it away from her. She was afraid at this thought, but at the same time she felt that she could scarcely blame them, and almost wished someone would take the basket from her.

Simone had grown up in comfortable circumstances in the Villa Monrepos. Since the death of her father ten years earlier she had lived there as a poor relative whose presence was suffered. She filled the place of a maid and worked hard but, on the other hand, she ate with the family and her guardian, Uncle Prosper, insisted that she be treated as one of the family. She accepted both duties and privileges as something natural and the attitudes and conditions of the Villa Monrepos were as incontrovertible for her as the alternation of day and night. Without open or even inner resistance she obeyed all instructions of Madame, Uncle Prosper's mother. It was self-evident that in these times a prudent housewife should look ahead and fill her larders with provisions. Nevertheless, without consciously giving way to the thought, Simone felt that the sense of guilt which had oppressed her all these days was connected with the heavy basket she carried.

She would have liked a good, relieving talk with someone about all her experiences of recent days. Only a short time ago, only last week, they had lived in the perfect security of the Maginot Line, under the protection of the strong army. In spite of the war, calm and order had reigned everywhere and daily life had gone on in normal abundance. And suddenly, overnight, in spite of the Maginot Line and the army, the enemy stood in the heart of the country and all France was a mob of pitiful refugees half crazed with misery. She was sick with pity and worry. She was depressed because every one had lived along stupidly and leisurely through this year of war. She was confused because she could not understand how all this was connected. She would have to talk about it with someone and ask questions of someone who was wiser than she. But she knew no one to whom she could open her heart.

Uncle Prosper, her father's stepbrother, was very fond of her. She was truly grateful that he had taken her into his home. He was kind, generous, a good Frenchman, a great patriot. But he continued to devote himself to his freight business as though it were still of major importance, and although the recent terrible events affected him, it seemed to Simone that they did not agitate him as much as her. At least what he said about these developments was not what Simone wanted to know; it explained nothing, it did not dispel her perplexity.

Madame, Uncle's mother, remained entirely aloof from current happenings. She erected a firm barrier about herself and her house, permitted nothing to enter, and examined everything for its possible beneficial or harmful effect on the Villa Monrepos. If, for example, a fugitive had taken away Simone's basket, Madame would have regarded him as a robber and criminal, and any attempt on Simone's part to excuse him would have seemed to Madame impudent and rebellious. Even Uncle Prosper, in spite of his good heart, would have no sympathy with such an excuse.

Of course, Simone would not mention the fact that she had given the Roblechon cheese to the refugee boy after all the trouble of procuring it. Her folks in the Villa Monrepos would regard her as mad. And then the boy had only given her an angry stare. Yet she would have done the same thing again.

Her head full of ideas, absent-mindedly yet with vigorous strides of her long legs she walked through the winding, hilly streets. Her errands were done. Now she had to go to her place of business, Uncle Prosper's transfer and trucking establishment, for her turn of duty at the gasoline pump. Her way took her past Etienne's house. If only he were here; but he was away at Chatillon, working in a machine shop.

Simone and Etienne were good friends; he was devoted to her and looked up to her. But after all, he was only a young boy and she felt older than he, although in fact she was a year younger. She could freely discuss all her thoughts and feelings with him, but she was certain that he could never explain the confusing events of the time. Still she wished he were here for he was Henriette's brother.

Her schoolmate Henriette was the only person to whom she had been quite close, and since Henriette had died a year before there was no one now in whom she could confide completely. As Simone with her heavy basket passed the house where Etienne and Henriette had lived she felt very much alone.

If she could have spoken with Henriette about the refugees, everything would have become clear. They would perhaps have quarrelled, Henriette might have become angry, but they would have understood each other. Henriette had been the exact reverse of Simone, quick, moody, always doing the unexpected. She had been quarrelsome and had enjoyed hurting people. She and Simone had once had a fight in school; that was when Henriette had made a disparaging remark about Simone's father. Then the otherwise quiet Simone had attacked her and had violently beaten and scratched the smaller, weaker girl. And after that, curiously enough, Henriette had asked her forgiveness and they had become friends.

Although Simone passed her house frequently, she had not thought of Henriette for many days. That often happened. For days, for weeks, she did not think of Henriette and then she reproached herself for lack of loyalty. Even now, while she ardently longed for a conversation with Henriette, she could not remember her friend's appearance. The gentle, waxlike face of the dead girl in her coffin had deeply engraved itself upon Simone's memory and she could recall it at all times. But it was hard to remember the living girl with her mobile, delicate, pale features. In Simone's memory this face constantly changed; it was sneering and comforting, it inspired hatred and greatest confidence. If only she could have a talk with Henriette.

Her father was the person whom she really needed. Although Pierre Planchard had been dead for ten years he was more alive to her than Henriette. Simone was only five when he died. The rumours concerning the manner of his death never ceased. Pierre Planchard had perished in the Congo on an expedition which he undertook to study the working conditions of the natives. He had always been an impassioned champion of the oppressed. His friends declared that he was preparing a book presenting first-hand evidence of the ruthless exploitation of the Negroes. Thereupon the concessionaires had done away with him in the jungle. Pierre Planchard's manuscript had never been found and the official investigation had revealed nothing. Old Madame Planchard, Uncle Prosper's mother, once said that he was dead and gone, but for his friends Pierre Planchard remained a hero and a martyr.

Simone's recollections of her father could not be very clear; she was not quite five when she last saw him. Still she believed that she remembered him well. She even declared that his voice was still in her ear, a resonant, deep, and very youthful voice. And she particularly recalled the time when her father took her up into the steeple of Notre Dame. They were in a good-sized company. Of course she could not climb the three hundred and seventy-six steps. The others laughed and advised her father to take her back down. But he, over their amused protests, carried her all the way up and showed her the evil, grotesque rain spouts, the gargoyles and chimeras, and he calmed her fears over all this strangeness until she felt only curiosity.

On the whole, Simone's memory was dependent upon pictures of her father, photographs, faded newspaper clippings. He had a lean face, large, deep eyes and bushy hair. Simone had been told that these eyes were blue-grey, that they could be very angry and very cheerful, and that the hair was reddish-blond. The pictures made Pierre Planchard appear older than he was. But whenever Simone recalled the incident of Notre Dame, she remembered her father as a very young man with a hearty laugh, and the many little wrinkles about his eyes did not make him older. Whenever she called upon her memory of him she saw him as clearly as though he stood before her.

The people of the Villa Monrepos did not like to speak of Pierre Planchard. To be sure, Uncle Prosper loved and admired his stepbrother in spite of their divergent views. But Madame spoke of her stepson Pierre with icy disdain and never let Simone forget that he left her without a penny. And Uncle Prosper never objected. But Madame's arrogant remarks only made Simone doubly proud of her father.

He ought to be here now. He would understand why her basket seemed so heavy today and why she gave the Roblechon to the fugitive boy.

She had now reached the Palais Noiret, a fine, old building in which Monsieur le Sous-Préfet had his offices. She was well known in the Deputy Prefecture and she left her basket in the bailiff's office so as not to carry it all the way to her uncle's transfer company.

Rid of the basket and with light feet she walked towards the Avenue du Parc that led out of the city and to the transfer office. But before she reached the avenue and the new section of town she changed her mind. She would visit Père Bastide. She simply had to discuss the things she had seen with some friendly soul.

The old bookbinder Père Bastide was not popular in the Villa Monrepos. Simone's folks did not approve of her friendship with him or with his son, Monsieur Xavier, the secretary of the Deputy Prefecture. Uncle Prosper and Madame turned up their noses at the political views of the two, and they blandly called the old bookbinder an idiot. Perhaps Père Bastide was a little ridiculous, eccentric, stubborn. He became excited over everything, he was unrestrained in praise and censure, and he often confused past and present; but he believed in France, even now when so many doubted, and she loved to hear him speak of France. But most important of all, he was a friend of her father, he had known him well, and he often spoke of him proudly and affectionately. Therefore Simone clung to the old man and after all of today's dark and sad experiences it would do her good to see him.

Père Bastide lived at the Petite Porte. On the outermost spur of the city hill, at the highest point, hung his ancient little house that had been patched up countless times and looked down on the one side over the variformed nut-brown roofs of the old town, on the other over the wide extent of the winding Cerein River valley.

Simone climbed up the worn stairs and looked through the glass door into the workshop. Although Père Bastide had long retired, he liked to putter and bind books for his own amusement and spent most of his time in the shop. He loved books and had a large library.

In this workshop, crammed with all sorts of junk and old-fashioned furniture, Simone saw him sitting asleep in his arm-chair. Above his head hung a picture of the great Socialist leader, Jean Jaurès, whom Père Bastide revered. Jaurès had been assassinated before the beginning of the last war by a fanatic instigated by the extreme rightist newspapers. For the bookbinder Jaurès was the symbol of the great past, the symbol of France. The picture showed him standing in front of a huge flag, on a platform, speaking to the masses. He stood there awkwardly, his massive, powerful torso resting on slightly bent legs; his neck was drawn down between the shoulders and his head with the broad, short, square-cut beard was covered with a hard, round hat. His hands were forming a gesture that seemed to invite the invisible multitude up to him. The man appeared colossal, patriarchal and prophetic, good-natured and yet irresistible.

For a little while Simone stood in front of the glass door looking at the old bookbinder sitting in his arm-chair dozing under the picture. He seemed changed. Formerly she had always seen him very lively, fidgety, full of fire; now he crouched there in the large arm-chair, tiny, shrivelled up, old as the hills. Simone looked at him sorrowfully and tenderly moved.

She supposed that he would not like to be surprised. She went down the stairs again, noisily slammed the front door, and came upstairs once more, her step as loud as possible.

As she had expected, Père Bastide stood there wide awake, his

head high with the ruddy face and the shining white hair.
"Hello, little one," he said gaily, walked to the closet, brought
out a bottle of his home-made nut brandy, and offered it to her.
She sipped it politely.

Then it came as she thought it would. "Listen," he said and
pushed her into a chair, walked back and forth, and let go excitedly about the events. "That's what we have come to," he
meditated angrily and pointed to the small window through
which one saw the Cerein valley. There, far down, crawled the
endless procession of the refugees over the sunny, dusty road.

"It is pure madness," he said, "that they fled; they only race
from one peril into a greater one. And instead of holding them
back, the authorities called upon them to go away. Now they
block the highways and our reserves cannot advance at any point.
One does not know whether our government is so incompetent
or whether there is an evil purpose behind it." The old man
looked excited, he gesticulated violently; Simone could scarcely
believe that only a few moments ago he had sat there, tiny and
bent and aged.

"The Prime Minister," Père Bastide meanwhile continued, "has
declared over the radio that entire army corps were not located
where they were supposed to be and that, contrary to orders,
bridges had not been blown up. He has dismissed sixteen generals. He himself has hinted that there was treason. Many say,
also my son Xavier, that persons in very high places, in the In-
dustrial Council, in the Comité des Forges, in the Banque de
France, had counted on a Boche victory from the very start, and
they say that such a victory would not displease them. I can't
believe that," he shouted with his clear voice in impotent rage.
"My old head won't believe that. I know what the fascists are
capable of. Since they murdered Jaurès I know of what the Two
Hundred Families are capable. I'll believe almost anything of
them, but not that."

He suddenly stopped in front of her, pointed at the picture of
Jaurès and quoted his fanatically revered master: " 'There is,' "
he said, " 'a historic structure called France. It developed out of
centuries of common suffering and common longing. To be sure,

there is class war, sharp social contrast, but that does not change the concept of the fatherland.' Do you believe," he asked Simone with a threatening gesture, "that there are Frenchmen who would actually betray France in her hour of danger? Who would send their fellow countrymen out on the highways like that?" He pointed down at the fugitive procession. "I don't believe it," he raged and struck the table with his fist.

Simone looked at him with her fine, earnest eyes. He was a piece of old France, and he would not admit that this France no longer existed. Small and helpless, brave and a little ludicrous, he stood there and fought for his dead ideals.

"The lawyers are to blame for all of it," he went on and resumed his pacing, "the politicians and the lawyers who rule France. They looked on while the Boches rearmed and while our financiers furnished the money. They looked on while our Two Hundred Families transferred their capital to America and peddled our steel to the Boches; they debated and argued and argued and debated; and there's the result." He pointed again at the road full of refugees.

Wickedly pleased, Simone listened to Père Bastide's indictment of the lawyers. The lawyers had prevented her father's name from being cleared and from being duly respected. The lawyers had dragged out the investigation of his death in the jungles of the Congo and had finally permitted it to lapse completely.

Père Bastide stormed at the lawyers a little longer. Then, practically in the middle of a sentence, he broke off, stopped in front of her, and smiled. In the midst of his grief and anger he even succeeded in producing a friendly, if somewhat forced, smile. "But, my little one," he said, "you probably didn't come here to listen to me scold my heart out. And you haven't even drunk my nut brandy. But wait. I have something else for you." And with his stiff, artificially brisk stride, he went into the adjoining room.

Simone guessed what he would bring. She was a passionate reader and spent all her meagre spare time over books. Père Bastide knew that, advised her, and lent her books.

Now he returned with books under his arm. With skilled hands he made a package and tied it up. She thanked him and said good-bye. She had remained longer than she had intended.

Père Bastide again stood in the little window nook and stared down at the distant highway with its caterpillar of refugees. "Disgraceful, disgraceful," he raged. "But," he added, consoling himself, "France has been in tighter spots, and has always pulled out of them. A miracle always happened."

His confidence touched Simone, but she asked herself from where the miracle would come if no one did anything except wait. Had he not himself only recently quoted a saying from the Orient: "When, if not now? And who else, if not you?"

II: The Loading Yard

HER doubts fled as she briskly descended the steep path that brought her back to the centre of the old town. It was a good thing that she had looked up Père Bastide and she felt more cheerful. France will recover.

The rock path debouched upon the Rue de l'Arquebuse, and here stood the stateliest house in the old town. It was number 97, and the number 97 was painted on it in huge old-fashioned, ornate figures. 97 Rue de l'Arquebuse. In school Simone had learned that this fine place had once belonged to the old noble family of Trémoille and later to the Montmorencys. Now a great, shiny copper sign proclaimed that the lawyer and notary Charles-Marie Levautour had his offices here. The stately house actually belonged to Maître Levautour, and Simone felt even greater resentment than ordinarily as she passed here today. Maître Levautour, a contemporary and schoolmate of her father, was one of the lawyers who had prevented the clearing of Pierre Planchard's name. He had continued to feed the press campaign against Pierre Planchard with new, poisonous material, and he had prevented the community of Saint-Martin from dedicating a tablet to Pierre Planchard's memory. Simone hated him profoundly. He was one of those against whom Père Bastide had raged. He was one of the lawyers with black robes and cap and white neck-frill who cheated the people out of their rights with a hundred tricks and who bore the guilt for the present plight of France.

Now she was back in the Avenue du Parc where the street turned off to the office. It was late and there was still a great deal of work in the garden and kitchen. She really should go home and omit the trip to the office. She actually would have had a good excuse: the errands had taken longer than usual. And besides, her job at the gasoline pump today seemed more disagreeable than ever. Moreover, she thought with disgust of the insolent glances and the dirty remarks with which the truck driver, Maurice, would certainly greet her.

So there she stood and hesitated in the Avenue du Parc where the way home and the way to the office divided. But then, in spite of arguments to the contrary, she went down the Avenue du Parc towards the office. She did not want to appear cowardly. If she did not take her place at the gas pump, the driver, Maurice, would think she was staying away because she was afraid of his remarks. But she was not afraid.

Although she walked briskly and the street went downhill, it took her a good fifteen minutes. The Planchard Transfer Company was located at the extreme west end of the new town where the main road to Saint-Martin branched off from Route 6 which made a wide curve around the city. The Planchard Transfer Company was not situated directly on the highway but covered a rather large terrain with an approaching road of its own.

Uncle Prosper had protected himself against being overrun with refugees. A chain closed the driveway to his business house, a huge sign proclaimed: "Private road, leads only to the house," and two of his workmen were on guard. At the closed gate in the wall surrounding the loading yard huge letters stated: "No gasoline, no spare parts, no repair work, no road maps."

Here again Simone entered by a private signal. She first reported in the office. After the wild disorder of the highway these rooms seemed empty and peaceful. The coloured travel posters on the walls looked strangely absurd today: huge trucks rolling along perilously steep roads, ocean liners pushing their mighty keels through foaming seas, scenic roads winding over rugged mountains.

For a fleeting moment Simone was aware of the scope of the business Uncle Prosper had built up. The Planchard Company not only had a monopoly on the extensive trucking business, especially in wine and lumber, of the entire Département, it not only operated several autobus lines, it had also built roads into the dark, romantic mountain range to the east and had organized a flourishing tourist trade.

Simone was astonished not to find Uncle Prosper at once upon entering. No matter in what corner of the big establishment one might be, the active proprietor could be seen or heard everywhere; he seemed to be at all places at once, in the offices, in the big garage, in the loading yard, giving orders or chatting in his deep, resounding voice. Simone had expected that in this time of trouble he would be doubly busy.

Monsieur Peyroux, the book-keeper, enlightened her. The boss had locked himself in his private office and did not wish to be disturbed. He was engaged with the Châtelain, the Marquis de Saint-Brisson. Since the telephone was not working, Monsieur Peyroux whispered reverently: the Marquis had deigned to come down in person from the castle to speak with Monsieur Planchard. The rabbity face of the book-keeper looked silly with deference.

Monsieur Peyroux was accustomed to speak frankly and confidentially with Mademoiselle Simone. He was attached to the firm, proud to be an employee of Monsieur Planchard whom he admired, and Mademoiselle Simone was a relative of the boss. He considered it self-evident that she would regard it as a great honour if a gentleman like the Marquis de Saint-Brisson was dependent upon Monsieur Planchard's help. But the other employees in the office smiled and winked at Simone; they were probably cracking malicious jokes about the business deals which "that fascist," the Marquis, was proposing to her uncle in his private office.

Simone asked for the key to the gas pump and went about her business. She crossed the yard which was ordinarily a hive of activity: tourist cars, buses, trucks came and went, were repaired, tested, loaded and unloaded. Today the big yard lay empty in the bright sunlight. On the bench in the shade of the wall sat the old driver, Richard, the packer, Georges, and two others. With relief Simone noted that the driver, Maurice, was not with them.

Simone had no easy position here in the truck yard. Uncle

Prosper treated his people jovially, kindly, even affectionately;
he was broad-minded in everything not concerning business. He
was well liked. But in matters of business he was not to be
trifled with and now, using the war as pretext, he made great
demands of his people. Sometimes that created considerable dis-
satisfaction. But they were dependent upon the boss since it was
up to him to decide whom among his packers and drivers he
would designate as indispensable and so save from military duty
at the front. They therefore did not dare to rebel. But they
thought they could release their pent-up wrath against Simone,
the poor relative. They did not regard her as a fellow-worker
but as a relative of the boss, they felt themselves observed and
spied upon by her, and they did not like it. In her presence they
particularly enjoyed airing their resentment against the boss.

For his part, Uncle Prosper liked to give her assignments he
did not wish to entrust to or require of his other employees. Her
job at the gasoline pump was of this nature.

The Planchard Company had hoarded great quantities of
gasoline to which it was not entitled under the rationing
regulations. Monsieur Planchard did not disdain small profits
and sold his black-market gasoline to people who were willing
and in a position to pay exorbitant prices. In these last few days
gasoline was worth more than the finest vintage wines, and
Monsieur Planchard's prices went higher and higher. He had
discovered that if he had an adult employee sell the gasoline,
embarrassing scenes occurred. The purchasers cursed and shouted
and there was gossip in town. So Monsieur Planchard preferred
to limit the sale of gasoline to one afternoon hour and to put a
little girl at the pump who knew of nothing and merely carried
out orders.

With a sulky, defiant look on her face Simone took her place
at the pump. There she stood in her neat light green striped
dress, and the red enamel of the pump gleamed in the sun.

A buyer came and when she named the price he recoiled. He
asked once more, pressed his lips together, hesitated, made up
his mind, swallowed hard, and paid. Another came and left
indignantly. A third came, swore abusively, and paid.

Simone had always detested this job. But the ten years she had
spent growing up in the Villa Monrepos had filled her with the
conviction that Uncle Prosper was a great, exemplary business
man, and what he did was right. If he put her at the pump, that
was right. If she did her duty at the pump, that was the least she
could do for a man to whom she was deeply indebted.

Today the job at the pump was particularly hard; the visions
behind her brow made it so. There were many visions and they
faded into each other: the stalled automobiles with their stolid,
miserable occupants; the lean, reddish-blond head of her father
with the merry, angry blue-grey eyes and the many little wrinkles; the refugee boy on the garden wall of the Hôtel de la
Poste, looking at her angrily after she had given him the Roblechon cheese; little Père Bastide standing in his window nook,
helpless, furious, touching, and ridiculous.

But her young, lean face showed nothing of the visions behind
her brow. The others looked at her disapprovingly, disdainfully,
as she went about her unsavoury business, the beggar princess
who earned neither thanks nor profit, the unworthy daughter of
Pierre Planchard. And she stood there and heard the words of
the exploited and tried not to hear them, tried not to hear the talk
of the packers and drivers and still she heard every word.

It was a blessing that Maurice, at least, was not there.

Back of her was the front of the big garage. Through the
open window near her came the splashing of the shower bath;
here was the drivers' washroom, much used on this warm afternoon. She heard the men snorting and puffing. It was quite
possible that Maurice was in there. In that case he might appear
at any moment and she would not be spared his malicious remarks.

The expectation tormented her so much that she was almost
relieved when he appeared in the garage entrance.

She stared straight ahead. But in fancy she saw every step he
took, she saw his strong, bulky face, his somewhat thick-set figure; she saw him strolling with long, lazy, rolling steps to the
others, saw him nodding to them and saw them make room for
him on the bench.

Maurice was young, he was insolent, his political views were opposed to those of Uncle Prosper. Uncle regarded him as an instigator; Maurice wrangled instead of being grateful that Uncle had saved him from front-line service. But he was the best driver for miles around. In his early youth he had been Citroen's truck-master and Uncle Prosper had paid a good price to get him from there. Maurice was popular with the other employees and to dismiss him would have caused trouble. So Uncle Prosper swallowed his wrath.

Now Maurice was sitting with the others, his blue shirt unbuttoned, and he listened to their talk. Of course the conversation concerned the refugees and the news from the front.

They would not believe that there actually was no longer a front; they would not admit the catastrophe. They spoke of the Maginot Line and said that Generals Pétain and Weygand must have a plan, and if they could not hold Paris they would defend the Loire River line. It would be impossible for France to collapse overnight.

"France?" interjected Maurice who, so far, had been silent. "What France? Will you please explain to me, what France? That of the Two Hundred Families? Or that of the two million small investors? Or yours? Or mine? People have talked so much about France that it doesn't exist at all any more. What is France, anyhow?" he jeered. "Is it the lady on the postage stamps, the lady with the cap?" His voice was high, almost squeaking, but he was not excited. He spoke calmly with a sort of sharp politeness.

Simone stood by her red pump and did not appear to hear what they on the bench were saying. But in her heart she was indignant at Maurice's words and that the others permitted him to speak thus. "What is this France?" Why don't they tell him? Every one knows what France is, every one feels it. France is . . . is . . . She was aghast. Suddenly she discovered that she herself could not have said what France is. But she brushed away the shock at once. Of course it is difficult to formulate it in words upon such a sudden demand. But one can feel it. One belongs to France, is a part of it. And if Maurice does not feel it, he is a poor, unfortunate creature, a creature without a heart.

Meanwhile Maurice was explaining to the others, and not for the first time, that what was going on out there was not a real war. It had never been a war. It was not true that the Boches had defeated France in a real war. The fascists within, the Cagoulards, the Flandins and Lavals and Bonnets, had delivered the country over to their partisans beyond the Rhine. They had prepared that long ago and Pétain, our old defeatist of Verdun, would not be able to change it. Maurice spoke of the connexion of French monopolistic capital with the German, of French industry with the German. One wolf does not devour the other. Of course Hitler who guaranteed our fascists, "these gentlemen," a 60-hour week, would be more convenient for them than Léon Blum who insisted on a 40-hour week. France was not overthrown by German tanks but by our own steel monopoly. Those were our good friends of the Two Hundred Families.

When Maurice, with his high, sometimes squeaking voice, spoke about "these gentlemen," it did not sound vague and general like Père Bastide. It sounded sharp and certain.

Simone, standing at her pump, confessed that a certain deliberate reality sounded out of Maurice's words. It was just this self-confidence that provoked one, and if one resisted this, then Maurice came with figures and facts and one would be the loser. A few times someone had doubted his figures but it had been proved that he was right.

But Simone did not dream of being convinced by his silly figures and facts. In her heart she passionately rejected them. He was not fair, he never saw the other side. For him there was only white or black, right or left. For him every one who did not agree with him was a fool or a knave or a fascist.

"Maybe we could have smoked out our Two Hundred Families," she heard him say now, "when we were united with the left-wing bourgeois party and had the majority. But when it came time to act our bourgeois friends showed no backbone. That is always so. When the going gets hard our allies of the other class always desert us, even the well-meaning ones."

The others were quiet. Maurice pointed up to the private office of Monsieur Planchard. "Joe Blow up there always pretended to be a patriot," he orated. "He always was an opponent of the Marquis, the fascist; but there you have it, now he is making a deal with him."

"Shut your dirty mouth," said the old driver, Richard, good-naturedly. "The boss talks a lot, I will admit, but when one needs him, he opens his purse. It was most noble of him to furnish two cars for the refugees."

"Yes," sneered Maurice, "the two old, shabby Peugeots. The refugees will be lucky if they get as far as Nevers with them. And now Joe Blow is a generous man and has taken precautions in case they demand more of him."

"You are not fair," the packer Georges contended. "You've got it in for him."

"I only see what I see," answered Maurice, "and you have let him talk you blind. The refugees need gasoline more than bread. He has his tanks full of black-market gasoline. I have not noticed that he gives any to them."

"Every one has black-market gasoline," said old Richard calmly, and spat. And: "He gave the gasoline for the two Peugeots," added the packer, Georges.

"I am no prophet," said Maurice, "but I tell you now, when it gets dangerous Joe Blow will tie himself to the apron strings of the Two Hundred Families."

"It's dangerous now," old Richard said.

Maurice turned his brown, intelligent eyes to the others, smiling slyly. "Right," he answered, "and I'll bet a bottle of Pernod and ten packages of Gaulois that in the end not the refugees will get his cars but the Châtelain, for hauling his wines."

Simone loved her Uncle Prosper. He had taken her in and replaced her father. She belonged to the family. He liked her and was attentive to her. When he went to the movies he took her along; when he went on a trip he always brought her something. Last year he had taken her along to Paris for two weeks. He was friendly to every one; he had a heart for everybody. All, even if they grumbled about him at times, liked him. Only

Maurice hated him, Maurice abused him out of hatred. It always hurt her when Maurice called him "Joe Blow."

The packer, Georges, was right: Maurice "had it in for him." Maurice had it in for everybody who had money. He was full of prejudice, a spiteful person.

He needn't open his mouth so wide, that Maurice, she said to herself. He is criticizing Uncle Prosper because he is making a deal with the Châtelain; but he himself hides behind Uncle Prosper to dodge the draft. Others fight and die under the tanks, and he stands under the shower bath and then sits comfortably in the shade and smokes and talks big. I won't listen to him any longer, I'll pay no attention to him.

But now she could not help hearing him state with provocative self-confidence: "In the end it's always we little fellows who pay the bill. We are always the ones who are sold out"; and she could not prevent this sentence from sinking into her consciousness.

She tried hard to take her mind off Maurice. But although she stared straight ahead she always saw only him as he sat there comfortably smoking, with his open blue shirt, and the others listening to him.

She had not noticed that he looked at her even once. Yet she was convinced that his words were intended for her, too. He did not count her among the little people, although she did not possess a red cent. If worst came to worst, he expected her, like Uncle Prosper, to crawl before the Two Hundred Families. And she was quite sure that he would soon say something nasty about her in his insolent tone.

Now he paused briefly. He was still not looking at her but she felt that he was putting his left hand on his hip; he always did that before he said something particularly vicious. Here it came, the insulting, nasty word which she feared and expected.

"Well," she heard his high impudent voice, "I see the honourable niece is out soliciting again."

Simone was rigid. She pretended to be deaf. She had never heard the expression "out soliciting," but she was quite certain

that what Maurice had just said was the worst thing that could
be said about any one.

What had she ever done to Maurice to make him hate her so?
She would have liked to start crying, but she controlled herself
and continued to stare straight ahead. Of course her face was
fiery red but that proved nothing. It was fearfully hot, she was
standing in the sun, and naturally her face was red.

Maurice was regarded as a good fellow. Everybody went to
him for advice; he was not stingy with his advice and his advice
was good. Maurice was a *débrouillard,* one who can worm out of
the most complicated situations. He racked his brain for others;
he helped many and was always concerned for others. But he
was not a good fellow where she was concerned.

And yet he was an adherent of her father. He, said Maurice,
was an idealist and a romantic like Jaurès, but still he was a
regular fellow; and that was probably the highest praise that any
one could expect from Maurice. Yet he derided and insulted her
at every opportunity. He did not regard her as the daughter of
Pierre Planchard but as a member of the Villa Monrepos family,
one of the high and mighty folk, one of his enemies.

What did he want her to do? In return for all his generosity
Uncle Prosper expected her to work for him. That was his privilege. It was vile of Maurice to jeer at her because she did her
work.

Why was she so hateful in his eyes? He was otherwise friendly
to girls; impudent but friendly. They say he likes girls. They say
he has many girls.

Sometimes Simone was tempted to corner Maurice and to ask
him why he disliked her. But she restrained herself and kept
silent. This time, too, she did not show him how much he
offended her.

With a defiant face she stood at her red pump and did her
duty. She was "out soliciting." Now more than ever. And tomorrow she would do it again. And the day after tomorrow. She had
her own pride. And some day, perhaps, Maurice would discover
that he had done her an injustice.

She looked at the big clock over the office entrance. If she wanted to keep her dignity, she had to stay until the full hour. She could not go until then and that was still eighteen minutes.

Eighteen long minutes. Her tanned, reddened, perspiring face seemed calm, but behind her broad stubborn brow pictures and thoughts became more and more tormentingly confused. Uncle Prosper and the Châtelain, "the fascist," with whom he was making a deal in his private office. The Roblechon cheese which she gave the boy on the garden wall. The steel monopoly, the Two Hundred Families, and the lawyers with their black robes and caps and white neck-frills and all their trickery. Maurice, who was friendly to all the girls and insulted her with poisonous talk. The picture of Jean Jaurès, the romantic and idealist, standing like a colossus before his huge flag and under the picture, nodding in his arm-chair, Père Bastide, helpless and aged.

Seven minutes more.

Finally, the time was up; she could go. With firm, hard stride she walked across the yard. "Good-bye, Mademoiselle," shouted Maurice with his high, impudent voice. It sounded commonplace and it felt like a blow. "Good-bye," she answered. She tried hard to sound commonplace, too, but her voice was deep and resonant; she had the beautiful voice of the Planchards and it sounded like a challenge.

She deposited the key in the office and left. She fetched her basket from the Deputy Prefecture. It had become cooler. And yet the way seemed long and hot and the basket very heavy.

III: Villa Monrepos

SIMONE entered the living-room; she had washed herself
thoroughly and prepared for supper. She was wearing her
brown dress and the little apron over it. While she ate with the
family, she frequently had to go to the kitchen to put the final
touches to the meal and to serve it.

Uncle Prosper would come home later than usual today; probably very late, he had announced in the morning. Madame, too,
was still up in her room. So Simone had a few moments of leisure. She sat there idly, her large, clean, work-roughened hands
in her lap. After all, she was quite worn out from trouble and
excitement. But now there was only the supper and the dishwashing left to be done.

The room was dusky and quiet. The large chamber—they
called it the Blue Room—was richly furnished with stately Bur-
gundian furniture. Formerly the Planchards had lived in the
old town, but a few years ago Uncle Prosper had built this comfortable house, the Villa Monrepos, out here, far from the office,
to the east of the city. It stood out in the open with a beautiful
view of the winding Cerein valley on the one side and of the
wooded mountains and the hamlet Noiret on the other.

Simone sat in a small chair, well aware of her inferior position in the Planchard house as one who had been taken in out
of pity. The large, portière-draped door to the dining-room
stood open, and Simone mechanically surveyed the supper table.
She had set it carefully, for the Villa Monrepos ate with tradi-
tional formality. There were many plates, many glasses, much
silver; everything had its exact place and its exact order; the
menu had been thoroughly discussed the day before. Simone
rapidly reviewed everything. The tongs for the snails and the
finger bowls were there; the Chablis stood in its ice-pail; the

plates for the leg of lamb had to be very hot; the Pommard lay in its basket so as to attain the right temperature. The salad bowl and its wooden implements were within reach in the kitchen; the chervil had already been cut. That really should have been done just before serving, but then the break between the roast and the salad would be too long. Anyhow it was not easy to keep the break between the snails and the roast short enough. The liqueurs and the orange marmalade for the crêpes suzette stood on the sideboard; Uncle Prosper made it a point to finish the preparation of the crêpes himself at the table.

The room became noticeably darker. Simone had already closed the shutters and lowered the shades in the other rooms to comply with black-out regulations. Here, in the Blue Room and the dining-room, she would do it when Madame came. Simone preferred the dusk to the electric light.

There comes Madame.

Simone was always astonished at Madame's soft tread although she was fearfully fat and heavy; her breath was louder than her step.

As usual, Madame wore a black silk dress and her hair was carefully arranged. It was not exactly white, but rather curiously mottled. Madame was probably in the early or middle sixties. Simone did not know exactly; Madame's age was never mentioned in the Villa Monrepos.

Simone had risen. "You might lower the shutters," said Madame softly. She was always polite, never excited, or at least she never showed it, and she rarely scolded. Yet every order she gave sounded like a reproach, and when Madame was in sight it always seemed to Simone that her every move was supervised by a stern eye.

Simone closed the shutters and switched on the light in both rooms. The bulbs were large and bright; Madame loved very bright lights. Then Simone sat down in the small chair again, but now she was no longer relaxed; her leisure was over, she was back on duty.

Madame also had sat down in the wing chair in which she awaited Uncle Prosper's return each evening. She was not tall but of enormous girth, and she sat there stiffly, her flesh confined in a corset. Her small, hard eyes were not directed at Simone, but her very presence made Simone feel small and oppressed.

Madame was not talkative. She sat there, breathing a bit heavily because of her weight, calmly, waiting.

But Simone knew that this calmness was simulated. Uncle Prosper was a bachelor and no saint; it sometimes happened that he made a call on some lady or another on his way home. Recently there had been all sorts of malicious and grinning gossip at the loading yard about his relations with the wife of Doctor Mimerelles who was in the army. Madame probably knew of this gossip. She did not see many people but she had the telephone, the newspapers, and her two friends in Saint-Martin, old ladies who visited her occasionally. With uncanny insight she put two and two together and usually knew about things before they happened. She loved her son and all her thoughts centred on him; every fifteen minutes she wondered where he might be and what he might be doing. Simone was aware that Madame did not approve of Uncle Prosper's mode of life.

Behind Madame's apparent calm Simone sensed her growing nervousness. To be sure, Uncle Prosper had prepared her for his late return. That was to be expected in times like these, and it was highly improbable that Uncle Prosper would choose today for a visit to his friend. And yet each minute Madame's suspicion grew stronger that Monsieur Planchard was keeping his mother waiting on account of this whoring Madame Mimerelles.

Madame sat in her wing chair, black and straight, in the brilliance of the electric lights. Her head was pressed down stiffly so that the enormous double chin projected even more; her stomach and thighs were a single swollen mass, her lower arms rested on the arms of the chair; person and arm-chair merged into one. Breathing heavily but without motion she sat there like a gigantic idol.

It was strange how different her son was from Madame Planchard. Uncle Prosper probably inherited much of his appearance and character from his father.

This father of his—the old Monsieur Henri Planchard, Madame's deceased husband, Simone's grandfather—had had a son from an earlier marriage, this Pierre Planchard, Simone's father. It was astonishing that Madame, the richest and most respected girl in Saint-Martin, had married him, a penniless engineer, a widower with a nine-year-old son.

Once again Simone reviewed what she knew about this Henri Planchard, her grandfather. They say he was a man of imagination, very attractive, versatile and interested in many things outside of his business, a spendthrift. Madame, stern, tight-fisted, stubborn, probably had no easy life with him nor he with her. The traits in Uncle Prosper which Madame opposed and which Simone liked probably came from this Henri Planchard.

"It's too bad that there wasn't any Roblechon," said Madame at length. "My son will miss it." She always spoke of Uncle Prosper as her son or as Monsieur Planchard. Simone did not answer; she did not even blush. Her slightly sulky face only became more expressionless. At this very moment she would certainly have given the Roblechon to the boy on the garden wall once more.

"How does it look in town?" Madame suddenly asked. Ordinarily she never directed such questions at Simone but made it a point to get all information from her own private sources. But now, since the telephone was out of order, her connexion with the city was cut off and her inner tension too great to bear in silence.

Simone was reluctant to tell Madame how deeply the spectacle of the refugees had moved her. Dryly and with awkward words she reported that the number of refugees had greatly increased and that they were suffering from hunger. Also many people had fled from Saint-Martin, Messieurs Amiot, Laroche, Raimu, and others.

Madame's features remained rigid in the strong light and her gigantic bosom continued to move gently. But: "Give me a cigarette," she commanded, and Simone knew how greatly the information had affected her; for Madame smoked only rarely, and only when she was excited.

"So they're fleeing," she repeated Simone's words after a while, "they're running away, they're taking to their heels." The voice came clearly, softly, and disdainfully from her massive face. "No discipline," she continued. "France of today has no more discipline. I am disappointed in Monsieur Laroche and in Monsieur Raimu, and particularly in Monsieur Amiot. A storekeeper who leaves his shop in the lurch in such a time of need is a deserter. He needn't be surprised if his customers desert him when the times are normal again. These people are as stupid as they are cowardly."

Madame smoked. Her small, bright eyes peered hard out of the rolls of flesh. Simone stared straight ahead. She was afraid that Madame might see the resentment in her face. She thought of the child that was carrying the cat over the hot, misery-laden highways of France; she thought of the exhausted soldiers with their bloody feet; she thought of the girl who, in all that crowd, was trying to scratch the crusted mud from the blue enamelled perambulator. "They're running away, they're taking to their heels. Stupid and cowardly"—that was all that Madame felt about these people.

"Don't be impertinent," she suddenly heard Madame's voice. Madame spoke calmly but Simone was startled and blushed deeply. It was uncanny how Madame guessed every insubordinate thought. Insubordination, "impertinence," were the worst crimes in Madame's eyes. Simone's father had been impertinent and he had perished. "Don't be impertinent" was the sharpest reprimand that Madame ever uttered.

They sat in silence. It was hard to sit so still in Madame's oppressive presence; she longed for Uncle Prosper's arrival. It wasn't always easy with Uncle Prosper either. He was very impulsive, he let himself go, and sometimes, when irritated, he said unjust things which made her angry. But he really liked Simone and usually he was sincerely friendly to her. Sometimes he spoke confidentially with her as to an adult, sometimes even so confidentially that it embarrassed her as, for example, in the movies when he expressed his frank opinion about the feminine qualities of the actresses. Nevertheless he was a person to whom she often, in fact most of the time, felt very near. But Madame remained strange and hostile; only to look at her made her cold.

"Turn on the radio," said Madame after a while. Simone did so. Out of the radio came the six notes of the "Marseillaise" which always came in the pauses between bulletins: *"Aux armes, citoyens."* They waited. They waited for Monsieur Planchard and for news bulletins.

Madame extinguished her cigarette. "Give me the paper," she demanded. "It's an old one," replied Simone. "I know," said Madame, not impatiently, only coldly. Simone brought the papers, a three-day-old *Dijon Dépêche* and an old *Echo de Paris* that Uncle Prosper had brought home yesterday. Madame took a lorgnon from her pocket and read the Dijon local news which she had repeatedly studied before.

Presently she closed her eyes. She still sat stiff and quiet, but the lorgnon and the paper had dropped to her lap. There she sat, evil and peaceful.

But Simone's discomfort did not decrease. She dared not even turn off the radio. Out of the instrument came those measures of the "Marseillaise" at brief intervals, preventing her even from thinking sensibly. She sat in her small chair under the bright light and found the sitting and waiting intolerable.

Steps in the garden. At last. She flew to the front door to help her uncle find his way in out of the dark.

As soon as she saw him her anxiety was gone. The house had changed. It was no longer like a coffin; it was now filled with life.

Uncle Prosper went over to Madame who remained seated. He had grown a little heavier in the past two years, but his movements were brisk and masculine, though perhaps the briskness was becoming more difficult. He looked well in his grey suit; he made it a point to dress carefully and tastefully. He embraced Madame and Simone noticed that she sniffed at him to see whether he had called on a woman.

"Of course I had to walk home," he reported. "It's out of the question to get through with the car. But the walk did me good," he continued with a smile, "and I've worked up an awful appetite. Let's eat right away. I'll only wash my hands. You've waited long enough. Now we deserve something good."

Then they sat down, and while Uncle skilfully drew his snails out of their wine- and butter-filled shells and ate them with relish, he spoke of the day's events. It was assumed, he said, that the alleged French official orders to evacuate additional territory really came from the Boches for the purpose of increasing the confusion. At any rate, the panic was contagious, half of France was now in flight, all roads were jammed, preventing military movements, and the government could not cope with the situation. He had seen heart-rending sights. However, it was his opinion that the authorities should not permit false pity for the fugitives to deter them from radical measures. If there was no other way, they would have to drive the refugees from the roads by force.

There he sat, distinguished, vigorous, handsome. Simone watched to see when he and Madame would finish their snails so that she could promptly remove the plates and serve the roast. At the same time she listened to Uncle Prosper's words.

"Of course I am glad," she heard him say, "that we are not the ones to take such harsh measures. It's a good thing that we, at least, are permitted to have human feelings."

He leaned back and his expressive, masculine features bore an embarrassed smile. "I must make a confession, Mother," he resumed. "I put two cars at the disposal of the Deputy Prefecture for the fugitives. I made no terms, but simply gave them the cars. I couldn't help myself."

Simone's heart grew warm. In Uncle Prosper's words she heard the sincere satisfaction it had given him to furnish these cars to save forty or fifty people.

His voice was deep and full. Her father's voice must have sounded like that. Indeed Uncle Prosper had much in common with her father: the heavy, reddish-blond hair, the lively, blue-grey eyes under bushy brows, the well-shaped lips. Many people said he looked like the full brother of Pierre Planchard and now, as he sat there, a little ashamed of his generous act, Simone was very conscious of this similarity.

Madame regarded her son with her small, prying eyes. "I fear you will get small thanks for it," she said at length. "You are too good, my boy. Isn't it indiscreet to give away two cars in these times?"

Uncle Prosper laughed. "Let me be indiscreet, Mother," he said.

Simone carried the dishes out and prepared to serve the roast. As she was bringing it in her uncle was just saying that it was the patriotic duty of every business man to keep cool. Simply by going about their usual business these men could do much to calm the populace. The very sight of an open store had a quieting effect. It was scandalous that so many storekeepers yielded to panic.

Red and juicy the slices of roast lamb lay on the hot plates, covered with dark brown, fragrant gravy; the heavy, deep red wine flowed into the wide, tall glasses.

Of course, continued Uncle as he ate, it could not be denied that there was serious danger. Although the territory around Saint-Martin had no strategic importance, the Boches might still occupy it. "Certain gentlemen," replied Madame in her low, hard tone, "seem to expect that. I have heard that certain gentlemen have left, have fled, have run away."

"Yes," confirmed Uncle Prosper. "Imagine, Mother, even the book-keeper, Peyroux, otherwise such a sensible fellow, quite innocently asked me whether I would not leave too."

Madame raised her lips in a sneer. "The common riff-raff," she commented, "is even more stupid than we think. I can't see why the highways should be safer than our homes. And even if the Boches should come, I can't see why it should be to their interest to kill us. It is certainly to their advantage to have life continue."

They had finished with the roast and Simone helped her uncle prepare the salad. He bent over the dish and his right ear was very close to her; it was pointed at the top and strangely thick. Suddenly she was aware of the great difference between her father and her uncle. When his eye became piercing, when he relaxed and slumped down heavily, he rather resembled Madame.

She carried off the plates. When she returned with the pancakes for the crêpes suzette her uncle was telling of the Châtelain's visit.

Simone knew that Uncle Prosper and the Marquis de Saint-Brisson differed politically, but that it was a matter of pride with Uncle to maintain social relations with the aristocrat. On the rare occasions when the Marquis appeared in the Planchard office, Uncle had always spoken of it as of a great event. So today's visit was probably also memorable. Simone was all the more astonished that he did not make much of this visit, just as if it had been a call by Monsieur Amiot or Monsieur Laroche. And Madame spoke in the same tone. "Yes, indeed," she said casually, "now the Châtelain comes running."

Still talking, Uncle Prosper skilfully prepared the crêpes suzette over the little spirit heater. He poured the liqueur on the pancakes and rocked the bluish flame back and forth. The Marquis, he elaborated, wanted to have his vintage wines carried out of danger to Bayonne, in the extreme southwest. Of course, in times like these, he said magnanimously, one did favours for an old customer, in spite of political difference. But the matter was not as simple as the Marquis imagined, he added with broad obvious irony.

Simone was happy. Evidently Uncle Prosper had roundly refused the Châtelain's proposal. She remembered Maurice's sneering challenge: "I'll bet a bottle of Pernod the Marquis will get our trucks for his wines." She knew all the time Maurice was a liar and a slanderer.

"That's what our little Simone likes," said Uncle Prosper now, pointing at the bluish flame and petting her. Simone blushed and recoiled the least bit. When she was a child her uncle had often taken her on his lap, and he had never given up stroking and petting her. Of late that sometimes bothered her.

Crusted with butter and sugar, sweetly fragrant, the pancakes lay on the plate. For a moment the scene at the Place du Général Gramont with the parked refugee vehicles stood vividly before Simone's eyes. It seemed unreal to her that she was seated in this bright, spacious room at the well-stocked table and that they were eating snails and roast lamb followed by pancakes, while they chatted calmly.

"I fear we will not be able to finish our meal undisturbed," announced Uncle Prosper. "Philippe is coming out." Philippe Cordelier was the deputy prefect of the county.

Madame looked up with some surprise. "Philippe came in to see me yesterday," Monsieur Planchard went on, "at the office. We agreed that it was wiser to continue our discussion privately. The government wants to rent all my trucks."

Madame succeeded in mastering her amazement. She took her lorgnon and scrutinized her son's face. "Oh lala," was all she said, and that with just a little derision. But Simone's face was silly with bewilderment, and it took a while before she absorbed the news. She drew her brows together so that her forehead and nose became wrinkled, and pondered.

At the loading yard there had been talk some days ago that, in case of extreme need, the authorities would requisition the trucks. Now the time had probably come for the deputy prefect to take over the Planchard establishment on behalf of the refugees. But Monsieur Cordelier had very good, even friendly, relations with Uncle Prosper. Uncle Prosper was the most prominent man in the county; he had rendered the government valuable service at elections. The deputy prefect was obligated to him and did not wish to offend this influential man. That was why he was making this long trip through the night to the Villa Monrepos. He wanted to get what he could out of Uncle Prosper in an amicable way.

The furrow in Simone's sulky young brow deepened; she looked far older than her years. Had she been mistaken when she was so happy over Uncle Prosper's gift of the two Peugeots? Unwillingly she recalled Maurice's vicious interpretation: "And now Joe Blow is a generous man and has taken precautions in case they demand more of him."

"Of course I expect to do my share to facilitate moving the refugees," Uncle Prosper declared. "But they'll have to leave the method to me. To take the whole establishment away from me is just a little thick. Don't you think so too, Mother? And where will Philippe get the drivers? Where will he send the various trucks? I am certainly a friend of the government, but in times like these the usual administrative routine won't do. In a catastrophe such as we are experiencing, the bureaucrats, the penpushers would do well to turn matters over to capable business men who know the local conditions."

His deep, plaintive voice sounded convinced and convincing. Simone had often heard such statements from him. He really believed that if he had his way he could do more about moving the refugees than the deputy prefect. But Simone could not forget Maurice's words, and the high, squeaky tone in which he always said "Joe Blow" accompanied everything that Uncle Prosper said.

Simone had the gift of visualizing events that might take place in the future. She saw the Châtelain's huge wine casks being loaded on the well-built trucks of the Planchard Company, she saw them drive through the stream of refugees, powerful trucks supplied with all essentials, with fuel, with spare parts, and guided by experienced drivers who knew the roads. She saw the fugitives, broken down at the roadsides, looking after the trucks with dull, dead eyes.

Uncle Prosper had stopped eating although a piece of pancake still lay on his plate. Simone got up to clear the table but he held his hand over the plate and poured himself a little more wine. With the crêpes they drank a light, sparkling Anjou. "Just a moment, little one," he said cheerfully. "Don't begrudge me the rest of my crêpes.

"You were at the yard today, selling gasoline," he continued approvingly. It had been worth while, too. The amounts that were taken in at the gasoline pump were not inconsiderable. He was now profiting from the prudence which he showed in buying plenty of gasoline in time. In these times one had to be especially careful to watch one's interests. He leaned back and played with his napkin. He gave Simone a pleased look and she blushed a little. Just in passing she thought of Doctor Mimerelles' wife who was blonde and plump. To Simone Uncle Prosper had said the other day: "You are skinny as a hound."

It was a real compensation for the day's troubles, he said comfortably, to open one's heart in the family circle in the evening. A cosy supper was the best recreation, he said, and politely raised his glass of very light-coloured wine, first to Madame then to Simone.

Just as he put the last bite into his mouth steps sounded from the garden. "Well," he sighed, "at least we finished the crêpes," and wiped his mouth while Simone went to the door.

Monsieur Philippe Cordelier, the deputy prefect, blinked in the light of the vestibule. The tall, lean, slightly stooped gentleman, who always looked a little worried, seemed particularly agitated today. Mechanically fingering the rosette of the Legion of Honour, he said a little absently to Simone who took his cane: "Good evening, my dear child. That was a difficult trip today"; and more to himself than to Simone he spoke of the hardship of this walk through the dark. At every step one stumbled over cars and people. It had taken him more than an hour. Once he had completely lost his way. His pale eyes were still blinking.

Simone led him to the dining-room. Monsieur Planchard greeted him verbosely. Although he sometimes referred to the deputy prefect as a not overly intelligent person, he always treated him with the respect due the highest official in the county. Sometimes, as tonight, his courtesy was mixed with a scarcely noticeable, ironically jovial condescension.

"The walk seems to have exhausted you, Philippe," he said and slapped him on the shoulder. "You'd better recover a bit first. We are still waiting for our coffee and you'll have it with us."

"We will take our coffee in the Blue Room, Simone," said Madame, politely and with frigidity. She was speaking to the maid, not to her husband's granddaughter.

Simone cleared the table and prepared the coffee. When she brought the glass coffee urn, the mocha cups, and the cognac into the living-room, the men were comfortably settled and smoking. Madame was smoking, too. That was the second time tonight and it wasn't good for her. Simone knew why Madame took that risk. Madame always smoked when important business was being transacted; that gave her a chance to bring pauses into the discussion and to think of sharper replies.

Although the old lady must have been very tired owing to the lateness of the hour and the long wait for her son, she sat up straight in her wing chair, her huge body confined in its corset, the great double chin pressed down, and showed no sign of fatigue. Obviously she found it desirable to supervise the conversation between the deputy prefect and her son. "Close the door to the dining-room, Simone," she ordered when Simone had poured the coffee and was leaving. It was clear that she did not want Simone to hear anything in the kitchen.

But in spite of the closed door the voices from the living-room penetrated to her while she washed the dishes. The high-pitched, hollow voice of Monsieur Cordelier was excited; he was evidently demanding the surrender of the trucks. Uncle Prosper also replied excitedly; he spoke loudly and rapidly; his voice was more ringing than ordinarily. Then again there was complete silence and Simone knew that Madame was speaking. When she spoke, no matter how softly, every one was silent and listened.

Simone could imagine the course of the discussion in there, and she knew how it would end. There had been differences between the Deputy Prefecture and the Planchard Company on previous occasions. But Monsieur le Sous-Préfet had never carried his point. Nor would he be able to do it today, especially now that Madame was taking part in the conversation. "I bet a bottle of Pernod the refugees will not get the trucks." The only reward that Monsieur le Sous-Préfet would have for his hard walk through the night would be his coffee and his cognac.

She really should not think so maliciously of Uncle Prosper. She should not see him through the evil eyes of Maurice, who jeers and speaks ill of everything. Uncle Prosper is regarded as a humanitarian, as the benefactor of Saint-Martin. And he is. He has always been a father to her. When she recalls the cheerful, companionable understanding with which he accepted all her childish fancies, her heart warms to him. And how magnanimous

he was that time in Paris. He spared no time, effort, or money
to make her sojourn pleasant. He took her everywhere, showed
her everything. She ate in the best restaurants, went to the opera,
and if she wanted something from a store he bought it. He
even gracefully accepted her whims. When they were in Notre
Dame, she recalls, he wanted to go up into the steeple and she
refused. Without a reason. She could not tell him that she did
not want to spoil the memory of her father, but he agreed without urging her. And if he wanted an evening to himself he saw
to it that she wasn't alone in the hotel. On one such evening she
went to the Louvre with the children of a business friend of
his; it was an evening when the statues were illuminated. She
will never forget how she stood breathlessly before the Winged
Victory, and how she lay awake all night wondering what the
head of the woman might have been like.

She really had a wonderful time in Paris with Uncle Prosper.
He did much for her. He is always happy when he can do something for others.

It's a queer thing: he likes her and yet he permits Madame to
treat her with coldness and hostility. Simone is unassuming and
has not even an inner resentment against doing menial work.
But Madame often assigns her unnecessary work, just to make
her feel that she is only a maid. Why does Uncle Prosper permit
that?

He probably shrinks from quarrelling with Madame. He re-
spects Madame for she is very shrewd. Uncle Prosper never
closes a deal of any consequence without consulting her. Madame
would never permit him to do otherwise. She still owns the
major interest in the company and, although she always stresses
the fact that her son is the head of the firm, she would not
dream of leaving the management of its affairs to him alone.

Simone understands Uncle Prosper's attitude. And yet she is
hurt that he does not defend her more vigorously against Madame. He is pleasant to her in Madame's presence but he gives
no indication of the true affection which he sometimes shows
her when they are alone.

She is ungrateful. All evening she has found fault with Uncle

Prosper in her heart. She is bitter when Maurice nags at everything, but is she different?

Of course her father was eternally dissatisfied too. That was
the charge against him, that he nagged and found fault with
everything. He was by nature insubordinate, this Pierre Planchard; he was "impertinent." He was so impertinent that he is
now dead and gone. His nagging and fault-finding meant so
much to him that he exposed himself to the danger of a mysterious death. And if people celebrate him today, then it is because he was a nagger and a fault-finder.

Maurice evidently assumes that she is not like her father.
Maurice evidently assumes that she is in agreement with the
Villa Monrepos, where impertinence and insubordination are
regarded as the worst of all crimes. But is she really in agreement? Isn't she one of the rebels, one of the insubordinates, like
her father?

The voices in the living-room became louder again; the voice
of the deputy prefect was shrill and violent. Monsieur Xavier,
the secretary of the Deputy Prefecture, who ought to know, once
said that Monsieur Cordelier was a decent fellow who spoiled
everything by his conciliatory attitude and his lack of decision.
Simone had had an experience in that regard. Monsieur le Sous-
Préfet had always declared that he admired Pierre Planchard;
but when the question arose of dedicating a memorial tablet to
him, he finally yielded to the opposition of the Notary Levautour. It ran through Simone's mind that Uncle Prosper acted
very "correctly" at that time, probably upon Madame's advice.
He declared that it was not proper for him, as Pierre Planchard's
brother, to vote and to work for the memorial tablet. He remained neutral.

So much was certain: Monsieur le Sous-Préfet was not the
man to win a cause over strong opposition. The Planchard Company would not deliver the trucks to him. Simone heard him
stopping in the middle of a sentence again; probably Madame
was speaking.

While these thoughts ran through her mind, Simone was nim-
bly washing and drying dishes, rinsing pots and pans, cleaning

knives and forks, polishing silver. There was a lot of work, the whole day had been a hard one, and while her strong, reddened child-hands mechanically performed their labours, her back hurt from exhaustion.

Before she had finished dishwashing Madame came into the kitchen. There she stood and filled the kitchen with her weight, and her hard, beady eyes looked at Simone, at the pile of clean, stacked dishes, and at the heap of dirty silverware. There was no sound except her breathing and the dripping of water into the dishpan.

Simone continued to rub the silver of the snail-tongs. She had done nothing which merited reproach, but still she felt uncomfortable while Madame stood and looked on. She wished Madame would finally say what she wanted.

"Leave the things as they are," Madame's soft voice at last issued from the heavy face, "and finish them tomorrow. It is late and you need sleep."

Simone was surprised. Madame had never before shown such consideration. "Thank you, Madame," she said and dried her hands. Evidently Madame feared she might hear too much of what was said in the Blue Room. "Good night, Madame," she said and went up to bed.

IV: The Books

SIMONE'S quarters did not exude the abundant comfort of the other rooms in the Villa Monrepos; it was a small, white-washed space with slanting roof, it was the servant's quarters. A few books stood on the chest; on the wall hung a yellowed photograph of Pierre Planchard, clipped out of *L'Humanité,* a large, badly reproduced picture. The printers' ink from the reverse side showed through. There also hung a coloured print of Saint Martin on his horse giving the beggar his coat; another print representing two bearded grenadiers of the Grande Armée, who stand guard at the open coffin of a highly coloured Napoleon while large tears roll down into their moustaches. Besides there was a fine large reproduction of the statue of the Winged Victory in the Louvre, a gift of Uncle Prosper.

Simone undressed, washed, and went to bed. She turned off the light. Downstairs the radio had been started, indistinct words, perhaps a news bulletin were audible, then again the interval signal, the two measures of the "Marseillaise": *"Aux armes, citoyens,"* also indistinctly, so that Simone could only guess at them. The alarm clock ticked softly, crickets chirped monotonously; it was hot. Simone was dead tired, but soon she became aware that she would not sleep.

The books that Père Bastide had given her lay enticingly on the chest. Should she turn on the light and read?

Madame did not like to have Simone read in bed. She did not approve of her reading at all. Madame was suspicious of all book-learning, of all "theory," and, although it was scarcely mentioned, Simone knew that Madame attributed Pierre Planchard's ruin to his exaggerated intellectualism.

Simone, for her part, would have liked to gain education and knowledge. Her teacher, Mademoiselle Rousseil, on the other hand, had regarded her as lazy and inattentive all through school. Not that Simone had been a poor pupil, but Mademoiselle Rousseil was of the opinion that, with a little more application, she could have achieved better results. But Simone was not lazy, only slow. What she mastered she grasped completely and knew how to use it.

Simone had always liked to read and Madame had always disapproved of this "mania for books." Madame had just now sent her away from her work so that she might get enough sleep, and Madame would certainly be annoyed if she should read in bed.

But Simone could not endure to be alone any longer with her thoughts in the dark, hot room. For the present Madame was detained in her conversation with Monsieur le Sous-Préfet. When she heard him leaving Simone would probably have time to turn off the light before Madame noticed it.

She switched on the light and took up Père Bastide's books.

These books all had to do with the Maid of Orleans.

Simone enjoyed reading about Joan of Arc; that pleased Père Bastide and he always gave her more books about the Maid.

Of the three books which he had given her this time, one was of fairly large format. Père Bastide had bound it in sombre, black cloth; it seemed to be scholarly and somewhat dry. The second he had daintily bound in red, with red leather back and red leather corners; it was easy to read, seemed fascinating, and was provided with many interesting illustrations. But the third was of small format, had an antique binding with much gilt and ornamentation; it was worn and had been frequently read. It seemed to be a collection of legends and moving anecdotes.

How essentially simple was the story of this girl, Joan of Arc, and how many books had been written about her. She only reached the age of nineteen, just four years more than Simone; her entire story was confined to three years and could be told in a few sentences. Nevertheless scholarship constantly added to the knowledge of Joan and her time, and constantly reinterpreted her character and her fate.

It sometimes seemed to Simone that she understood Joan of

Arc better than all the learned writers. Still she eagerly read everything she found about the Maid and the story always moved her with the same mysterious power.

She had a good, reliable memory and retained all dates.

Joan, born in 1412, the daughter of a fairly well-to-do peasant, Jacques d'Arc, in Domremy, was a gentle, cheerful child, strong and apt in farm work. But then she heard the voices of saints and set out to the Royal Governor of her district, and he sent her to the Dauphin, Charles the Seventh, to advise him according to her voices and to anoint him as king. And the Dauphin entrusted his armies to her, and with these armies she freed the besieged city of Orleans, and defeated the English, and took Troyes and other cities, and crowned the Dauphin king at Rheims, as the voices had commanded her. Then, however, she seemed undesirable to the court, and they curtailed her powers and dismissed her soldiers. And she tried to attack Paris with insufficient troops, and she was wounded, and the attack failed. And she tried to liberate the city of Compiègne, but while she was fighting outside the walls, her own partisans closed the city gate behind her and raised the drawbridge, and she was captured by the Count of Luxembourg, an ally of the English. And he sold her to the English for ten thousand pieces of silver, and they handed her over to the Inquisition for trial. And the trial took place in 1431 and lasted from January 9 to May 24. And she was sentenced to be burned alive. And that took place on May 30 of the same year, and she was nineteen years and four months old.

There lay Simone Planchard, a healthy, somewhat skinny girl of fifteen, on the good, coarse linen sheet of her bed; she lay on her stomach in her short night-gown, propped on her elbows, and read in the books about the Maid of Orleans. On the whitewashed walls about her were Saint Martin, her father, Pierre Planchard, Napoleon's grieving grenadiers, and the Goddess of Victory from the Louvre.

Since Simone was well acquainted with the story of the Maid, she did not, as usual, read page by page, but skipped about and picked out what seemed of particular interest to her.

She read of Joan's naïve pleasure in the splendour amid which she lived at the Dauphin's court. She read of the fine materials in which she was clothed, of her royal stable, of the glitter of her armour, of the costliness of her flags. The Scotch painter, Hamish Power, had painted two flags for her at the price of twenty-five livres: the large one was of white satin and represented Christ on the throne, behind Him the lilies of France; the small one showed the Annunciation, and the angel was handing a lily to the Madonna.

Simone read that Joan had been strong, rather large, but not beautiful. She inspected the picture of the Maid which she found in the red-bound, exciting book. It was a reproduction of the statue in the museum of Domremy. The book said the sculpture had not been made until several decades after Joan's death, the dress was not authentic, and the statue was crude and clumsy, without artistic worth. But Simone particularly liked this picture. Joan must have looked just like that, she imagined—a little clumsy, and not at all out of the ordinary.

Simone read that Joan, contrary to the wishes of her circle, insisted upon wearing practical, masculine clothes, trousers. She read that she frequently did not lay aside her armour for days at a stretch, that she was always with men and appreciated crude jests. On the other hand, it was repeatedly stated that this clumsy girl in masculine armour spoke with a beautiful, round, entirely feminine voice.

For a moment Simone lowered her book and pondered.

She picked up the book once more and read of the awful misery that had befallen the land in the days when Joan heard the voices. She read of the sufferings of the peasants of France. "What shall we do, we people of the soil?" they complained. "There is only one profession left: war. God is on the side of the soldiers; we can go to the Devil. What concern of ours is all this slaughter? On account of bad government and treason we must leave our wives and children and hide in the woods like wild beasts. Not a year or two but for fourteen or fifteen years this painful dance has gone on. Most of the great lords of France have died by the sword, poison, or treason, without benefit of extreme unction. We would be better off serving the Saracens than the Christians. Let us give no further heed to the orders of our masters. What can happen to us except to be captured and slain by the Godons?" That was the name they called the English, on account of the oath they constantly uttered: God damn.

And she read on: Near Meaux there stood a great elm on which the Bastard of Vauru, a nobleman from Gascogne, had all peasants hanged whom he could catch and who were not able to pay ransom. He had them tied to a horse and dragged there at a gallop. And at times he even hanged them himself.

On one occasion he caught a young peasant, tied him to his horse, and dragged him at a gallop to Meaux. Then he had him tortured. Racked with pain and in the hope of saving his bones, the young fellow promised to pay three times as much as he owned. He sent for his wife to bring the money; they had only been married that year and she was about to have a child. Since she loved her husband, she came in the hope of touching the heart of his tormentor. The Lord of Vauru said: "If you do not bring the ransom by a certain day, I will hang your husband on my elm." Cursing her fate, she raised the money as quickly as possible, but she only succeeded a week after the fixed day. The tyrant, however, had hanged her husband on his elm as soon as the day had passed, without mercy and without respite. The young woman came and asked for her husband. She wept, for she had come the long way on foot and could scarcely stand on account of her pregnancy. She fainted. When she revived she again asked for her husband. They replied: "You tramp, pay the money and we will show him to you." But as soon as she had paid the money they said: "Your husband has, of course, been hanged, like the other tramps." Then her heart was filled with such pain and rage that she broke out into wild curses. When the deceitful villain, the Bastard of Vauru, heard her imprecations he had her whipped and dragged at a gallop to his elm. There he had her stripped naked and bound. Above her in the branches some eighty to a hundred men were still hanging, some high, some low. Those dangling low touched her head every time the wind swayed them and filled her with such fear that her legs gave way. The ropes with which she was tied cut into her flesh. "My God," she cried, "when will this pain cease?" The poor, tortured creature cried so loud that she could be heard in the city of Meaux; but any one who might have gone to help her would have been killed. Amid such grievous pains night fell. And as she cried, and as she was shaken by rain and wind and cold she gave birth to her child. She screamed loudly, and the wolves scented flesh and they came and devoured the child and the mother. So this miserable creature perished and it happened in the month of March, in Lent, of the year 1420.

These were the things that Simone read about conditions in France, occupied by the enemy and his allies, at the time when Joan of Arc heard the voices.

She read about these voices. They came to Joan most often when she was in the forest. They were the voices of the Archangel Michael and, especially, the voices of Mesdames Sainte Cathérine and Sainte Marguérite.

And Simone read how Joan, obeying these voices, with the help of old Durand-Lassoir, a relative, set out to find the governor of her district, the Field Commander Robert de Baudricourt. She was wearing a poor, patched, red dress. As soon as she arrived in the castle she went fearlessly to Sire Robert and said: "I have come to you, sir, at the command of Messire, that you send word to the Dauphin he should remain quiet and not engage in battle. Before Mid-Lent Messire will send him aid."

The commander grinned. "Who is this Messire?"

"The King in Heaven," answered the Maid. "He has ordered me to lead the Dauphin to the unction and coronation. I must go to the Dauphin, even if it wears my legs off to the knees."

At this statement Sire de Baudricourt broke out into resounding laughter and told the relative to take the girl back to her father and tell him to box her ears. And when Joan refused to go, the general asked his soldiers whether they wanted to have their pleasure of her. But when the soldiers saw her, they had no inclination for her. That, Simone read, was the report of witnesses. The popular legend, however, pretended that among the brutal soldiers there was not one who dared to touch her.

Simone, with her gift of vivid imagination, pictured the scene how the great Lord Robert de Baudricourt received Joan and had her go soliciting among his soldiers, and how perhaps some Maurice tried to make indecent advances to her. And it filled her with satisfaction that the words stuck in his impudent mouth.

Then she pondered over the further course of Joan's life after she had returned home from the unsuccessful interview with the great lord. It was probably not too easy. If, for example, Simone were now to go to Madame and tell her that she was about to leave for the Congo to continue her father's work, to instruct the concessionaires how to treat the natives, Madame would certainly send her about her business. The records stated that Father d'Arc said he would rather drown Joan before he let her be a soldiers' whore. At the very least Joan's parents must have regarded their daughter as high-flown and adventurous. And her father certainly took the commander's advice and boxed her ears thoroughly.

Therefore it was probably a good thing for Joan that right after her return the enemy threatened her home, and the entire population had to seek safety in the neighbouring fortress of Neuf-Château. There her parents probably had little time to worry about her visit to the commander. And then, when the whole family returned to Domremy, they found their village almost completely burned down by the enemy. And it was not safe at all, for the enemy still lurked near by. It was not the first time that they had fled to Neuf-Château, and they expected to leave Domremy again quite soon.

At that time, too, there were fugitives in France, thought Simone. They fled, and returned to false security, and fled again. Things looked as desperate then as today. No, not as desperate. Joan did not experience such horrors as Simone did today. Or perhaps she did. That affair with the wolves. We are sold out, we poor people, they complained then as now. But Joan did not give up. "I have come to comfort the poor and humble," she said, and she believed in her mission and carried it out.

Simone read about the self-assurance with which Joan moved about the army camp, the only woman among men, a little country girl amid great lords. She read how Joan, relying upon her mission, ordered these great lords about, these Constables and Marshals, without fear of their ancient names and great titles. Withal these lords were at heart her foes from the start, envious of her successes, and not at all willing to be supplanted by her.

Simone read about the man who worked most violently against Joan, the Duke Georges de la Trémoille. He was the Dauphin's favourite and always near him. He was powerful and very wealthy, and the Dauphin was in his debt. The Sire de la Trémoille was a portly man, cruel, fond of power, at the same time a sycophant, careful in his speech, and skilled in all trickery.

Simone read that Joan had few friends in court and camp, no matter how jubilantly the people acclaimed her. These friends were mostly very young gentlemen. The most interesting among them was Gilles de Laval, called De Rais. He was the richest man of France, had the title of Maréchal, and was extremely handsome. He was regarded as the sensualist of his time, surrounded himself with proverbial splendour, passionately loved the arts; he took his orchestra, his selected choir boys, and his actors into the field with him. He was a great snob. He perfumed himself with exotic aromas; he dyed his moustache blue and thereby earned the popular nickname "Bluebeard." Simone wondered why he should have been particularly drawn to Joan and she to him. That they were good friends is certain. In camp she slept in the same tent with him and with other generals, and in Orleans, in the house of the ducal book-keeper, Jacques Boucher, she and he occupied adjoining rooms.

Suddenly Simone listened. It seemed to her she heard doors open and close. Monsieur le Sous-Préfet was probably leaving. Quickly she laid her books aside and extinguished the light.

Yes, she heard voices, but could not tell from where they came. She lay in the dark, in the heat; from without came the chirping of crickets, in the room was the ticking of the alarm clock. Simone waited for Madame to come upstairs and withdraw to her room. Then she might continue to read.

Now voices issued from the hall. And now she heard steps in the garden, and the crickets were silent.

Simone lay and waited.

V: The Commission

THE doorbell rings. Simone runs to open the door. It is Monsieur Reynault, the mailman, who wants a signature. "I'll call Madame at once," says Simone. But Monsieur Reynault makes a queer face, and: "No," he answers importantly, almost solemnly, "*you* must sign, Mademoiselle Simone," and he shows her a letter.

The letter looks like a mobilization order, but it is very large and continues to grow larger as Monsieur Reynault holds it out. The envelope is made of heavy, expensive paper, a seal hangs from it with the words, "Liberty, Equality, Fraternity"; it is the coat-of-arms of the Republic.

"That's something very important," the mailman repeats and clears his throat. "You see, it says here: 'Official Business.'" Simone looks and her heart beats violently. Allured, yet timidly, she reaches for the letter. "Is it really for me?" she asks. Monsieur Reynault stands at attention and raises his hand to his cap as he answers: "Here it stands, clearly and plainly. That has never happened to any one here before; that is a great honour for all of Saint-Martin."

Simone stands and holds the letter in her hand. The experience has given her a great scare; her knees tremble and she sits down.

She must read the letter undisturbed. It will be best if she reads it out here in the hall before Madame surprises her. She is hot with expectation, yet she hesitates. A wave of joy flows over her, but at the next moment she is oppressed with fear of the contents of the letter. Again and again she shrinks from opening it. Moreover you can't just use your finger to tear open such a valuable envelope.

But there is suddenly the large, ivory letter opener that lies on Uncle Prosper's table, and now she must not hesitate longer. She opens the letter.

The letter is written in antique characters; the initial of each paragraph is blue, red, and gold. And the letter says she is to report to the headquarters of the Dauphin on a special mission. "On a special mission" is underlined.

She trembles from head to foot and perspiration stands on her brow. To the headquarters, on a special mission. She is terribly frightened. Mademoiselle Rousseil has always said she is not a good pupil and Simone is aware that she has no special talents. "On a special mission"; how will she acquit herself?

"What kind of a special mission is that?" she asks the letter. And here it is written already, clearly and unmistakably: "Mademoiselle Planchard is to show the Dauphin where the real enemies are. Mademoiselle Planchard is to warn the Dauphin to fight these enemies. Mademoiselle Planchard shall not put her sword into its sheath until the Two Hundred Families are definitely and permanently defeated. Only then may Mademoiselle Planchard lead the Dauphin to Rheims and crown him king. Signed: The Mandator."

Simone drops the letter into her lap and sits in complete dejection on the bench in the hall. She is filled with a tremendous fear. All have perished who have tried to conquer the Two Hundred Families. Joan was burned, Jaurès was assassinated, her father was killed in the jungles of the Congo, and she is only fifteen years old, small and insignificant, a poor relative, a serving maid, who is pushed around politely, cruelly and inexorably by Madame. How shall she accomplish such a momentous commission?

The more she thinks about it the more heavily it oppresses her. Why has the Mandator chosen her, of all people? The commission rests on her like a stone, becomes heavier and heavier, and crushes her.

"From whom do you come?" she asks the letter. "And are you good or evil?" And again the letter answers. There it is plainly in a postscript: "Don't be afraid. Your loving Father."

At once the weight falls from her. She is a little fool. She should have finished reading the letter before she yielded to panic. Her father requires her to continue his work where he had to drop it. It is a disgrace that she didn't see this for herself. It really is lucky that he sent her the letter. It is a great honour. "When, if not now? And who else, if not you?"

Suddenly the truck-driver, Maurice, looks out of the garage window and grins. Of course he knows nothing. He still believes that she belongs to the Villa Monrepos where impertinence and insubordination are regarded as the worst of all crimes. She is strongly tempted to tell him about the letter. But she has pride. When she executes her commission he will see it.

But he grins harder and harder, and now he shouts something to her; she can't hear it, but she knows it is something nasty. She does not restrain herself any longer; she goes to the garage, seizes him by the sleeve of his leather jacket, and says: "Listen, Maurice, just wipe that smug smile from your face. I have received a letter from the Chancellery of the State. I am ordered to headquarters on a special mission." She says this very calmly, as though it happened every day.

Maurice is stunned for a moment; the smile vanishes from his bulky face. But then he grins again and says in his usual disdainful manner: "Tell that to your grandmother, Mademoiselle. A letter. To the headquarters. Anybody can come and say that." Simone is enraged; she reaches into her basket to show him the letter. But the letter is gone. Then the driver, Maurice, laughs; good-naturedly and contemptuously he says: "You see," and goes to the shower with his broad rolling gait.

Simone is crushed with humiliation. She can't have only imagined all that. She read the letter—the characters were blue and red and gold. She put the letter in the basket herself and the basket became quite heavy because the letter was so large and weighty. And now Maurice probably imagines that she was putting on a silly act and despises her more than ever. There he goes into the shower room and behaves as though she were not there at all, as if she were a mere nothing and leaves the door open. She does not know where to turn for shame. And to top it off Henriette looks into the window and says: "Shame, shame," and laughs at her.

Maurice stands under the shower; his whole body is covered with spray so that one can see nothing; besides, Simone did not look at all, and the waterfall says jeeringly: "Such a silly flapper. And she wants to go to the Dauphin. She ought to go back to the Villa Monrepos where she belongs." But suddenly a man enters, in slovenly dress, and he has a lean face and heavy reddish-blond hair and countless wrinkles around his shrewd blue-grey eyes. And he sits down on the bench and crosses his legs and says pleasantly to Maurice: "Listen, Monsieur, you are doing my little girl an injustice. I really sent her the letter. And now don't be stubborn, but ask her pardon, like a good fellow." Maurice has quickly wrapped himself in a bath towel. Behind it he tries to hide his shame.

But Simone is proud. He has always misjudged her, has always said derisively: "You can't tell by looking at this Simone that she is the daughter of Pierre Planchard." You couldn't tell by looking at her that she was anything but the poor niece and the little maid of the Villa Monrepos. The General de Baudricourt made dirty jokes about her and wanted to turn her over to his soldiers. But now the Mandator has picked her of all people, and now no one dares even to think of anything indecent that he would like to do with her.

She sets out for the Headquarters. The Dauphin has his headquarters in Chinon—that she knows out of her books. She knows the road well; it goes through Saulieu and Autun. But she sees at once that progress on the clogged roads is hopeless.

She clenches her teeth, she uses her elbows, she must get ahead, she has her commission. But the fugitives don't let her through; they are all against her. One especially blocks her road, stiffly and stubbornly—a boy of about fourteen. She hands him the package of Roblechon cheese that she has taken along for her lunch. But he only gives her an angry look.

She must tell the fugitives that she belongs to them; she must speak of her commission, she must show them her letter. "I have come to comfort the poor and humble"—that is what the Maid said, that is in her book. She must prevail upon the refugees to let her through.

But she cannot speak; she seems to have a gag in her mouth. Nor can she raise her head to show them the letter. And those round about her are also dumb and motionless. That is almost worse than her own muteness. The entire procession of refugees stands still as a painting: the motors do not hum, the people do not speak, the horses do not neigh. This is unbearable, this silence, this deadness in her and about her; it cramps her heart.

Where shall she get the strength to overcome such resistance? She clings to her letter. She thinks of the Mandator. She summons up her strength and lifts her foot. And behold, now she can advance it, now she can walk. She even gets ahead very quickly, the road clears, the crowds divide wherever she steps.

She has arrived; she is in Chinon.

But in her present state, perspiring and in the light green striped dress, she cannot possibly go to the Dauphin. First she must have a good wash and then she must buy a respectable suit of armour and order a flag. The flag is to cost twenty-five livres. How much is that in current money? It is hard to figure out, surely several thousand francs; but in such an important matter you must not pinch pennies.

She is a little afraid of going into the hotel alone, but she summons up her courage and at the reception desk she says in a perfectly natural manner: "A room, and everything is at the expense of the government; I am travelling on official business," and she shows her letter. The desk clerk is the one from the Hôtel Bristol in Paris from the time when she lived there with Uncle Prosper. As he sees the letter he becomes very deferential. The proprietor rushes up; it is Monsieur Berthier of the Hôtel de la Poste. He executes a bow, fitting for the richest Englishman and leads her at once to the Napoleon room. The chambermaid immediately turns back the bed; it is the one in which Napoleon once slept, but of course it has fresh linen on it. And then, exhausted by her long journey, she lies down for half an hour and closes her eyes; and the alarm clock ticks and the crickets chirp.

Then Messieurs L'Agréable et L'Utile come in to measure her for armour. Monsieur L'Agréable measures all around her. "Chest 34," he says, "Hips 32," he says, and Monsieur L'Utile diligently writes it down. At the same time he chatters interminably: "Mademoiselle shall have a top-notch suit of armour. All made to order. It's hard to do with all the iron but we know what we owe to Pierre Planchard's daughter."

Monsieur L'Agréable occasionally squeezes and feels round a little bit too much while he measures her, but she only needs to look at him; then he hums innocently to himself and pretends that it was someone else. And then they start hammering round on her to make the armour fit well. It resounds, and it is strenuous to stand up so long; moreover she is still tired from the many errands that she had to do for Madame. But finally everything is finished.

She stands in front of the mirror. Now she needs only the helmet and the flag. And here comes the flag. And it is Henriette who brings it.

That is really nice of Henriette. Henriette is vindictive, and Simone was always afraid that she had not forgotten the licking that Simone gave her when she insulted her father. But now it is plain that she is a good friend after all and that she comes when you need her. There she stands and smiles and waves the big banner and she looks exactly as she did in her coffin, very pretty and waxlike.

And then Simone tries on the helmet; it is more like a three-cornered cap such as the soldiers wear, and Henriette gives her the banner and smiles at her in the mirror.

And then Simone stands at the steps to the Headquarters. They are the steps of the Elysée and President Lebrun lives upstairs. In Paris she often passed here; her Hôtel Bristol was close by.

Sentries stop her and ask for her identification. She shows her letter and the sentries present arms and say: "Go right up, Mademoiselle. You are expected. This is a great day for France." And they look at her reverently.

Simone goes up the steps. At first it is quite easy; but the steps are endless, and now they are no longer the steps of the Elysée but those of the steeple of Notre Dame. They wind and they wind and she asks the people coming down: "How many more steps are there?" and the people reply, "Three hundred and forty-two, Mademoiselle. You really ought to know that." And she goes on climbing and when she has climbed another fifty steps she asks: "How many more steps are there?" And again they answer reproachfully: "Three hundred and forty-two." And again and again, no matter how high she climbs, there are still always three hundred and forty-two steps.

She stops, she has to catch her breath, her back hurts, she has pains in her sides. She is very much afraid that she will not reach the top.

Again she goes on, but the armour is too heavy and the flag presses her shoulder; it would have been much wiser to have ordered a cheaper, smaller flag; and she simply cannot carry the basket with the letter any longer. When she looks through the little windows she sees below the nut-brown roofs of Saint-Martin, and on them squat the gargoyles and monsters of Notre Dame, and they always remain at the same height no matter how high she climbs; they just will not sink lower. She will never arrive in time. And when the Dauphin asks her: "Why are you so late?" she will not be able to answer. Yet she started at once when she received the letter.

But there stands the Dauphin. She recognizes him by his black and silver uniform; it is the one that the deputy prefect wears at festive occasions.

"Now just sit down for a while and catch your breath, my dear little girl," says the Dauphin. He has a high, hollow voice, he looks a little absent-minded, but he has a friendly manner and does not inspire fear. "Nice of you," he continues, "that you came at once when we sent for you. Did you get my letter all right? I was afraid it might get lost; the conditions in the country are so bad now, in the Postal Administration, too. We need you very badly, Mademoiselle."

She talks with him as with an equal. "You knew my father, gracious Dauphin, didn't you?" she asks trustingly. And: "Of course," replies the Dauphin. "I used him a great deal, he rendered me important services. But then, when I sent him to the Congo, he didn't come back. That is mysterious. My police have been unable to find out anything. I fear they are corrupt, too. Between you and me, I believe the Two Hundred Families, the gentlemen of my Banque de France, and my big industrialists and the nobility had him poisoned because the results of his investigations displeased them. I am always having trouble with the Two Hundred Families, especially with Family Number 97. All they can think of is poison and concentration camps; all they can think of is fire and sword against the poor people. It is not my fault. I should so much like to earn the surname, 'the Well Beloved.' If it goes on like this, however, I shall always have to remain simply Charles the Seventh."

Simone looks at him kindly, almost sympathetically. Monsieur Xavier told her the truth: the Dauphin is at heart decent, only he is undecided, weak, and cannot carry out his good intentions.

She is just about to say something comforting and encouraging to him when the telephone rings. Annoyance on his tired, sad face with the surprised eyebrows, the Dauphin lifts the receiver and begins a conversation. It is endless, and he is speaking in a strange language. At first Simone believes it to be Latin, but then it seems to be either English or German. She is very anxious to know with whom he is speaking. It is probably one of the gentlemen of the big monopolies. They have many ears; they know everything. Very likely they have gotten wind of this audience and would like to sabotage it. Now she is almost sure that she hears the creaking voice of the Châtelain in the telephone, the wicked General La Trémoille who would like to overthrow her so that his wines will reach Bayonne safely. She listens hard. But then the Dauphin interrupts his conversation, looks at her angrily and says: "Don't be impertinent," and she is ashamed of herself and blushes.

Finally, he hangs up the receiver, sighing, and turns to her again. And now it's up to her. Now Simone must fulfil her commission and get his consent to a fight to the finish against the

Two Hundred Families; and in this fight there will be only victory or death.

She stands there and considers the best way of persuading the weak, evasive Dauphin to make a clear-cut decision. But while she stands there and thinks, she sees to her dismay that he has obviously forgotten that she is here. He has seated himself and has begun to eat his crêpes suzette. She comes closer to him to remind him of her presence. Then all at once she recognizes that his right ear is pointed at the top and strangely thickened and a great terror seizes her.

But she must not lose heart so quickly. She thinks of her great mission and makes a start. "Gracious Dauphin," she declares resolutely, "things can't go on as in the past. You must tackle your Two Hundred Families quite differently. The way you do things you'll never get anywhere with them. They are smart devils, downright crooks. There's no question that they would prefer a Hitler, who gives them a 60-hour week, to a king of France, who promises his people a chicken in every pot and a 40-hour week. There's no sense in making nice Latin speeches about liberty to those birds. You have to give them a good trimming. You simply have to forbid the export of capital, and the Comité des Forges must not peddle its steel to the Boches any longer. That's the very least I demand of you. Yes, indeed, that's the way it is; don't look so surprised. I have come to comfort the poor and humble. You mustn't only plunder the poor people all the time, gracious Dauphin. You must also exploit the rich for a change. You have to smoke them out. Everybody at the loading yard says that, especially the driver, Maurice, and he knows the exact figures. If you don't do that ʸou'll be sold out in the end, just like we."

The Dauphin is displeased. "That's not for me," he says. "I'm not interested in matters of economy; that's what the experts are for. I am the king and I have to act the part. Shoemaker, stick to your last. I speak many languages. Didn't you hear me telephone in Latin a while ago? But if I tried to teach my gentlemen of the Banque de France their business, that would be impertinent. No, no, you take your request to the driver, Maurice, of whom you seem to think so much. Here you're barking up the wrong tree," he concludes sulkily.

Simone reproaches herself. She did not intend to offend the Dauphin. He means well, only he is so cautious because he is dependent upon Madame. He is good to look at as he sits there with his thick reddish-blond hair, his fine blue-grey eyes and the bushy brows. And he has always been especially kind to her, the Dauphin. How much attention he showed her during their stay together in Paris!

Now he seems to regret that he answered her so indignantly. "You know, little one," he resumes and speaks familiarly with her as with an adult, "that business of the Two Hundred Families is not as simple as your Maurice thinks. They are full of fight, especially Family Number 97, and if I am too strict with them they make use of their international connexions and, first thing you know, I'll lose my royal salary."

But now Simone has overcome her attack of unwarranted sympathy. She seizes her banner more firmly—it is now the red flag of Jaurès—she plants herself resolutely in front of the Dauphin, and with a very definite tone in her fine, deep voice she advises him: "Punch them in the nose, gracious Dauphin. If you just give your cursed Two Hundred Families what's coming to them, you'll see how fast they'll come to heel. After all, these gentlemen are not only business men, but also Frenchmen."

This argument, however, is of no avail with the Dauphin. "Frenchmen," he repeats with weary irony, "Frenchmen. France. What is that, France? There are as many Frances as there are classes. My peasants and my workers and my Two Hundred Families, they all speak to me of France all the time, and each one means something else. This much I know: my Two Hundred, when they say France, mean higher profits and lower taxes."

Simone stands in front of the Dauphin, fervently, ardently. To overcome this slackness, this despondency, that is her duty. She must transform this Joe Blow into King Charles the Seventh of

France. That is why the Mandator sent her the letter. "No," she calls to him. "You must not say such things. You must not even think such things. France is not an empty word, you know that very well." She points at her flag and enunciates in a clear voice: "Our fatherland, France, grew out of centuries of common suffering and common longing. To be sure there is class war, sharp social contrast, but that does not change the concept of the fatherland."

These words make a visible impression on the Dauphin. He walks up and down with brisk, manly steps, so that the crimson robe over the black and silver uniform streams behind. "You are very eloquent, Joan," he says and looks at her approvingly.

Simone blushes; he seems to believe the sentences were her own. She must not permit that; she must not strut in borrowed finery. "But that's not mine," she says earnestly. "That's by Jaurès."

"But the effect comes from your beautiful voice," answers the Dauphin and pets her in a friendly manner. And: "You're going to the front," he announces magnificently and fondles her once more.

Simone is embarrassed that the Dauphin pets her. But her embarrassment changes to satisfaction. So it made no difference that she was skinny as a hound. She succeeded in getting this difficult man to make up his mind.

Then she is at the front.

All the generals that she has read about in books are there, the Constables, the Marshals, the admirals. Negotiating with them is easier than she had expected. She talks right ahead according to her lights, and no one takes offence that she doesn't know the rules of etiquette that are customary among these gentlemen of great names and titles.

It is much more difficult to prevail upon them actually to wage war. Simone knows exactly what is to be done and she states it clearly, and the generals say yes. And then nothing happens. Everything is done differently; they say they didn't understand her; she talks herself hoarse, and they simply will not understand her. She senses that they all oppose her. Surely many of the generals have been bought by the Two Hundred Families and would rather have the Nazis win. She knows it, but how can she prove it?

Moreover she sees with her own eyes how some of these gentlemen are constantly trafficking with the lawyers. The attorneys come, clad in their black robes and caps and white neck-frills; and there is Maître Levautour, too, who, with his trickery, was her father's downfall. He acts very importantly now, also. Fat, oily, well dressed, he goes from one general to another. In front of his fat stomach hangs the copper shingle with the inscription: "Charles-Marie Levautour, Attorney and Notary," in the first place, so that everybody may know who he is, and in the second place, because it saves him the cost of a suit of armour. Simone asks him sternly: "What do you want here, Monsieur?" He replies, however: "But, Mademoiselle, the Duke de la Trémoille, the Field Marshal, has personally deigned to send for me," and he shows her his huge universal passport.

The Duke de la Trémoille smiles with malicious friendliness. Of course, she knew all the time that he is really the Marquis. She whispers it to the Dauphin and tells him that this fascist is making deals with the gentlemen of the steel monopoly across the Rhine, and that he lets the English sign over the best vineyards to him as a bribe. But: "What do you expect me to do, Mademoiselle?" asks the Dauphin. "If I were to throw out all who are crooked, . . ." and he shrugs his shoulders eloquently.

Simone looks for the faces of her few friends. She knows them well; she knows from her books who are her true friends. But one is missing, one whom she was most eager to see. That is Gilles de Rais, the great, infamous, pampered sensualist, with his choir boys and actors and many women and books. He simply isn't there and Simone hesitates to ask the others.

She will ask Henriette. She has always asked Henriette about great secrets: how it is about men, and how you get children, and Henriette always whispered and knew the answers. She knows this time, too. "He is here at the Headquarters," she whispers. "He is very curious about you; he'll be here presently."

And there he comes now; you can recognize him by his blue

moustache. He strolls over from the garage with a rolling stride. He's probably coming from the shower; he takes very good care of himself and certainly takes seven or eight showers a day, and he smells like Monsieur Armand's barber shop. But really he smells more like leather. That's because he is wearing a leather jacket.

The sight of this jacket is a blow to Simone. Of course she guessed that it was the driver, Maurice, and in a moment he will make one of his dirty remarks.

He stops in front of her. Brazenly he rests his hand on his hip, looks her up and down, and says: "Well, young lady, how's everything? How about a little moonlight stroll? But, of course, Mademoiselle won't go out with the likes of me. She belongs to the other crowd, to the Villa Monrepos."

Now she ought to tell him plainly that she has come to comfort the poor and humble. But she can't do it. She wasn't a bit afraid of the great generals. But in front of this man she can't open her mouth. She stands there in great distress and everybody waits to hear her answer, and Gilles de Rais stands impudently in front of her with his heavy face, his arm propped on his hip, and the generals smile at her embarrassment, and if she doesn't say something quickly she can kiss her authority good-bye for ever.

But presently Etienne takes a hand. Without ado, with more courage than she had expected of him, he steps up to Gilles de Rais and says to him: "What do you wish of this lady, Monsieur? Have you ever been introduced to her?" He looks terribly young beside the huge Gilles de Rais; after all he is only a little boy of sixteen, very thin, although very tall, and Gilles de Rais will probably not stand for his conduct.

But no, Gilles de Rais doesn't think of starting a row. He laughs, puts his arm about Etienne's shoulder, and says genially: "But, my dear friend, doesn't she belong to the Villa Monrepos? You belong where you sleep. And where does she sleep?"

And then they all go to sleep. Simone sleeps in the same tent with several generals; that is customary at the front. She is glad that she is wearing her green slacks, without regard to Madame

who thinks that that is improper in war-time. But if she had on
a skirt during the night, in the tent with all these men, that
would be highly embarrassing.

Simone is very tired. There was so much work today, the errands for Madame, the discussions with the Dauphin, the work
in the garden, and the Council of War. She is afraid she might
snore and that might create unfavourable comment. She notices
that the generals do not snore. That is natural; as gentlemen
they have learned not to snore. However, they are constantly
pitching from one side to the other because it is uncomfortable
to sleep in full armour, and their armour jangles, and through
the jangling her snoring probably could not be heard anyhow.

She feels that she will have to step out right away. That is embarrassing; the generals will probably all look after her, just as
the men do when you go to the powder-room in the Café Napoleon. She wishes she could at least take Henriette with her; it is
always better when two go out together, but unfortunately Henriette is not there. So she sneaks out alone, softly and inconspicuously through the ranks of the sleepers, but she cannot keep her
armour from clanking. At once they all wake up, and Gilles de
Rais twists his blue moustache and smiles. But luckily Etienne is
there again. And he says to her: "Don't be scared, Simone. If he
makes a dirty remark, I'll beat him to a pulp."

Simone stretches. The crickets chirp and the alarm clock ticks.
Simone rolls over on the other side.

Then it is daylight and there is a battle and Simone is in the
midst of it with her banner. The tanks approach lurching clumsily, all enemy tanks; there must be many thousands of them
and they are all built of French steel. The sky is black with
enemy aeroplanes and they are all built of French aluminum. But
Simone waves her flag and no matter how many enemy tanks
come, the poor people of France do not yield, and if hundreds
are crushed down, two hundred more arise, and Simone continues to wave her flag.

And then there is a council of war, a very great council of
war. Uncle Prosper's private office is not large enough; the room
grows and grows—it is the Deputy Prefecture, then Saint-Lazare

church, then Notre Dame. The Dauphin presides, again in his black and silver uniform. Tall and lean, he sits there, slightly stooped, looks at the assemblage with his pale, helpless eyes, and fingers his rosette. All the generals whom Simone knows are there, even Marshal Pétain, and, of course, not only the generals but also Monsieur Berthier of the Hôtel de la Poste, and Messieurs Amiot and Laroche and Raimu and Peyroux; and Monsieur Grasset of the Café Napoleon goes from one to the other, bows, and asks about their health. Again there are countless lawyers in their black robes and caps and naturally Maître Levautour is present also. They are constantly running in and out and show scripts to each other, and talk importantly to the generals, and bring them documents and checks, and whisper.

The Dauphin opens the session with a speech in Latin. He reports that Mademoiselle Planchard, at her father's behest, wishes the war to be waged energetically to an end without delay. He says many learned things and opens the subject for debate. At once the Duke de la Trémoille rises, and this time the Marquis is particularly unpleasant. "No one can admire your genius more than I, Mademoiselle," he says in his creaking voice and switches his riding crop against his boots. "But the art of war is subject to laws that cannot be learned overnight, while our ancestors have laboriously studied them for centuries. It would be simple enough just to attack all the time. But even my great ancestor, before he defeated the enemy on the Catalonian fields, first wore him down with a carefully and subtly planned policy of non-intervention. 'Make haste slowly' is the motto of all military experts. Isn't that your opinion, Field Marshal?" he turns to General Pétain. And the old general rises, and with his cracked, venerable voice he announces: "Yes, comrade. We are done for, we must surrender. That's what I said in the Hundred Years' War, that's what I said at Verdun, and that's what I sav now. I'll pledge my military word of honour on that."

And immediately Maître Levautour rises and declares with feigned regret: "Mademoiselle has inherited that impetuosity from her father. And she is wearing her dark green slacks again, too. In spite of the fact that Madame has expressly declared that slacks are improper in war. But Simone simply has no respect for high traditions. It is her nature to be impertinent. Her late father, too, is dead and gone as a result of his impertinence."

And they all crowd around the Dauphin and they all whisper eagerly in his ear and the people from Saint-Martin, Messieurs Amiot and Laroche and Messieurs L'Utile and L'Agréable and all the others look with disapproval at Simone; but Uncle Prosper says distantly: "I am a business man and as such reserve my vote."

Simone feels left alone. Again she experiences how enormously difficult it is to fulfil her mission and to protect the poor people against the powerful union of the Two Hundred Families and the two million small investors. Constantly they crawl round the Dauphin and whisper in his ear, from the right side and from the left and from above and below. And his face grows continually more tired and his eyes paler and paler and his brows higher and higher, and now he turns to her and says: "I hear we have no more money to continue the war. If we continue to fight, I would have to order new taxes, and of course the poor people would have to pay them. The Two Hundred Families tell me that they are bled white and cannot possibly pay more." And: "Entirely impossible, out of the question," protest the Duke de la Trémoille and the Notary Levautour and all the Two Hundred Families, but loudest of all Family Number 97. And the two million small investors scream bloody murder and throw four million defending hands up into the air. And Marshal Pétain stands there, old as the hills and awe-inspiring and: "Always surrender," he demands.

"There, you see," says the grieved Dauphin to Simone, and plays with the rosette of the Legion of Honour. "France doesn't want to fight. France wants to end the war."

But there Gilles de Rais steps in. He puts his hand on his hip and declares: "France, gracious Dauphin? What you see there is not France. The France of these gentlemen is not ours," and his voice sounds especially clear and squeaky. And Père Bastide steps forward; small and sprightly he walks up and down, his valiant head high with his ruddy face and the shimmering white hair and quotes lines from Victor Hugo and the sentences of Jean Jaurès. Yet they all only smile with pity and shake their heads and say: "Poor fellow, he is getting senile."

But Simone is enraged. She knows that Père Bastide is right in spite of the fact that he is old and maybe a little foolish and she knits her brow and frowns at the Dauphin and says: "You should be ashamed of yourself, gracious Dauphin. You certainly know that France is something different from what these people are talking about," and she makes a scornful gesture at the Two Hundred Families and the small investors. "The Two Hundred Families are the ones who have bled the country. They catch the farmers and if they cannot pay the mortgage, they hang them on the elm tree until the wolves come. And you should certainly not listen at all to this poisonous Notary Levautour." But now Maître Levautour gets very excited and pushes forward and many other lawyers with him. All at once the whole cathedral of Notre Dame is full of them; their black robes flutter, one sees nothing but their black robes and white frills, and Simone becomes fearfully aware that many of them have heads like birds and if one looks closely they are the gargoyles on the roof of Notre Dame, all dressed up in robes and caps.

But Maître Levautour pulls out a large paper from under his copper shield and announces in a croaking, birdlike voice: "This is a peace offer from the enemy. It just arrived. It is very favourable. It would be a crime to refuse this offer and to continue the war. France wants peace," he screams with his croaking bird's voice, and all the monsters from Notre Dame flutter with their black robes and croak in unison: "France wants peace." And the Dauphin looks very tired and very yielding and he shrugs his shoulders regretfully and in a moment he will say: "All right, let's make peace."

But now Simone grips her flag and plants herself firmly and shouts: "France wants peace?" and she feels that the whole cathedral resounds with the furious contempt in her voice. And she faces the lawyers and the Two Hundred Families and the two million small investors and she bursts out: "France? What do you know about France?" And all at once she can express what she has never been able to put into words before. All at once she knows exactly what France is and she can say it. The lawyers look at her fearfully with their birds' faces and hack at her with their sharp, gigantic beaks, and the Two Hundred Families rattle their swords against their golden armour, and the small investors raise a shrill, wailing howl that penetrates to the very marrow, and behind them appears Uncle Prosper with a frightened, imploring face, and farther back the fat masklike face of Madame stares horribly. Yet Simone does not fear any one or anything; she does not even fear to hurt Uncle Prosper. She has the mission to give strength to the Dauphin so he will not weaken and make a tragic peace, and she knows now what she must say, she knows now what France is.

She starts to speak. She is not prepared, she does not know what she will say next; at times she does not even know in what language she is speaking. But she knows that now the words come easily, that it is now given to her to speak with a gift of tongues.

She speaks of the Two Hundred Families. Here is this noble vineyard, France, and then they came, the vermin, and moved into this lovely vineyard, and they ravaged it, and they attracted all the rest of the vermin in the world. "Do not tolerate it," Simone shouts. "Smoke them out. And if there is no other way, then tear out the infected vines, root and branch, and burn them, and save the beautiful vineyard, France. Do not spare the axe, do not spare the fire."

Simone speaks with dark and ardent fervour, and all fall silent; and Mademoiselle Rousseil, her teacher, is there, and at first she shakes her head violently, but then she becomes quiet and listens with enthusiasm. And the foes become smaller and smaller; Madame's bulky face disappears, and the two million investors drop their hands, and the golden armour of the Two Hundred Families fades, and the lawyers draw in their black robe-wings and silently sneak back to the roof of the cathedral.

More and more exalted faces Simone sees about her. All her friends are suddenly present; Etienne looks up to her admiringly, and Père Bastide's ruddy, wrinkled face shines with joy, and Gilles de Rais twirls his moustache and says in his high, squeaky voice: "Oh lala, she really did give it to them. Now their goose is cooked. Now you can tell that she is Pierre Planchard's daughter."

And the Dauphin has his crimson coat on again, and his face is very manly and his eyes are grey-blue and they gleam under his bushy, reddish-blond brows, and with ringing voice he proclaims: "You have convinced me, my dear Simone. Of course I'll give you the money and the troops. And I don't care what Madame says."

And then the advance begins, and Simone is in the very first tank. But before her floats a great, bright figure; it flies ahead impetuously, its dress billowing with the speed of flight. And Simone sees that it is her goddess, her Winged Goddess of Victory. But this time she will not let her escape; now she has the opportunity to see her head and to find out who she is. Simone trembles with impatience. She forces her tank to its highest speed, but the clumsy vehicle rocks and lurches and cannot catch up with the flying figure. Sometimes Simone almost reaches her, but the goddess has only slowed her flight to accelerate it more than ever. It is plain—the winged creature is teasing Simone. But now at last she turns her head in flight, she smiles at Simone, almost sportively, and—Simone knew it all the time—it is the pale, delicate head of Henriette.

A great bliss fills Simone, a happiness that almost breaks her heart. She feels light as a bird; she feels—victory; she feels—France; she feels—Liberty, Equality, Fraternity.

And then she is sitting in a movie, watching the newsreel. She watches a serpentine arrow on the screen that marks her advance from one town to another; she watches children exultant with joy because they have a school holiday on account of her victory; she watches all the world putting little flags on maps to mark the places she has taken, and they have to move the flags so quickly that they can't keep up with her. But Simone sits in the very last row of the movie theatre and sees all that, and hides, hot with joy.

And then the alarm clock ticks more and more loudly and

finally grows into a tremendous tolling of bells. That is because the Dauphin is being crowned in the cathedral at Rheims. The cathedral is badly riddled from shell-fire, and the sun shines through the roof, and every one perspires in his Sunday clothes. But that makes no difference. The bells ring, the aeroplanes fly through the blue, the crickets chirp, the band plays the "Marseillaise," and all join in singing.

But Simone stands there in her armour and her dark green slacks, and waves her banner. Now it is clear that it was a good idea to pay the twenty-five livres and not pinch pennies.

She looks round for her acquaintances. Sure enough, there comes Gilles de Rais, and he plants his fist on his hip and says: "You belong to us, Mademoiselle. I have misjudged you. Pardon me."

She is very curious whether Uncle Prosper is here. Madame will certainly have forbidden him to attend. But there he is. He has a proud, sly, embarrassed look on his face, and he comes closer, and stealthily plants a cheerful slap on her dark green slacks. And she is a little confused, but very glad that he came.

He beams at her with his radiant, grey eyes amid the many little wrinkles, and with a sweet shock she sees that it is not Uncle Prosper at all, but her father, Pierre Planchard. And her father says: "You did very well, baby. I am satisfied with you. You are really my daughter." And she is unbelievably happy, happier than a human dares to be.

PART TWO

ACTION

I: The Incident at the Bridge

SIMONE sat on a stool in the kitchen, a little stooped over, her thin, strong hands in her lap. As usual she had taken her noon meal in the kitchen with Madame; then Madame had retired while Simone washed the dishes. Now she was finished and, for the first time in many days, had nothing to do. She did not need to go to town as on other afternoons; there was nothing to order, nothing to pick up. The coming hours belonged to her.

That was an unaccustomed sensation. With an empty, slightly astonished look on her face she sat and stared absently into the garden, which lay there well tended and pretty in the glare of the noonday sun.

Then sharply and suddenly came a realization of this strange condition. There she sat idly; about her was the quiet, well-ordered house, before her lay the beautiful, peaceful garden, every shrub cared for, every rose protected, while all France round about was shattered and bruised.

So she sat for quite a while. She could not grasp this novel situation of being unhurried, of having no chore that had to be finished in a brief space. Finally she rose and stretched, and went up to her room.

Up here it was stifling in the early afternoon. She sat down on the edge of her bed. In front of her, on the chest, lay her books, the three which Père Bastide had given her on top. Should she read? She stretched out her hand but then hesitantly withdrew it.

She was almost dissatisfied that there were no errands in town today. To sit here and wait was unbearable, while the country teemed with wild, great happenings. In the city one was so much closer to everything. The things one saw and heard there were painful, but it was worse not to see and hear anything.

Madame apparently considered it self-evident that she would stay at home today. But suppose she went over to the city after all? Suppose she tried on her own to make a few purchases? They were almost out of pepper, and a few cans of condensed milk would be useful, too. Perhaps she might find something at the Café Napoleon or at Beaumont's. So she decided to go to the city.

Having decided to act on her own initiative, she became bolder. Madame regarded the wearing of slacks in these times as improper. But who would pay any attention to that now, in the midst of this general dissolution? And besides, slacks were much more convenient; you could get through the crowds more easily, you felt safer. Simone took the slacks from the closet.

These dark green slacks were a gift from Uncle Prosper; he had brought them along for her from a trip to Cannes. The slacks had been too large for her; she had had to grow into them. From the beginning Madame looked at them with displeasure, but since they were a gift from her son, she was reluctant to interfere. Simone had worn them only a few times, for when the war broke out Madame had a welcome pretext for prohibiting the wearing of the slacks.

Today, however, without regard to Madame's wishes, Simone took out the dark green slacks and put them on. Then she picked up her large wicker basket and went to town.

She went through the narrow, winding, hilly lanes. Every stone of the old colourful houses was familiar to her; even the fugitives who wandered through the streets in busy idleness were no longer a novelty; and yet the city seemed somehow changed today. Most of the former inhabitants were no longer there. They had left the city to which they belonged like the stones and the gay façades and the sloping, nut-brown roofs. Simone had been accustomed to an exchange of greetings with them, to a few casual words. These words generally had meant little or nothing, but today Simone felt the pain of not being able to give and to receive these meaningless phrases.

Suddenly there came a report which drove those that had remained in the city out of their houses; and now it appeared that there were still some of them.

The news which drove them out into the streets was the message of the horrible incident at the bridge across the Cerein River.

The road across this bridge was the only one which led to Highways 7 and 77. For hours the crowds stood before the bridge and on it, closely jammed, hopelessly entangled. They were always full of fear that German flyers might dive down upon them here, but those who had declared that there was no danger here had, so far, always been right. The district was strategically unimportant, military actions were not to be expected, and the cities had not yet been bombed. Notwithstanding that, German flyers had now been there and had shot at the fugitives on the bridge. The result had been fearful. No one knew how many were dead; it was only known that there were many. And the wounded were in a bitter plight. The ambulances proceeded very slowly on the crowded roads, the hospitals were hopelessly overfilled, the wounded had to be transported as far as the region of Nevers.

That the war had in this way come into the immediate vicinity of Saint-Martin sent the inhabitants who had decided to remain into a new panic. There was general talk of blowing up the bridge across the Cerein River. If that were done the city was definitely cut off from the southbound roads and the people were trapped. Many had weighed the arguments for and against flight a hundred times and had finally decided to remain. Now they weighed them again. Wouldn't it be wiser after all to leave like Messieurs Amiot and Laroche and many others? The choice remained open for only another day, perhaps only hours. They asked themselves, they asked the others, every one asked every one else, they even asked Simone.

In her mind there was no doubt. If they fled they only stopped up the highways and hindered the troops. They would have to stay. So far there was still hope that the Boches could be kept away from Saint-Martin, and, if not, the people of Saint-Martin could be more useful here than anywhere in the south.

Simone perceived that the incident at the bridge affected the refugees in a different manner than the inhabitants. In past days the fugitives had had only one wish, to get along, the farther the better, in the direction of safety. Gradually, however, this wish was strangled in grim resignation. The incident at the bridge confirmed the embittered indifference of the refugees. It was senseless to crawl farther, it was immaterial where they awaited the Germans; danger was everywhere. The incident at the bridge only proved anew that they were in greater danger on the road than here in Saint-Martin. To be sure there was nothing to eat, to be sure all necessities of life were lacking, but still they decided to remain. Indeed, having passed two or even three nights here, they had almost come to love the miserable little spot which stood at their disposal. They were familiar with the straw bedding in the corridor of the Hall of Justice or with the little corner of the Place du Général Gramont. They did not want to go farther.

They sat in front of the cafés, the refugees, under the red and orange awnings, in the sultry heat. They drank their brandy or wine; they dozed or talked wearily, always the same things.

Simone walked with her basket across the platform of the Café Napoleon. The tall girl with the wilful, tanned face did not look unattractive in the dark green slacks, and the men looked after her. She squeezed through between the tables and listened to what was said.

At one of the tables they were arguing when the Germans would come. No one could know anything about it but every one held wearily and tenaciously to his opinion. One of them declared they could not possibly arrive here in less than four days; they had more important things to do than to occupy this strategically unimportant region. Another maintained that they were unbelievably fast and thorough, and if they advanced along roads 7 and 77, they would certainly also occupy this eastern portion. A third, an elderly man, said that it was entirely out of the question for the Germans to come here at all; not only the Maginot Line but also our positions on the western Loire were completely impregnable and the Germans could certainly not scatter their troops by sending some of them here. The others remained silent and contented themselves with making incredulous faces. But one of them said: "If they were only here now, so that this miserable waiting and wondering would stop."

Meanwhile new rumours about the incident at the bridge were constantly circulating. Every one contradicted every other one. Numbers were quoted. There were 214 dead, one man reported, and they had counted 89 ambulances. Another, with a very virile face, asserted that there had been 168 dead and 98 ambulances. The first clung to his figures, the second, morose and angry, to his; they were actually on the point of fighting about it.

Simone stood and listened quietly but intensely.

Across the platform came a young fellow, tall and lanky, with a long, broad-browed, pointed face. Simone's heart leapt; Etienne had come into town. At the same moment he saw her and pressed through between the tables towards her. Red with joy and a little awkwardly he took her hands in both of his and urgently asked her to sit down with him inside the café.

That was an unusual, an unheard-of invitation. But it was also unusual that she had gone away from home without telling Madame, and it was unheard of that she was loitering about on the platform of the Café Napoleon, alone and in dark green slacks. The times were to blame for it. She did not hesitate to accept Etienne's invitation.

The interior of the Café Napoleon was dusky, almost dark; it was empty and after the heat outside it was pleasantly cool. You could see the platform with its red and orange awning and beyond it the square, basking in the glare of the sun, and you could hear the subdued noise of the platform and the square. The two young people sat at the little marble-topped table, each with a glass of apple cider. They were good friends, they belonged together, and dusk and coolness stood about them like a protecting wall.

Even in peaceful times the face of the sixteen-year-old Etienne was thoughtful. Today he looked troubled and he found it hard to speak as precisely and sedately as usual.

He had come over from Chatillon with great difficulty be-

cause he did not want to leave his parents alone. His parents had
no idea what to do. At one moment they thought they should
leave by all means; the next moment they were just as sure that
they should stay; and when Father was in favour of remaining,
Mother argued for leaving. They packed; they found they had
packed the wrong things; they repacked; they decided to remain; they unpacked again.

It was unbearable, he said, and moved his head close to hers.
"I myself, just between you and me, I have hesitated a long time
what to do," he confessed. "I have more reason to run away than
the others. They all say that the Boches are thorough and carefully investigate whether civilians of military age are not actually soldiers who have exchanged their uniforms for civilian
clothes. They lock up countless civilians who appear suspicious
to them, and when they once have you, they will scarcely let you
go. I look older than I am," he continued with a mixture of
pride and dejection. "I don't want to be caught by the Boches.
I don't feel very safe here."

He looked straight at Simone and something like a smile ran
over his face. "Now I know what I will do," he said with sudden decision. "It is strange; since we have sat here together I
know it. I will not be driven to panic. I am staying. Perhaps
something can still be done when the Boches come."

Simone's heart grew warm at his words. There they sat together and spoke together like people who made their own decisions and who had to find their own way. With her large dark
eyes she looked kindly at him and: "Of course you must stay,"
she said eagerly, "and certainly you will be able to do something
here. But it has not come to that by a long shot," she continued
almost furiously; she had to make an effort to lower her ringing
voice. "There is still the Maginot Line, and our positions on the
western Loire are impregnable. At the Marne, in the last war, we
were in a much worse fix before the great victory came." She
spoke forcefully and with conviction.

Etienne looked at her with friendship and respect. For quite
a while they said nothing. From outside came the subdued noise
of the talking of the refugees and the clinking of glasses. Some-

one had turned on the radio and again and again came the two measures of the "Marseillaise": *"Aux armes, citoyens."*

"I dreamed about Henriette last night," Simone suddenly began. She did not wish to say that but she couldn't help it. He, Etienne, and Henriette had always played together in the Parc des Capucins when they were children; they had had innumerable secrets together; these three had been an inseparable group among the others. Henriette had tormented her awkward brother, she had mocked him in the presence of Simone; he had put up with it and had looked up to her as a creature out of a more delicate and more alert world. He and Simone had again and again exchanged thoughts of love and admiration about this strange creature Henriette. Since her death, however, as though by agreement, they had avoided talking about her.

Now Simone unexpectedly related: "Last night I dreamed about Henriette." Etienne looked up and glanced at her attentively. "I rarely think of her," Simone continued, "but sometimes I dream about her. Just imagine, last night I dreamed that Henriette was Joan of Arc."

Etienne drank his apple cider. "Strange," he said. She waited for him to ask questions; she wished it, she dreaded it. But he did not pursue the subject. "Do you still have such a hard time at home?" he asked instead.

"Yes," she answered, "it is not always easy."

"You are a brave girl," said Etienne. "The true daughter of Pierre Planchard." She blushed.

They left. He accompanied her a short distance. They passed the Palais Noiret where the Deputy Prefecture was housed. A long line of refugees stood in front of the beautiful, old portal; three policemen stood guard.

Simone was not infected by the panic round her. But she wanted a confirmation of her faith. If any one could have reliable information about the actual events, then it would be her friend up here, the secretary of the Deputy Prefecture, Monsieur Xavier Bastide.

Monsieur Xavier had the ruddy face and alert, good-natured brown eyes of his father. It was Simone's opinion that he also had his stormy temperament, but he had noticed in his early youth how much misunderstanding and unpleasantness this temperament brought his father, and he had made every effort to curb his own impetuosity. He had succeeded. When he walked about in the Deputy Prefecture with sedate step, very well but inconspicuously dressed, always wearing sleeve protectors, and when he listened thoughtfully to the arguments of litigants, he did not look like a man who, in the depth of his character, was like his father. Simone particularly admired him on account of the strength with which he restrained his violent temper.

Monsieur Xavier had gone to school with Pierre Planchard and Charles-Marie Levautour. He fought against Levautour with the same fervour with which he had loved and honoured Pierre Planchard, and he was very fond of Simone.

Simone saw the long line of waiting refugees. She was well aware that Monsieur Xavier would be very busy today. But she longed to hear his friendly, ironic voice and she hoped that he would have time for her even today.

She bade Etienne good-bye and succeeded without difficulty in entering the Deputy Prefecture.

Confusion reigned behind the fine peaceful façade of the old Palace. Although the portal was well guarded, the doors of the offices within were open; every one had access to all offices and the fugitives went from one official to another. The officials urged them to leave the city. There were no longer any provisions to be had, and they should try to get farther south where the supplies were more plentiful. Moreover, the roads were less crowded than before and the rumours that the Germans were already beyond the Yonne or even in Le Creusot were pure nonsense. The fugitives, however, were gloomy and suspicious. In order to get farther they would have to cross the bridge over the Cerein River, and the officials were powerless against the terror which the catastrophe at the bridge had caused. "You simply want to get rid of us," the people said. "It is all the same to you if we get knocked off at the bridge."

The deputy prefect, Monsieur Cordelier, walked about anxiously amid the crowd and confusion, absently trying to comfort the people. But they did not want general comfort; they wanted bread and lodging for the night, they wanted milk for the infants, medicine for the sick. Simone knew that the deputy prefect would have liked to help them, but she also knew that he could not and that he was just as helpless as the people themselves.

Simone was well aware that it was not Monsieur Cordelier but Monsieur Xavier who actually took care of the business of the Deputy Prefecture. Unfortunately, however, Monsieur Xavier had very little authority; he had to content himself with carrying on a quiet, tenacious battle against the weakness of his superior, and it grieved him that he accomplished so little with so much effort.

Simone went into his office. He smiled at her but indicated by a gesture that he was busy. He was arguing with a police officer. He seemed a little astonished that she remained but he apparently had no objections. Moreover, there were three other people in the office, obviously fugitives, who were standing against the wall and listening. Simone joined them.

It appeared that the police officer, with his men, traffic officials from Paris, was on the way south. The Paris officers were noted for their training and ability. The officer had been ordered to assign men at particularly dangerous points in order to direct traffic. Monsieur Xavier wanted him to leave two officers at the Cerein bridge. If that were done, he argued, a part of the refugees could be persuaded finally to leave Saint-Martin. The community was no longer in a position to supply the barest necessities. The fugitives had to leave but they were afraid of the bridge.

The police officer was unwilling to leave any of his men. He had only a small number at his disposal, and although he had considerable authority, his orders were to regulate traffic farther in the south. Moreover, he feared that any men whom he left here would eventually fall into the hands of the Germans. In his elegant, rapid Parisian he uttered many objections, and he looked at his watch repeatedly; he was in a hurry.

Simone stood quietly in the corner beside the three fugitives.

She listened silently and tensely as they did, and her eyes were glued to the face of the speakers in turn. She knew Monsieur Xavier's features thoroughly. She observed that the big birthmark on the right side was swelling and reddened, and knew that Monsieur Xavier was angry and that he was exerting every effort to remain calm. He wanted to save the lives of hundreds of miserable people; he wanted to spare his city, Saint-Martin, still greater misfortune. He had to be shrewd and he dared not speak as he wished to the gentlemen from Paris. With strange insight, however, Simone also understood the Parisian's motive. He had been sent out to restore order at certain danger spots farther south. He wanted to perform his task as well as possible; he did not want to scatter his men up here in middle France. That was understandable. But Simone with her plastic imagination also realized what was going on in the heads of the refugees who stood next to her. She did not need to look at their faces to sense their grim resignation and their tenacious hopes. In spirit she was fighting Monsieur Xavier's battle to save hundreds or at least a few dozens of these refugees by skilful persuasion of this man from Paris.

Monsieur Xavier was making great efforts. The police officer gave indifferent answers, anxious only to leave quickly. The three fugitives and Simone with her basket stood against the wall and listened.

The deputy prefect came in. "Have you gentlemen not come to an agreement yet?" he asked sadly and politely. He had some new information regarding the incident at the bridge. What had happened there, he said, must have been horrible beyond conception. "If any spot is in danger," Monsieur Xavier summarized emphatically, "it is the bridge over the Cerein River."

But the police officer was now obviously tired of the argument. "Why don't you apply to the Staff," he said coolly, "and have them finally blow up the bridge?" Besides, he added, the first reports of such catastrophes were usually unreasonably exaggerated; and he put on his gloves.

Simone followed his every motion. Now he is about to go, she thought, but he must be stopped, he must be persuaded at all cost to leave some of his men here. "There were 214 dead," she said suddenly. In her mind's eye she saw the refugees who, under the red and orange awning on the platform of the café, were quarrelling over the number of dead; she plainly saw the man with the very virile face who had gloomily and angrily defended his figures. "There were 214 dead," she repeated. "Eighty-nine ambulances drove to Nevers and they had to leave most of the wounded." Inconspicuous and thin she stood against the wall, the big basket on her arm, but her fine, strikingly full voice rang valiantly and decisively. She herself did not know why she spoke with so much assurance; the police officer and the officials of the Deputy Prefecture probably knew the figures much better than the man on the platform.

All looked at Simone with astonishment. She stared straight ahead, as if it had not been she that had spoken. There was a brief silence. The gentleman from Paris was still busy with his gloves. Then, without looking at Monsieur Xavier or Simone— he probably thought she was one of the fugitives—impatiently as to an importunate petitioner, he said to Monsieur Cordelier with a sigh: "Very well, I will leave you two of my men," and he walked out, accompanied by Monsieur Cordelier.

Monsieur Xavier walked over to Simone with rapid tread and stood in front of her. Suddenly he looked very much like his father. He put his hand on her head, looked at her with a broad smile, shook his head and said in a very kindly manner: "What the deuce has gotten into you, Simone?"

Simone herself did not understand how she had dared to open her mouth in the presence of these gentlemen and to make such questionable statements with so much assurance. But her figures had not seemed questionable to her when she named them, and she was aware that she had had to speak even though it cost her her life.

"And now we will see about moving the fugitives," said Monsieur Xavier. Simone prepared to leave. "You are a plucky girl," said Monsieur Xavier. "Your father would have been pleased with you."

II: Monsieur le Marquis

THE time had come to return to the Villa Monrepos. But Simone could not bear the thought. She walked through the crooked, hilly streets; she was numb and in a fog. It had cost her no effort to speak. She had spoken involuntarily and the effect had been immediate. She was happy but she was confused.

She was looking for someone with whom she could speak; she was looking for Etienne. She did not want to go to his house for she could not have spoken in the presence of his parents. She walked through the streets, she passed the Café Napoleon; he was not there.

For some time she roamed about the city. Then suddenly she set out for the Avenue du Parc, to the loading yard, to the Planchard Transfer Company.

She walked rapidly, a little smile round her curved lips. To-day she will not stand at the red pump; today she will not be "out soliciting"; today there is no red pump and no one will be sitting on the bench in the shade. Today the trucks are rolling out to move the refugees. An hour has passed since she left the Deputy Prefecture. Surely by this time the deputy prefect and Monsieur Xavier had sent word to Uncle Prosper and the trucks are probably on the way.

And she need not be afraid of Maurice today. She has done something to prove that she does not belong to the Villa Monrepos. Today she has the right to laugh aloud if Maurice makes one of his impudent remarks.

But he will not. He will probably not be there at all. He will, like Etienne, have heard that men of military age are in danger when the Boches come. And Maurice is not like Etienne; Maurice will not await the Boches. A man who continues to work in the hated Planchard firm simply to dodge the draft, such a man will make himself scarce under the circumstances. He will run off; he will flee; he will take to his heels, as Madame puts it.

Now she was at the office. "I wasn't able to get anything," she said and deposited her empty basket with the book-keeper Peyroux, trying to make him and herself believe that she had gone to town on her daily errands. "I am sure, Mademoiselle, that you couldn't get anything," Monsieur Peyroux replied sadly and grimly; his rabbit face looked even unhappier than usual. "Everything is in dissolution," he complained. "I don't understand why Monsieur Planchard sits here and waits for the terrible things that are bound to come. Most of the employees are gone, even old Arsène. Just imagine, the loading yard without a concierge. But when I asked the boss whether he really intended to stay here he gave me an awful calling down. Of course, I understand that he feels responsible for the firm." He moved his head closer to Simone and, although the office was quite empty, he whispered to her in confidence, "I'll tell you, Mademoiselle, he is hard and brave like an old Roman, the boss. Think of it, Madame Mimerelles was here and implored him to go away with her. But he is staying on the job. A Roman."

Simone pictured the blonde, pretty, plump Madame Mimerelles. It must have cost the gallant Uncle Prosper great self-restraint to let her go alone.

"And the bureaucrats," raged the book-keeper, "have the impudence to make more and more demands of him. Yesterday he gave them the two Peugeots, today a Renault, but they want the whole establishment. There," and he pointed to a document on his desk, "just ten minutes ago Monsieur Cordelier sent me another such rag. He claims to have found the means of moving the greater part of the refugees and he insists that we finally deliver our trucks and gasoline to him. They dare to make such a proposition to a man like Monsieur Planchard. Old man Jeannot, the bailiff, is sitting out in the yard waiting for an answer. He'll have to be patient, the bailiff. I don't dare bring this rag of paper to the boss now." And, whispering, he confided to Simone: "The Châtelain is here again."

Simone looked silly with surprise. "Is it still about his wines? ..." She did not complete the sentence.

But Monsieur Peyroux was not listening to her. He had a sudden notion. "Perhaps," he meditated aloud, "it will help him in his dealings with the Marquis if I show him the letter." Painstakingly he picked up the letter and went up to Uncle Prosper's private office.

Simone also left the office. She stood in the doorway. The loading yard lay white and empty in the glare of the sun. She looked over at the bench in the shade. There sat three men, the packer, Georges, the driver, Richard, who was really much too old and was only being kept on account of the shortage of men, and the wobbly old bailiff, Jeannot. Maurice was not sitting there.

It afforded her some satisfaction that this impudent fellow, who was constantly criticizing others, was a coward himself. At the same time, however, she was disappointed. Today it would have been a secret triumph to hear his insolent remarks.

Suddenly, without knowing why, the feeling of elation which she had experienced until now was gone. She would have liked to turn back. But there sat the three on the bench and looked at her and it would have appeared very foolish if she suddenly made an about face. The men on the bench would think she had been looking for someone, probably Maurice. All at once she blushed, and with pretended nonchalance she walked diagonally across the yard to the gasoline pump.

There she stood. The men looked at her mildly astonished but not interested. It was fearfully hot and Simone felt empty and exhausted after all the excitement. All at once she was filled with fear at her own boldness with which she had again and again transgressed the rules of the Villa Monrepos. She had gone to town on her own responsibility. She had worn her dark green slacks contrary to Madame's specific orders. She had impertinently interfered in the affairs of the Deputy Prefecture. What would Madame say, what would Uncle say when they heard of it?

Buyers came and asked for gasoline, more buyers than usual,

very many. Evidently word had gotten round that the bridge and the road were passable.

Someone strolled out of the gloomy interior of the garage. Simone's heart stood still: Maurice. He was still here, he had remained; she had done him an injustice.

Now he was with the others. He pretended that he had not noticed her before. "Oh, lala, Mademoiselle Planchard," he said in his high voice, propped his hand on his hip and grinned at her. "Mademoiselle Planchard has put on her attractive slacks and is out soliciting again."

He sat down by the others, yawned, and smoked. "Here we sit and wait for the Boches," he said. "The others," and he scornfully indicated Simone with a little jerk of his head, "they at least know what they are waiting for. They are at least consistent, those ladies and gentlemen. They stick it out to the end. The refugees on the Place Gramont are starving to death because they can't be moved and upstairs the Marquis and the proprietor are making a deal about the transport of wine barrels. Business as usual. The world is on fire but they are not afraid. They use the fire to cook up their little deals."

Simone stood at the pump. There was a grain of truth in Maurice's words, with a lot of poison added. He twisted and exaggerated everything. Uncle Prosper would probably be happier if the world were not burning and if everything were going its orderly way as before. Uncle Prosper would probably prefer to forgo "cooking up his little deals," as Maurice called it, and would probably prefer to be with his Madame Mimerelles instead. Uncle Prosper was good-natured and would certainly like to help the refugees. But he believed in his business, he was attached to his business; he had built it up. And that Maurice counted Simone among the people who profit by the general misfortune was both stupid and vicious.

The men on the bench were meanwhile poking fun at the boss. They had seen Madame Mimerelles coming and going and they put two and two together. Yes, indeed, they said, the rich had their problems, too. Poor Monsieur Planchard had had to make up his mind whether he should go away with his lady love or remain here to keep up his profits and to guard his trucks. "When they face a choice between lewdness and greed," the packer, Georges, said philosophically, "greed always wins."

Then they began to discuss the Châtelain. He had as much money as a dog has fleas, they said; he did not need to worry about a few truckloads of wine. But over in England and America they paid more for his wines than the Boches and therefore, conceited as he was, he came down from his castle and whined to a common Monsieur Planchard for his trucks. "I bet a bottle of Pernod and ten packages of Gaulois," declared Maurice, "when the Boches come the Marquis will be hand in glove with them."

Old man Jeannot, the bailiff, had held his job for many years and had learned tolerance from his boss, the deputy prefect. He said that it was going a little too far to believe the Marquis capable of such treason; of course it could not be denied that the Châtelain was perhaps a little fascistic. "A little fascistic," mocked Maurice. "The girl is a little pregnant." And: "How about it, Jeannot," he urged, "will you take up my bet?"

"I am not a gambler," the official refused with dignity.

The old driver, Richard, turned to Maurice. "I am surprised," he said, "that you are still here. If I looked as hundred per cent 1-A classification as you do, I certainly would not wait for the Germans." Simone could hardly await Maurice's answer.

He yawned; it sounded a little artificial. "Oh hell," he said, "the Boches will have more to do than to look at the clothes of all men between nineteen and fifty-five. And here in Saint-Martin I can most easily prove that I am a civilian."

"The Boches don't fool round," persisted the old man. "If they once get you they send you straight to Bochie."

"All rumours," Maurice rejoined scornfully, "all nonsense."

It seemed to Simone that Maurice knew exactly that these rumours were not nonsense and that it was a serious risk to stay here. Why then did he stay? Probably because he was enormously proud and conceited. He could not bear the suspicion of cowardice, not even the shadow of a suspicion. Now that was decent of him, that he concealed his courage and his pride behind rude and embarrassed excuses.

From the office Uncle Prosper and another gentleman came walking across the court in the bright sunlight. The gentleman was rather small but he carried himself very erectly; his skin was sallow, his hair very black, and he had hard, agile, brown eyes over his slightly hooked nose. He was wearing riding clothes and as he came across the yard he was switching his riding crop lightly against his boots. Simone had never seen the Marquis de Saint-Brisson from close by; she looked at him critically and spitefully. The nearer he came the more her hatred grew. "A little fascistic." She regretted that Uncle Prosper had engaged in business with this man.

With idle, suspicious curiosity the men on the bench saw the two gentlemen approach. When they had come very near, the bailiff, Jeannot, stood up; the old driver, Richard, also rose slowly; Maurice and the packer, Georges, remained seated. The two gentlemen stood in front of the bench. There was only a little shade. Uncle Prosper stepped into the shade; the Marquis stood so that part of his face was shaded and he continued to switch his boots with the crop.

The employees were silent and waited. Presently Uncle Prosper cleared his throat and said: "My friends, I have a contract with the Marquis. I have assumed the obligation of taking a shipment to Bayonne. It is a matter of property which is not to fall into the hands of the Boches. This shipment is of great importance to the Marquis and the Planchard Company would like to carry out its contract. Whether that can be done depends upon you."

The men were silent.

Simone could not believe her ears. Uncle Prosper had spoken with friendly persuasion as the fatherly head of the firm, in a casual tone as if the whole thing were quite natural. Simone could not believe that he seriously wanted to have the wines transported and not the refugees. It was only his weakness in front of this distinguished gentleman, the Châtelain, that prompted him to speak this way; he was not serious; he expected his men to say that it was impossible.

The bailiff, Jeannot, an upright man, said: "I had a letter for you from Monsieur le Sous-Préfet, Monsieur Planchard. Didn't

Monsieur Peyroux give you the letter? Monsieur le Sous-Préfet is waiting for an answer."

No one said a word. Then, without looking at the people, the Châtelain said: "I will pay a high premium if the shipment arrives safely in Bayonne. I will pay ten thousand francs." And Uncle Prosper added: "You must understand that Monsieur le Marquis' sole concern is to save French property from the Boches." But the Marquis with his rasping voice said: "Don't talk so much, Planchard. My motives concern only myself."

Simone at the pump swallowed hard and wiped off the perspiration. Uncle Prosper should not have gone so far. He should not have taken the part of this man so emphatically.

Maurice, with his high voice, said slowly, to the point: "I believe it will hardly be possible to bring the shipment through. What will the likes of us do if the Boches snatch us? On the road it is hard to prove that one is a civilian. Here I can do that. Here you can testify for me, Monsieur Planchard." He spoke thoughtfully, as though seriously weighing all these arguments, but he looked boldly into Uncle Prosper's eyes.

The Marquis, still looking into space and switching his riding crop, said: "Yes, it will take some courage." He spoke softly. It sounded unspeakably arrogant.

Maurice, just as softly and coolly, said: "Yes, it takes courage. These refugees are strange people. They only think of themselves. They think the cars should only be used to transport them and they have no respect for French property. It could very well happen that they would simply throw the barrels out of the trucks and get in themselves."

Everybody was quiet.

Only the soft cracking of the riding crop against the boot was audible. Simone stood at her pump, filled with wild emotions. "You mustn't let Maurice speak all alone," her inner voice told her. "You mustn't act as if you belonged to the other crowd. You must say something. You must prove it."

She swallowed, and all at once she said, not loudly but valiantly into the sultry heat and into this unpleasant silence: "What else can the refugees do?"

They all looked over to the pump. There stood Simone, slender, fairly tall, in her dark green slacks. Her tanned, bony face was red and perspiring; she pressed her long curved lips together, she gazed into space meditatively and a little stubbornly.

"Eh?" Maurice's voice from the bench sounded clear and astonished.

The Marquis turned away suddenly and sharply: "Come on, Planchard," he said. "You haven't trained your men well." With bewilderment and rage Uncle Prosper looked from Simone to the others and back again at Simone. He wanted to explode, but he thought better of it, turned round likewise and followed the Châtelain. As they walked towards the house the latter added: "Whatever might happen in this country, discipline will be restored again. There are some people who will discover that."

After the two gentlemen had disappeared into the office building, old Richard, the driver, cleared his throat with much ado, spat, and said to Maurice: "Now it's high time that you disappear. The Châtelain is not to be trifled with."

Maurice grinned all over and answered: "Well, wasn't I right, old fellow? The refugees would knock my head off if I transported his wines. Even the half-baked brat over there in her dark green slacks grasped that. So the stuck-up, dirty swine of a fascist must understand it, too."

"I still think you ought to get out of here in a hurry," the old fellow repeated stubbornly.

But Simone was proud. In spite of his disdainful words, Maurice knew very well that it had taken courage to speak as she had done.

III: Nutmeg in the Cream Gravy

IN THE evening the dining-room was brilliantly lighted, the
table, as always, ceremoniously set. It was of great importance
to Uncle Prosper to dine even now with the usual formality; since
his nerves were so taxed, he wished that at least his home life
should run smoothly and peacefully as always.

Simone's eyes followed her uncle as he peeled radishes, ate his
sardines, spread pâté on a roll. She waited for him finally to
make some remark about her brazen behaviour. But he acted as
if nothing had happened. He didn't even mention the visit of the
Marquis or the new pressing demands by the authorities. Instead
he talked in detail about minor happenings and wasted many
words on those who had fled and those who had stayed.

Simone did not take her eyes from him as he ate so that, when
he had finished, she might quickly serve the next course. But her
thoughts remained with the events of the afternoon. It had been
foolish of her to speak so freely at the loading yard. What did
she wish to gain by voicing her opinion right in Uncle's and the
Châtelain's faces? Madame was right: she was arrogant, unruly,
impertinent.

But at least Maurice had seen now where she stood. He knew
now that she did not belong to the others and that she did not
only "go soliciting." After all, she had accomplished something.

It had been painful to listen to Uncle Prosper echoing the opinion of the Châtelain. It had been painful to see how he had
turned round and obediently trotted after him into the house.
She had not thought him capable of so much subservience.

He was her father's brother. He was the half-brother of her
father. Such reddish hair, such full, shapely lips her father had
also had. And also the voice, they all said, was very much like her
father's voice. But Pierre Planchard had urged the country to

establish justice for all and Prosper Planchard urged his men to transport the wines for the Châtelain.

She ought not to listen to the talk of those at the loading yard. She had to try to justify Uncle Prosper. He was humane; he did many good deeds; he had also done many kind things for her. If he did not weigh all his acts of commission and omission to the smallest detail now, one had to remember that he stood in the midst of a hard battle. The whole great establishment that he created was suddenly in the greatest danger. And he shielded it and did not take to his heels like Messieurs Amiot and Laroche.

However these friendly feelings did not last. The memory of her uncle walking across the yard with the Châtelain drove them away.

She was waiting for him to tell Madame of her unruly conduct, and it tormented her because he did not do it. Was he making an effort to understand her? Did he realize that, as her father's daughter, she could not have acted otherwise?

Nothing in her attitude indicated her rebellious thoughts. She served Madame, she served Uncle Prosper, and ate a little herself. Then she carried out the dishes and prepared the next course; it was a roast loin of veal with mixed vegetables.

While she served it Uncle was speaking again of the many people who had fled from Saint-Martin. Yesterday, he declared, he had thoroughly disapproved of such flight. Today he would have to admit that those who fled now had certain reasonable arguments in their favour. There was reliable information that Highways 7 and 77 were less crowded now. If, for instance, he himself would now try to salvage some of his trucks by taking them to the south, there was a chance of success. Moreover, it was generally reported that the Boches were arresting hostages in the occupied towns in order to give emphasis to their demands. If that were done here, then he, as the most prominent man in the community and as a well-known patriot, was in serious danger.

Simone had stopped eating and looked at him intently. He sat there with his expressive, manly face; he spoke with his full, ringing voice—and he wanted to take to his heels. He wanted to evade the problem of the refugees; he wanted to dodge the demands of the Deputy Prefecture; he wanted to escape the obligation of continuing the battle against the Boches.

"I am not saying that I want to go away," he continued. "On the other hand, if I did it, it would not be from fear. It would be from well-considered regard for the interests of the firm. Isn't it, in a certain sense, my duty to save the trucks and the head of the establishment? Don't you think so too, Mother?" With a little sigh he poured gravy over his meat and vegetables.

Madame sat there, black and immense. So far she had spoken very little; she was even more sedate today than ordinarily. Now she said: "*If* you did it, if, if. I should think, my friend, that these times confront us with so many real problems that we don't have time to dally with such idle thoughts. If, if." She managed a little smile. "It is true in case of an emergency," she continued, "I believe I could deal with the Boches alone, despite my age. But it is a good thing that Saint-Martin has a man like you, my friend, who can show the Boches and the population how a big business man acts in difficult times." She sat there, her double chin pressed against her breast, stiffly and very erectly; she breathed with difficulty.

Simone admired the cleverness with which Madame had rebuked Uncle by means of praise. Uncle, too, forced a smile. "You are right as usual, Mother," he replied. "It was an idle thought." And he raised his glass towards his mother and bowed his head. Then he cheerfully spoke of unimportant matters; that the leather saddles, which the army had refused to accept, were still on display in Monsieur Binet's store, and other things of this sort; and he continued to eat. Simone was pleased at the self-restraint with which he accepted Madame's reprimand.

Suddenly he pushed his plate away. "Haven't I said a hundred times," he exploded, "that there shouldn't be any nutmeg in the cream gravy? Nutmeg in the cream gravy! And I am expected to eat that after such a day as I have had. Doesn't any one have the slightest consideration for me? I won't eat that; that is slop."

Simone looked at him shocked beyond words. It was true that he had once said he did not like too much nutmeg in the cream gravy. But it was customary in the Villa Monrepos to put some nutmeg into the cream gravy, and this time she had put in just as much and just as little nutmeg as the last two times, and the last two times he had fully approved. Besides Madame had tasted the gravy.

Meanwhile his rage still increased. "You have only done that to spite me, you brat," he thundered. "That is my thanks for taking you into my house and keeping you as my daughter. In return for that you not only incite my men, but you also spoil my food."

Simone had lowered her head while Monsieur Planchard raged. It was not because she was afraid to look at him, but she had to figure out, undisturbed by the sight of his face, what had suddenly got into him. She was a little ashamed on his account. Apparently he was deeply confused by what she had done in the loading yard; that was why he was abusing her without rhyme or reason. She looked over at Madame. Madame knew all about the cream gravy. Wouldn't she defend her?

Madame, in turn, had looked up when Monsieur Planchard had begun to rage. She moved her eyes from him to Simone and back again. At the moment when he blurted out the true reason for his anger: "In return for that you incite my men," Simone believed that she saw for a fraction of a second an enormous, deadly hatred rising in Madame's small hard eyes. But no, she was probably mistaken; she had probably imagined that. Madame sat there in complete calm.

Uncle Prosper had finished; he was still casting furious glances at Simone and was breathing hard. Simone awaited what Madame would say. Would she help her? Would she reprimand her son? At long last Madame opened her mouth. "Give me cigarettes and a light, Simone," she said with unmoved voice. And after Simone had given her cigarettes and a light, Madame said just as calmly: "And clear the table."

Simone cleared the table. As she was in the kitchen attending to her small duties, she heard Uncle's muffled voice evidently now reporting to Madame. She was sure he would not describe what had happened in a kindly manner; he would, at best, tell only a part of the truth. Simone would have preferred to discuss the matter with him alone. She still believed that she could make him understand her, for he was her father's brother. But Madame was not related to her; Madame had never liked her stepson, Pierre. Now, since Madame was drawn into this affair, it was impossible for Simone to talk things over with Uncle Prosper.

She was excited. A bad quarter of an hour lay ahead of her and probably bad days. Nevertheless she was not afraid. She knew she had done the right thing.

When she returned, Madame had moved from the table and sat in the corner in the big wing chair. It rarely happened that she got up from dinner before the dessert was served. This time she had done it. Dark and bulky she sat in her wing chair and smoked.

She took her lorgnon and eyed Simone for a little while. Madame's glance was fixed on her and penetrated through and through her but Simone did not waver. Then Madame lowered the lorgnon and brushed the ash from her cigarette. And all at once Simone knew with certainty that she had not been mistaken when she had seen that tremendous hatred flaming out of Madame's eyes.

"So it was all quite useless," Madame began with her soft, high, harsh voice. "I have done everything that was possible for an old woman to check your impertinence and to put you in the right way. I have talked in vain. As soon as the discipline in the loading yard began to break—not through our fault—you displayed your impertinence and you dared to insult your guardian, who has done so much for you, in front of his employees. You have joined his enemies, you stabbed him in the back, and this now, of all times, when the decent people should stand together against the riff-raff."

She was silent for a little while, breathing heavily. Simone stood there, motionless. She suffered Madame's words; she let them pass over her. It was not she who was being abused. What Madame uttered in her low, mean voice was her resentment against Pierre Planchard and against his father, her husband. Simone knew that Madame welcomed this opportunity at last to let loose upon her all the bitterness and poison pent up during these years and decades.

"If these were not such hard times," continued Madame, "that you would certainly come to a bad end if you were elsewhere, I would advise my son to throw you out; today rather than tomorrow. I would advise him to put you somewhere and to pay for you. Good riddance, by all means. In more peaceful times I would not dream of suggesting to my son to bear the sight of your obstinacy and ingratitude any longer. But as things are, my son will have to endure you in his house. I warn you for the last time. You are depraved through and through. You have bad blood. We knew your father. We warned him. He was deaf to our warnings. He is dead and gone."

Simone stood there, her head slightly lowered, her fine mouth tightly closed, obedient, but not at all submissive. "Of course now she won't look me in the eyes," said Madame, softly and very scornfully. Up to this time Simone had been looking at Madame, although she stood with bowed head. Now she raised her head a little higher, calmly, not defiantly.

Uncle Prosper began to walk up and down with heavy but rapid step, as was his manner. "You are quite right, Mother," he said angrily. "As she was standing there at the pump in her slacks, and was inciting the men against me, I had to think of Pierre, too. That's just the way he was from youth on. Who told him to go to the Congo and to stir up the Negroes against us? But that's the way he was. He could not refrain from stirring up the masses, from inflaming the unbridled greed of the masses. He fouled his own nest because he played no part in it. Because he could not get anywhere in Saint-Martin, he had to go to the Congo."

Simone stared at the excited man as he walked up and down. Confusion lay in her dark, large, deep-set eyes; she was aghast at so much intentional blindness, intentional stupidity, so much hatred. Wasn't he ashamed of himself to utter such horrible, criminal slander before her, who knew better?

"Don't look at me like that," Uncle Prosper suddenly burst out. He walked towards her, and with his hairy, fleshy hand he

seized her shoulder so violently that it hurt. He shook her.
" 'What else can the fugitives do?' That's what my niece throws
into my face," he shouted loudly. "Rob my trucks, steal my
trucks, what else can they do? That would suit you, you and
your father. You want anarchy so that you will be great and
popular." His flushed head was very close to hers, his breath
smelling of wine and food blew into her face. His manly features
were twisted, drawn out of all form, distorted into a caricature;
his grey eyes were veiled, savage, and helpless at the same time.
Suddenly Simone no longer thought it peculiar that he had the
strangely thick, pointed ear. "I was too good to you," he raged,
but now more softly again and more repressed. "I ought to beat
you black and blue so that you will lose your appetite for arrogance and for mutiny."

He let go of her. Again he walked up and down. Simone had
stood quite still. She was ashamed for the furious man; she almost felt sorry for him.

"You should not get so excited, Prosper," said Madame. Uncle
Prosper sat down at the table, still snorting with rage, staring
straight ahead angrily. "You ought to eat," said Madame. "You
have eaten practically nothing."

Hesitating, indignant, Monsieur Planchard sliced off a piece
of cheese, ate it and took a swallow of wine. Then, mechanically,
he continued to eat.

IV: The Aviator

THE next afternoon Simone again went to the city as though it were a matter of course. This time she took her bicycle. Again she carried her market basket, and again she was in slacks.

The streets were no longer so crowded; the majority of the travellers now were soldiers. Simone went straight towards the loading yard. For a while the road led rather steeply up hill; Simone had to push the bicycle and it was very hot. Nevertheless she moved rapidly, as if the time for her arrival were fixed.

After yesterday's excitement she had slept soundly and well but in the morning she had recalled all the events of the preceding day and she had looked forward to meeting Madame and Uncle Prosper with a little fear and much defiance. She was all the more surprised when Uncle Prosper acted at breakfast as if nothing had happened. He was friendly, spoke about unimportant things, and left for the office as usual. Madame also was as calm and polite as ever; there was no trace of the wild eruption of the night before.

Simone thought it all through for the tenth time as she pushed her wheel towards the loading yard. She couldn't understand it. With her own ears she had heard Uncle Prosper abuse her father absurdly and vulgarly; she had seen unrestrained hatred flare in Madame's eyes; her shoulder was still black and blue from Uncle Prosper's hard grip. They must both have discovered that she, Simone, was the daughter of Pierre Planchard. Did they think that after last night they could continue to live with her as before?

She had arrived. It was strange to find the little glass house at the entrance of the loading yard empty. Old Arsène was as much a fixture there as the chair and the bench.

The loading yard lay white under the hot sun. Maurice, the old driver, Richard, and the packer, Georges, were lounging on the bench in the shade. "Good afternoon, Mademoiselle," said Maurice with the same slightly mocking tone as usual in his greeting.

Simone leaned her bicycle against the wall and started for the pump. "We are not selling gasoline today," said old Richard. "The boss has locked up. Maybe he is through with the gasoline pump for good. Or maybe it is only for just now while the deputy prefect is here."

"France is dying very slowly," commented Maurice. "Government authority, in the form of Monsieur Cordelier, has still not given up trying to get the trucks that are coming to him and the necessary gasoline from the boss. Even the Deputy Prefecture has no more automobiles. But that did not deter Monsieur le Sous-Préfet. Monsieur le Sous-Préfet came dashing up on the back seat of old man Jeannot's motorcycle. The fatherland, on the back seat of the motorcycle, heroically clung to the shoulders of the tottering old bailiff, in order to perish with its rightful claims on its lips."

"Don't talk such high-sounding nonsense," the old packer, Georges, remarked quietly.

"I am not talking to you, you dirty so and so," replied Maurice. "I am talking to Mademoiselle Planchard."

Since the pump was locked up Simone had no business at the loading yard and she might just as well have left. But she hesitated and finally, still uncertainly, walked over to the bench in the shade. She was aware that what she was doing now was another act of impertinence. In times of mutiny and danger she was consorting with the employees; she increased the gap between herself and the Planchard family; she transgressed Madame's final warning.

Although there was plenty of room on the bench, the three politely moved closer together. Maurice grinned. Simone sat down with them.

She expected them to speak of yesterday's occurrence. She was a little afraid of it; she did not want to spoil what she had done yesterday with a lot of talk. But when the three did not mention it she was sorry after all.

Richard related that at the Café Napoleon they had heard on the radio that the city of Tours was still holding out. The city was being defended by a small garrison against enormous odds. They were now holding out for the fourth day. Simone beamed with joy. That proved it. We will hold out. The Loire line will hold. But Maurice said: "What good is all the courage of the little fellows if the higher-ups don't want to fight?" And he wiped Tours away with a gesture.

Then he spoke of the visit of the deputy prefect. The subject of the discussion in the private office no longer had to do with the moving of the refugees. Joe Blow had let loose of two more trucks with loud lamentations, and a large part of the fugitives had already been moved away. So they were probably talking about something else. It was too bad that the bailiff, Jeannot, was not there; he knew what was going on. But he seemed a little embarrassed today; he did not sit down with them but sneaked off to the office. Nevertheless he had dropped some hints to his friend, the packer, Georges. It seemed that orders had arrived to destroy all transport material as soon as the occupation by the Boches was unavoidable, so that it would not fall into the hands of the enemy. The civil authorities had been ordered to assist the military in this matter. The deputy prefect had made the journey out here in this uncomfortable manner in order to make the necessary arrangement with the boss. Awkwardly and bit by bit the packer, Georges, reported these facts.

"I am not worried about the boss," Maurice remarked. "I'll bet ten packages of Gaulois and a quart of apple cider that our hoarded gasoline and our truck yard will be safely kept. Joe Blow will talk himself out of it. He will negotiate with the deputy prefect until the time comes to negotiate with the Boches."

"No," cried Simone, "not that."

Maurice looked her up and down with impudent amusement. "How about it, Mademoiselle?" he asked. "Will you take my bet?"

Before Simone could answer, however, the bell at the locked

gate of the garage sounded long and stridently. Simone ran and looked through the peep-hole.

The man who stood outside was an aviator in English uniform. Simone had trouble understanding him for he spoke a queer French; but she understood him. He was very insistent. He had to find some means of getting away, getting away quickly, very quickly, and he had been told that if any one could help him it would be here at this Planchard Transfer Company. Simone admitted him.

He walked through the dark garage and out into the bright yard; he blinked, he walked with difficulty, he limped. He looked haggard; bristly stubbles covered his face. The three men regarded him silently. Simone asked politely: "Now what can we do for you, Monsieur?"

He had to get away, he declared again and again. He had to report to the nearest air corps detachment. Aviators were now doubly important, he said, awkwardly and blushing, and he must not under any circumstances fall into the hands of the Germans. He became tangled in his speech, his face quivered at times; he was very young. Simone made up her mind to do what she could.

The men were still silent. Simone was irritated because they were so impolite. "Are you hurt?" she asked. He replied that his plane had been shot down, he had landed by parachute, and he had been bruised a bit. The three looked up but they still did not say a thing. It was a dialogue between Simone and the Englishman.

Simone, after a pause, said: "We will help you, Monsieur," and to the others: "We will help him, Maurice, won't we?"

Maurice looked at the stranger, he looked at Simone, he smoked, then he said lazily: "If you want to help him, Mademoiselle, I won't put a thing in your way." And without raising his voice, in fact pleasantly, he continued: "What has gotten into you? How do you get to play the boss here? Only yesterday you put in your two cents' worth unnecessarily. When we have something to say we'll open our own traps. Greenhorn. France is falling and you only think of getting a thrill out of it."

Simone blushed deeply and gulped. Old Richard said: "Well, well, leave her alone." And the packer, Georges, a bit uncouthly, said to the stranger: "Come into the shade, Monsieur. Would you like a glass of apple cider? We have good, cold apple cider."

The stranger had probably not quite followed Maurice's words. He said: "If it's a matter of great expense to get hold of gasoline and transportation, I have money. It is English money but I suppose now it will be worth more than French. And I must get to the south; I must get to Bordeaux. You understand that, Messieurs, don't you?"

The packer made an inviting gesture and the aviator sat down with them. Simone stood there, half in the sun, half in the shade. She looked at Maurice. He smoked.

Old Richard said: "If you gave him your motorcycle, Maurice, he might be able to get there."

"Sell my motorcycle now?" mocked Maurice. "You don't think I'm nuts, do you?"

"So you want to leave after all?" asked the old fellow in his slow, obstinate manner.

"I didn't say that," objected Maurice. "I haven't made up my mind yet. I'll have to see how the situation develops. In any case, to give away my motorcycle under such conditions would be crazy."

The packer brought the drinks. He poured some for himself and the others. "To your health, Monsieur," he said to the aviator. Simone was still standing half in the sun. The old fellow said deliberately: "If you want to scram, Maurice, then you'd better do it today. Otherwise it will be too late. I'll tell you something. Take your motorcycle and take the gentleman along."

"Keep your trap shut," Maurice said crossly. "I told you before, I am not leaving. I want to see first what's going to happen."

"But then it will be too late," insisted the old man. "And then very likely the Boches will take your motorcycle. In your place, Maurice, I would either pull out or sell my motorcycle. English pounds aren't so bad."

Simone, her lips slightly parted, looked with great tension at Maurice. He suddenly fired off at her: "You keep quiet. You keep your impudent mouth shut." He put his hand on his hip and looked her contemptuously up and down. Then, slowly, stressing every word, with his high, squeaking voice, he continued. "But that's the way the well-to-do are, those from the Villa Monrepos. Joe Blow hoards and makes millions for himself and sabotages the war. And then Mademoiselle pretends pity for a bruised English leg, and with that they have salved their conscience and are patriots. Damn silly brat! Why don't you go and sleep with this fellow if you insist on being so charitable, and leave us alone with your two cents' worth of sentimentality." He drank his apple cider.

Simone felt as though he had struck her. She got up, staggering a little, tears in her eyes, gulping, and walked towards the garage.

Maurice meanwhile said to the Englishman indifferently: "How much would you invest, Monsieur, in a first-class motorcycle?"

Simone stood still. She felt a sharp pang in her heart; the change had come too suddenly. But at once joy closed over her like waves. This Maurice. What a man! She feared that they would all notice her joy and that must not be. She walked fast, she almost ran, she ran into the garage.

There she sat in the dark, hot and flushed with joy. "That Maurice," she said to herself with a smile, and once more, "that Maurice. What a man!" He was thoroughly decent and was ashamed to be decent. He had abused her, he had thrown the dirtiest obscenities at her, only to conceal his decency. Fortunately the Englishman had not understood any of his nasty remarks, and with the two old men it made no difference.

She heard Maurice explaining to the others out on the bench why he was accepting the Englishman's offer. He said that, in the first place, he really had to stay here; only here he could prove himself to be a civilian and essential in the trucking business. In the second place, if there were serious danger, it would be better for him to escape into the mountains, and he could get along better there on a bicycle than on a motorcycle. In short, circumstances being what they were, the English money was of more use to him than a motorcycle.

Of course that was pure nonsense. He knew it; the others knew it. Simone knew it. He simply did not want to admit that he was doing it out of decency.

In the gloom of the garage Simone joyously heard Maurice outside bargaining with the Englishman, who understood him with difficulty. She heard him drive the poor fellow from hope into fear and make fun of him, until he finally promised to give him the motorcycle, get him food, gasoline, road maps, and get him started on his way.

She took her bicycle and her basket, and without going out into the yard to say good-bye to the others, she left through the office entrance and started for home.

On the road the motorcycle from the Deputy Prefecture passed her. In front sat old man Jeannot, the bailiff, and on the back seat, his hands on Jeannot's shoulders, sat Monsieur le Sous-Préfet. He looked sad and had trouble hanging on. It was evident that he had failed in his mission with Uncle Prosper. Simone almost felt more annoyed with Monsieur Cordelier than with her uncle. She looked after the disappearing motorcycle and saw it with the eyes of Maurice; she felt how grotesque it was for government authority to beat such a hasty and undignified retreat.

V: The Action

ON THE following day when Simone pushed her bicycle up to Saint-Martin her tanned, bony face with the broad, obstinate forehead was very calm and without any trace of emotion. But behind this collected forehead was passionate excitement.

She trembled with impatience to carry out her decision, and at the same time she looked for excuses to postpone the deed. Again and again she groped in her pocket for the keys and the lighter. Again and again, without willing it, she pictured in her mind the course of the action and the consequences it would produce. It cost her great efforts to suppress her emotions.

She recalled the moment when she had made up her mind. It had been yesterday at dinner while Uncle Prosper was telling of his conversation with the deputy prefect.

Uncle Prosper had certainly exaggerated his report and had described the conference from his point of view. Nevertheless Simone was convinced that she knew exactly what the deputy prefect had demanded, how he had argued and what Uncle Prosper's attitude had been. She could well visualize, as though she had been present, Monsieur Cordelier's urgent requests and Uncle Prosper's angry, ironical responses, the long oratorical debate back and forth, until finally the deputy prefect started on his dismal retreat, which she had witnessed.

Obviously an army officer had called earlier to see Uncle Prosper and had demanded the destruction of the trucks and the gasoline. "If the Captain left without accomplishing his foolish purpose," Uncle Prosper claimed to have said to the deputy prefect, "you might just as well spare me your silly, unreasonable demands." And: "Don't interfere in my business, old man," he claimed to have declared. "Do you actually believe that I took the trouble to scrape my gasoline together only to have it stolen by the Boches? I am no greenhorn. You can be sure they will not steal a mud-guard or a drop of gasoline from me. But what has to be done and when, only I will determine and nobody else. I insist on that."

When Uncle Prosper had quoted his final, definite answer, it was then, just then, that Simone had decided to take this matter into her own hands and to go to the loading yard. Just then, at that moment, she had decided on her action. Because then, at that moment, she had told herself: "Uncle Prosper is obviously ready to destroy his materials before the arrival of the enemy. It can't be otherwise. He is the leading citizen of Saint-Martin, the best patriot, and he is a Planchard, a true Planchard. He objects only to the pressure. He wants to remain master of his own establishment. He will not accept orders and threats from others."

That's the way it was and without the unfortunate conversation with the deputy prefect everything would have been all right. But now, through his clumsy interference, Monsieur Cordelier had spoiled everything. Uncle Prosper would now have to find the right method to save his self-respect. And that might take a long time. And the Boches might arrive in the city at any moment. And what a disaster, what undying disgrace for the house of Planchard, if it should be too late and the material should fall into the hands of the Boches.

That's why she would have to take over for Uncle Prosper, that's why she would have to take it into her own hands, she, the daughter of Pierre Planchard. And when the action had once been accomplished, then Uncle Prosper would breathe freely; then he would have thanks and praise for her.

Since the night before she had reviewed these considerations a hundred times, but with all her ups and downs and pros and cons the decision had been plain and final in her mind from the first moment. The whole action was clearly defined in her heart even before Uncle Prosper had completed that one sentence in his report.

Madame's comments about the report of Uncle Prosper had only strengthened Simone's determination. "That's the way they are, these pen-pushers," Madame had remarked. "They only want to destroy property just to satisfy their bureaucratic arrogance." And: "What good are your few drops of gasoline to the Germans? Does this Philippe believe they have to depend on your gasoline for their tanks?" But Simone had answered immediately in her mind: Because so many thought so, that's why we're in this fix. It was clear to her that Madame's arguments were no less dangerous than the enemy tanks.

The steep path came to an end; ahead of Simone lay a stretch of level road. She climbed on her bicycle, she rode, she rode fast. She felt free and happy; she was filled with solemn serenity. It was her big day today; her life had a meaning. Her mission, her action stood before her, great and glowing.

She had prepared herself as for a ceremony. Before she left, she had for the second time that day given herself a shower bath with the garden hose and had put on clean clothes. She smiled. She recalled the rapture she had felt as the water sprayed over her. Everybody had always looked down upon her; she was nothing but the poor niece and the little maid of the Villa Monrepos who "solicited" at the red pump. And now she had been selected to prove that Saint-Martin was a respectable city which would not surrender to the Boches without a struggle.

The road began to curve sharply upwards in a steep grade towards Saint-Martin. Long ago, when Simone was still a child she had sometimes ridden part way up in spite of the grade; occasionally she had challenged Henriette to see who would endure it longer. Today, too, she did not dismount, but rode on. It was perfectly absurd; everybody pushed his bicycle up this road. But she felt so full of energy today. She rode on, she pedalled, the bicycle ran zig-zag. It was very hot; she panted; it was sheer bravado, but only a little piece more, and still another yard, and just to the corner. Thus she rode upwards, a blank, strained, and contented smile round her lips.

Only when it was quite impossible to go on and her heart throbbed in her throat, did she dismount. For a moment she leaned against the saddle of her bicycle and wiped off the perspiration, the same smile still on her face. All at once, however, her joyfulness was gone. She was exhausted from the effort of this unnecessary ride and happy that the way to the city was not long any more.

She pushed her bicycle the rest of the way. A few soldiers sat on a bench, dead-tired, and looked at her dully. For a moment she doubted whether it was possible to carry on a war with such soldiers. But at once she visualized how they fought in the city of Tours against tremendous odds, and yesterday they had held out for four days and probably they were still holding out today.

Faster, and with more strength, she pushed her bicycle. Her mission stood clearly before her. "When, if not now? And who else, if not you?"

She had reached the Porte Saint-Lazare. What did she really want here in the city? Why hadn't she ridden directly to the loading yard? Oh, yes, she needed an alibi. She would have to be seen in the city at the time of the action; she would have to be seen at the Deputy Prefecture. They all should believe secretly that the act had been done by the Planchard family, but nobody should really know it, so that no one would be entangled in it. That was very simple; she had calculated all that minutely.

If it had not been necessary to establish an alibi, she would have been at the loading yard long ago. She thrilled at the thought of it. She was racked and torn with impatience yet she feared the moment of the action and was glad of the excuse to postpone it.

Aimlessly she pushed her bicycle up and down the winding, irregular lanes. Once more, since yesterday, Saint-Martin had changed. Only a few, scattered people appeared in the streets; the city was quiet as the grave, paralysed in expectation of the enemy. The houses stood lifeless, the shutters were down. It was unbearably hot. With heavier and heavier step she went on through the leaden heat; the realization of the ghostly emptiness pressed heavily on her heart. Because the houses looked so bright and colourful, their desolation was all the more depressing. It seemed to Simone as if the walls were closing in about her. She walked on and on, her breath came painfully. The heat of the pavement and of the cobbled squares seemed to burn the soles of her feet, and the wheel that she pushed was heavy as stone. And, although she did not see a single familiar face, only an occasional, strange, indifferent soldier, it seemed to her that the whole city was watching her and was aware of her intentions.

The worst of it was that even those inhabitants who had remained were not visible. Simone had come to the house of her schoolmate, Adrienne Voisin. With a sudden decision she seized the door latch. The door was not locked. Perhaps the Voisins were still here. She climbed the stairs. No one was there. The house was in disorder, there were signs of sudden departure, the air was musty and unbearably hot. Simone walked into the living-room. Monsieur Voisin had kept a number of small, brightly coloured, exotic birds in a large cage. The cage stood there; the colourful birds were there but they were dead and reeking.

For a moment Simone was nauseated. She left the house and went on, pushing her wheel through the streets. So far she had seen no one whom she knew and could therefore not tell whether any one had seen her. She sighed with relief when a voice hailed her from a shaded bench in the Place Saint-Lazare.

It was Maurice. He sat under an elm, his face freckled with shadows, and he was not alone. He was sitting with a girl; she was curvilinear and Simone thought she looked rather vulgar. At the loading yard they said he ran round a good deal with girls. But she was glad to see him. "Are you still hoarding for the seven lean years, Mademoiselle?" he called out lazily. She thought of the action for which she had come. She even reached instinctively for the key and the lighter that she had in her pocket, and she felt a sort of satisfaction at his cruel injustice.

With her large dark eyes she looked at him reproachfully and a little scornfully. He laughed. "No harm intended," he resumed, and: "Come, join us, brat," he invited her good-naturedly. "You were very helpful yesterday in that business with the aviator. I mean, you played right into my hands. The fellow paid me a nice little chunk of dough. And now you'll get your commission. Let's go to the Napoleon and drink a glass of beer before the Boches come."

Simone hesitated. What would Madame say if she went to the Café Napoleon with Maurice and this vulgar-looking girl? It's a monstrous idea; two days ago she herself would have considered it absurd even to her. But today it was different. She wanted to be seen here in the city, and therefore it could only be of advantage to show herself in the Café Napoleon. And besides, if she did not go with him, Maurice would again think her cowardly and arrogant. She took a few steps in the direction of the bench.

Maurice arose with a good-natured grin. "This is my friend, Louison," he gestured, "and this is Mademoiselle Simone, my boss's niece."

They went into the near-by café. They sat down on the platform under the red and orange awning at one of the little marble tables. A few soldiers were there and a few refugees; of the local people the only one was the eccentric watchmaker, Darieux. Maurice's blue shirt, as usual, stood wide open. Monsieur Grasset, the proprietor, seemed to be astonished to see Simone in the company of the driver, Maurice, and of the girl, Louison. At any rate, he would be able to testify that he had seen Simone.

When the three frosty glasses of beer stood before them Maurice asked: "It seems to me that we were interrupted yesterday in our discussion of a difference of opinion, weren't we? Now we will soon see what will happen to our gasoline and our trucks."

Simone looked at him with startled eyes. Had he guessed her purpose? He continued: "Or do you still believe that we will 'hold out'? You can believe me: within twenty-four hours, probably within the next few hours, we will know exactly who will do what with our loading yard. If you will open your beautiful eyes, Mademoiselle, you will perceive that the soldiers of our courageous army are not only coming in from the east and from the north but also from the southwest. That shows that they have also met the enemy in the southwest. Do you know what they call the situation in which we are? They call that—encircled."

Encircled. Probably within the next few hours. Panic seized Simone. She had no time to lose. She set herself a time limit:

within two hours she would have to complete what she had to do.

"Now I will have to go," she said abruptly. The thought came back into her mind: "When, if not now? And who else, if not you?" At the same time she was annoyed at the manner in which Louison looked at her; she probably believed that Simone was another one of his girls.

"Don't be so unpleasant," Maurice replied. "Why don't you at least take a drink?" She drank. "Well, and how about our bet now?" he teased her. "I am willing to increase the wager. I will bet a bottle of Pernod and twenty packages of Gaulois." He looked at her. He grinned in a superior manner. She returned his look. "I will take your bet," she said and her voice sounded decisive and challenging.

He looked surprised. He surveyed her critically for a fairly long time. "It's easy to see that Mademoiselle is a rich girl," he resumed. And: "It's a bet, *tope, commère,*" he said and extended his hand. For a moment she looked at the strong, open hand over the little marble table. Then she grasped it. Louison laughed. "But now I do have to go," Simone said and got up.

"But for heaven's sake, why?" he replied in astonishment. "You don't have to be in any hurry today. There certainly isn't anything more to be hoarded today, not even for the people of the Villa Monrepos."

"I have to go to the Prefecture," she said and since he looked at her with a little suspicion she lied: "I have a message for Monsieur Xavier."

"Oh, you are busy all the time," Maurice grumbled ironically. "Well, run along, brat," he added.

She left. She pushed her wheel towards the Palais Noiret. She felt that Maurice was looking after her and she heard Louison laugh; now they were probably making dirty remarks about her.

Presently she had arrived at the Palais. The great old gate was locked. She did not ring the bell. Her own nervous expectation made her sensitive for the state of mind of others; she told herself that the people behind this gate were awaiting the Germans and that the sound of the bell would startle them. She preferred to push her bicycle to the side entrance and today, as she had expected, she saw the familiar face of the concierge through this window. She knocked and he admitted her.

"What on earth do you want here?" he asked in some surprise. Simone was glad that he commented on her arrival. "I have to speak with Monsieur Xavier," she explained. "May I leave my bicycle with you?"

In the interior of the building all the officials were assembled; they wore their best Sunday clothes; each one sat at his place. No one spoke. They sat there solemnly and sadly, with rounded shoulders and heavy faces.

But the apparent idleness of the waiting group did not conceal their tortured nervousness. The deputy prefect could not control his agitation. He roamed about, he went from one office to the next, he twiddled with his rosette, he sighed, he made gloomy and kindly and meaningless remarks. Now and then, with an absent-minded expression, he put his hand on the shoulder of one or the other of his officials.

As a result of her friendly relations with Monsieur Xavier, Simone was quite at home here. This time, to be sure, she felt strange and uncomfortable. Perhaps one of the reasons was that she was wearing slacks; that was out of place today, Madame was right, and every one looked at her with some astonishment. But she could not imagine how she might carry out her project dressed in anything else but slacks. She made an effort to impress herself upon all the officials; it was very important that they should all have seen her.

She walked into Monsieur Xavier's office. He sat at his desk. He had propped his cheek on one hand, and the other hand lay loosely on the arm of the chair. His customary vivaciousness had given way to fatigue; Simone recalled how she had involuntarily surprised his father sitting in his arm-chair and looking old as the hills.

Monsieur Xavier looked up when Simone entered. He tried to be friendly, he even attempted a little joke, but he did not succeed. "What are you doing here?" he asked her.

"I could not stand it at home," Simone explained vaguely.

"Won't Madame be annoyed?" Monsieur Xavier asked.

Simone shrugged her shoulders. "Is it very bad that I am wearing slacks?" she asked.

Monsieur Xavier was playing with the letter-opener. "I don't know whether the Boches will be offended by your slacks," he answered with gloomy irony. She stood in front of him and looked at his sad face; it was obvious that he could master his excitement only with the greatest difficulty and the birthmark on his right cheek was swollen. She looked at him intently. Now, at this very moment, she would have to start on her way and she wanted to take the bright memory of his kind friendly face with her. He noticed something strange in her look. "Is anything the matter?" he asked with a trace of suspicion and worry in his voice. Simone hesitated a brief moment. Would it be better perhaps to tell him everything? He had loved and admired her father; he was very fond of her. No, she was not permitted; she dared not involve him, an official, in her undertaking; she had to bear the danger alone. "No," she said with pretended nonchalance. "What could be the matter?"

"Well, we all have our worries now," said Monsieur Xavier.

A protracted, strong peal of the bell shrilled through the house. Simone, and even Monsieur Xavier, started; every one looked out of the windows. Before the gate stood the Châtelain. He had driven up in front in his auto; the big car stood there blue and gleaming, well fed with Monsieur Planchard's hoarded gasoline. The liveried chauffeur sat elegantly at the wheel. "This is a good time for rats," said Monsieur Xavier.

He went over into the office of the deputy prefect and Simone followed him. Other officials came in, discipline was relaxed. Every one wanted to hear what the Châtelain had to say. Monsieur Cordelier received the Marquis de Saint-Brisson without concealing his astonishment. The latter greeted him and hesitated. The door of the office stood open and officials stood in the ante-room and even in the doorway. The Marquis probably expected that the deputy prefect would want to speak with him without witnesses. Since, however, Monsieur Cordelier made no move to send his officials away, the Châtelain began to speak.

"I have reason to assume," he said with his creaking voice,

"that my name will mean something to the German gentlemen who will probably appear here in the immediate future. I believe, Monsieur le Sous-Préfet, that I can be of some assistance to you in the reception of the Germans. In the interest of the county I regard it as my duty to be present here at the arrival of the German troops." He looked even more arrogant than ordinarily; he stood even more erectly, his brown eyes above his slightly hooked nose stared hard and contemptuously at the deputy prefect. He seemed unaware of the presence of others.

Every one waited for Monsieur Cordelier's answer. He meditated. It was easy to see that he had a sharp answer on his tongue but that he swallowed it. Finally, he said weakly: "If you think so," and pointed to a chair.

Simone saw the sallow, haughty face of the man; she saw the pale, helpless eyes of the deputy prefect; she saw the furious countenance of Monsieur Xavier. She was glad that she had made her decision. Saint-Martin would have the right answer for the fascists.

She left. She flitted by the office of the concierge and luck would have it that the concierge did not notice her. She left her bicycle there; she wanted every one to assume that she had stayed here at the Prefecture the entire time.

She went towards the Avenue du Parc. She was in a hurry. One-fourth of the time limit which she had set herself had already passed; she had a long way to go and she was on foot. She walked hastily so as not to be seen. She was supposed to be at the Deputy Prefecture; she crept along close to the walls.

Now she was in front of Etienne's house. She could not refrain from whistling the old signal which they had used as children. She decided to wait half a minute but before the half-minute was up he came.

He beamed when he saw her and seized her by both hands, as was his habit. "All day long I've been wondering whether you were coming," he said. "I was afraid they wouldn't let you go out there." She did not reply. Suddenly and vividly she thought of Henriette. How brave she had been, even bold, and then again filled with inexplicable fear. She clearly remembered a moment when they had been near the cemetery at night and Henriette had not even dared to pass there. And then Simone had laughed at her and had forced her to walk through the cemetery with her, and Henriette had been soaked with perspiration. Four or five such reminiscences came to her at the same time. With Henriette she could have discussed her action. Henriette would have understood perfectly why it had to be done. Henriette would have joined her.

Etienne walked along beside her. Close together they strolled in the shade of the old colourful houses. He led the way towards the Parc des Capucins; when they were children they had been there countless times together with Henriette.

The park was quite deserted. A few little girls were running about; they probably belonged to the fugitives. They were noisy, their cries sounded strange in the midst of all the silence; and they soon stopped as though paralysed.

Simone and Etienne sat down on one of the low benches. Only for three minutes, Simone told herself. They did not speak; it was very hot; a sleepy bird twittered in a near-by bush. They felt very close to each other.

After a while Etienne asked: "Did you dream of Henriette again?"

Simone answered—and for the life of her she could not have told why: "Yes, she gave me a commission to do." That was foolish and perfidious; she should never have said that. Now he probably expected her to tell him what sort of a commission it was. Now he would ask her and he had a right to ask. But of course she would not tell him under any circumstances.

However Etienne did not ask; he only looked at her, seriously, friendly and attentively, and she was grateful to him for not asking. She sat there in silence and confusion, embarrassed by her own indiscretion. Then at last she shook herself out of her lethargy, arose and said: "I must go on."

Etienne continued to look at her with the same serious friendliness and said: "That's too bad. I should have liked to talk with you a little longer, today of all days."

No, no; she dared not linger a moment longer. Suddenly she

had an idea. "Listen, Etienne," she said. "I am in a hurry and I left my bicycle at home because I thought the roads would still be crowded. But now I would surely get along faster on a wheel. Could you loan me yours?"

"Why, of course," he answered.

They walked back the short distance to his house. She waited. Everything was working out perfectly. Now she had a bicycle and no one except Etienne would know anything about it. He brought her the wheel. "Many thanks, Etienne," she said. She wanted to say more but she restrained herself. They looked straight at each other for a moment. Then she gave him her hand, quickly mounted the bicycle, and rode away.

There she rode, young, serious, happy, filled with her mission, at one with her mission, solemnly certain that her way was the right way.

At first, in order to attract no attention, she did not ride very fast. Then, however, as soon as she had reached the Avenue du Parc, she pedalled with all her might. She rode along, bent over the handle-bars, a deep furrow between her heavy, dark-blond eyebrows, her lips firmly pressed.

The road was quite empty. On her left ran the white line that divided the road and that had been put there at Uncle Prosper's instigation. It was uncanny to see the highway so deserted while only a few days ago it had been a dark, creeping caterpillar of people and vehicles. There it lay, greyish white and deserted, in expectation of the Boches. And so it was only for the Boches that Uncle Prosper had had the road so well repaired last year.

Simone was all alone. Nobody saw her on her perilous journey. No; one person almost certainly saw her: Père Bastide. He was surely standing in his window nook, waiting for the Germans and staring down at the road. She had a clear picture of him, standing motionless, full of grief, impotent, furious. His eyes would be following her as she rode along. But for him up there she would only be a tiny, hurrying speck; he would not guess who was so hastily moving along the highway and what was about to happen.

It was hot but she felt nothing of the heat through the speed of her motion. Now the road dropped downhill and she could coast; she sat up straight. Round about her a vast silence reigned; all about her everything was quiet. The immobility, the complete hush of the landscape oppressed her. It seemed to her as though she had been riding since time immemorial; it seemed to her as though this ride would never end. And it seemed to her as though she had experienced all this once before, this rapid, silent, and wild ride to a wild and great goal.

She dared not lose herself in dreams, she dared not permit herself to digress, she had to think of her task, only of her task. She had planned everything with great care. Some time ago a small fire had broken out in the garage and at that time the drivers had expertly discussed the possible origin and course of such a fire; they had conversed at great length about the likelihood of a fire and an explosion, and she, in her quiet manner, had listened and had remembered everything. Last night, on the basis of her knowledge, she had carefully considered her plan of action. Now she quickly reviewed it as she had done ten times, twenty times, before. Again she reached into her pocket and felt for the key and for the lighter. The only thing that she still needed was a stone which she would have to pick up along the way. She picked up a suitable one. Now she had everything.

It was a good thing that the establishment lay in complete isolation far away from the city and from other houses. The explosion would endanger no other buildings. And everything would be timed right. If she set the fire in the basement it would not be discovered in time to extinguish it. She, on the other hand, would have ample opportunity to reach a safe distance before the trucks and the great gasoline tank would explode.

The road again levelled out; it even began to rise a little and Simone had to exert herself. And for the first time she saw some people. They were a few soldiers, lying at the side of the road in the shade of the bushes. As she pedalled past them they called to her. "Hello, Mademoiselle," they shouted, "won't you join us? We are waiting for the Germans," and they lifted a bottle. They were drunk and they were waiting for the Germans. Simone rode faster.

Now she had reached the point where the private road branched off to the Planchard establishment. The entrance was still blocked by the chain. Simone and her bicycle slipped under the barrier. She stood in front of the locked main gate of the loading yard. She had arrived in time.

No one would be able to stop her now. Now the gasoline and the loading yard belonged to her, not to the Boches. Now Maurice had lost his bet.

She leaned the wheel against the wall and climbed over into the yard.

The loading yard lay empty and white and dead. It was depressing to stand as the only living being in this hot expanse. She looked at the clock above the office entrance. There was not much time to spare. She would have to make the best use of the next few moments; she would have to think of nothing but her purpose; she would have to attend to her business precisely and in the exact sequence in which she had planned it.

She took a firm grip on the stone that she had gathered up on the way and smashed the glass pane of the door leading from the yard to the offices. There was a sharp crash that startled her. She removed the fragments of the broken pane and pushed back the bolt that barred the door on the inside. In doing so she injured her hand; it was a slight injury, a scratch, nothing at all. It only annoyed her a little that she stained her slacks with a little blood.

She climbed the stairs to the private office. They were awkward stone steps and they seemed endless. Her feet were leaden; every step cost an effort.

At last she had reached the top.

She took the key from her pocket. It was the key to the door in front of her, the key to Uncle Prosper's private office. He was accustomed to take it home with him and to keep it in his bedroom. She had taken it from there.

She unlocked the door. The dead, confined air, the sultry heat, the silence of the little room oppressed her. Suddenly the forbidden, adventurous character of her situation overcame her like a physical force. There she stood in this room in which Uncle Prosper kept the letters and the things that others were not to see; she had broken into this room illicitly. For a moment she stood there paralysed.

Then she quickly put the notion aside. She was here to look for another key, the key to the gasoline tank. She knew where it was kept. Uncle Prosper had frequently given it to her and he had frequently put it away here when she had returned it. The key was kept in the second drawer of the desk on the upper right-hand side. She was sure of that. But what if it should not be there after all? The tiny moment while she opened the drawer seemed an eternity of tense torment.

Now the drawer was open. And there lay the key.

She took it. It felt cold and the chill of the metal was pleasant to her perspiring hand.

Presently, however, she drew up her shoulders uneasily. She seemed to feel the hard, small, wicked eyes of Madame upon her and she seemed to hear her soft, high, harsh voice: "I have spoken in vain. I have not succeeded in checking your impertinence and in putting you on the right way." No, she was not doing this out of impertinence. She was doing it because she was Simone Planchard, the daughter of Pierre Planchard.

The rest was easy. She went down into the basement of the garage; she distributed oil-soaked rags; she distributed them carefully and precisely, in the basement, on the stairs, in the garage. It would require some time for the fire to reach a point where it could no longer be extinguished, but she had prescribed its course and it could not possibly be discovered early enough in the bright sunlight.

Then she walked over to the tank. She unlocked it, lifted out the one small lid and then the second one. With tightly closed lips and distended nostrils she breathed in the slight odour of gasoline.

Now everything was ready. There had been much to do and she had done it with undivided attentiveness; now she was exhausted. It must have taken her an endless time, surely more than an hour. She looked at the clock. It had taken four minutes.

Now it remained only to light the first rag. She returned to the basement. She stood there with the lighter in her hand. It was not too late yet; she only needed to ride back to town and nothing would have happened. No, something would have happened after all. The Boches would come and she would have played into their hands, she would have helped the Boches to get the prized trucks and the gasoline.

"When, if not now? And who else, if not you?" The lighter sprang into flame; the oil-soaked rag flared up.

With her dark, deep-set eyes she stared in fascination at the flame; her long, thin, shapely lips were opened in a blank, avid smile; she breathed the odour of the fire. Tensely she watched the board beginning to smoulder; she watched the fire eating its way to the next rag.

It was still not too late to extinguish it. Even now. The flame came nearer. It was no longer smouldering, it was fire, and now the fire seized upon the second rag. But it could still have been extinguished.

Simone walked towards the exit, with small hesitant steps; she walked backwards, staring, staring at the flame. She walked up the stairs, backwards, step by step, holding to the railing with her hand and staring at the flame as it ran its prescribed course.

Then, in sudden flight, she ran from the basement.

In the garage she stopped once more. She went into the washroom and washed the scratch on her hand. With expert eye she examined the blood stain on her slacks to see whether it had dried. It was only a tiny stain and it had dried in the heat. She brushed it off. She was seized with a sudden uncontrollable desire to take a shower bath. It was too bad that there was no time.

She left the loading yard. She took Etienne's wheel. She rode away.

Her heart was filled with a great joy. Now the fire was running its prescribed course. Now Uncle Prosper's name was safe from disgrace. Now Maurice had lost his bet. Now the gasoline and the trucks would not fall into the hands of the Boches.

VI: A Night of Expectation

BEFORE dinner on the evening of this day Madame and Simone were waiting as usual in the Blue Room for Monsieur Planchard. Simone sat erectly in her uncomfortable chair. Madame, in her black silk dress and neat coiffure, had seated herself in the wing chair, enthroned stiffly, in massive dignity.

Simone had returned to the Villa Monrepos and performed her customary tasks in the garden and in the kitchen. Uncle Prosper was not at home. Madame informed her that it had been Monsieur Planchard's original intention not to show himself in Saint-Martin. But when the explosion took place he could no longer stand it in the Villa Monrepos and had driven to town.

When Simone heard that, she breathed a sigh of relief, and yet suffered disappointment. She had wanted ardently to be present at the moment when Uncle Prosper was informed of the action. She had wanted to see his face at that moment, his surprise, his shock. She had wanted to see his secret, no, his shining joy; for certainly his joy that now he need not reproach himself for having brought disgrace upon the name of Planchard would eclipse his shock.

Now he would hear all about the occurrence while in the city. He would guess, of course, that it was she who had done the deed. He would be torn by conflicting emotions. She could hardly wait to see his face when he returned and looked at her. He would be clever enough to pretend that he knew nothing. But at heart he would be grateful to her and would make some oblique comment and caress her.

The room lay dusky, cool, and quiet. Madame sat calmly in her wing chair. But Simone was quite sure that it was only a surface calmness. She wondered whether Madame knew of her excursion to town. It was possible. The roads were passable now and one of Madame's two friends might well have come out and have told her. Madame always knew more than one expected.

"Imagine," Madame said abruptly, "my son could not find the key to his private office today. That's the first time in twenty-five years. It may be that in the excitement over the argument with Philippe he left it at the office. But he was quite certain that he brought it home with him and he even thought he saw it this morning."

Simone did not budge and did not answer. She tried to maintain a placid face and not betray herself by a sudden start. She was glad that the room was so dusky.

"Turn on the radio," Madame demanded after a while. The radio was working. It was the Dijon station, now obviously in the hands of the Germans. The radio told of the progress of the German armies. It told of the destruction of English troops that were trying to flee back to England. Then came instructions regarding the sections of Burgundy newly occupied by the Germans. All public utilities would have to function within twenty-four hours, likewise all establishments concerned with the production and sale of foodstuffs. From nightfall until six o'clock in the morning the population were not permitted to appear outside their houses. Then followed items of local news. It was reported from Saint-Martin that the Planchard Transfer Company plant had burned to the ground along with the entire fleet of trucks; the authorities of the Army of Occupation had started an investigation in collaboration with the French authorities.

Simone, overcome by the magnitude of the news, had jumped to her feet. Her action had been a complete success. And she had acted in the very nick of time. She forgot that she was not alone in the room. Her face distorted, both hands clenched on the back of her chair, she stood there. She was filled with fierce earnestness and with great, consuming joy.

Madame sat slumped; she had given up the effort to appear composed. "So that was it," she said. "My God, my God. So that's the way it is. That was it. That is it." She panted so hard that Simone became frightened. She stepped closer to Madame; wanted to help her but did not dare.

Very gradually Madame became calmer. Simone did not dare to ask anything, to say anything.

Three minutes later, however, Madame had regained a semblance of composure. "My son had the right instinct," she said. "Under these circumstances the only thing he could do was to show himself in town."

Five minutes later Madame was the calm and poised lady whom Simone had always known. "Maybe the telephone is really working," she said with a trace of grim irony. "The Germans seem to be sticklers for law and order. Try it. Call up Monsieur Peyroux."

Simone tried to get the connexion. The telephone did not work. Madame was not particularly annoyed. "Lower the shutters," she ordered, "and turn on the lights." Simone did as she was bidden. Then Madame meditated aloud: "The Germans have directed the population to stay off the streets at night. My son knows well enough to obey the order. We cannot expect him tonight. We will begin to eat," she decided.

Simone served the meal. They ate. Simone knew that Madame was filled with anxiety for her son. Her own thoughts, too, centred on Uncle Prosper. Had the Germans arrested him? Whatever had happened it would not take long to prove his innocence. He could produce evidence of his violent opposition to the order of the deputy prefect. And if the Boches should not believe him, she would be ready to testify that she was the one who did it, entirely on her own and without any accomplice.

It was quite possible that they had arrested Uncle Prosper. In that case they had probably held him in the Saint-Michel prison, near the Hall of Justice. This prison had played a great role in her childhood. It was near her school and she had always passed it timidly but mysteriously attracted. Dangerous, venturesome men lived behind those walls. She had been especially terrified at the bandit and killer, Guitriaux, who was imprisoned there before his transfer to Francheville, the capital of the Département. Countless times she and Henriette had discussed the Saint-Michel prison; Henriette had been even more interested than she in the ancient building. They had often loitered about it in the hope that they might some time catch sight of a notorious criminal. She shrank from the idea that Uncle Prosper might be locked up in this prison. A man who loved the good things of life as he did and who was accustomed to respectful treatment would suffer doubly.

Madame sat at the table as though nothing had happened. She did not speak of the events of the day nor of Uncle Prosper. She ate only a little, but she ate.

Later, while Simone was preparing the salad, she raised her lorgnon, watched her, and asked casually: "You were in town today, weren't you, Simone?"

Now Simone had to be careful not to say too much and not too little. "Yes," she replied.

"What was going on in town?" asked Madame.

Simone became very much occupied with the mixing of the salad. "The city was quite deserted," she said, "all the houses were closed. I didn't see anybody, only a few soldiers. The city was never so deserted before. I was at the Deputy Prefecture. They were all waiting for the Boches there. They all had their Sunday clothes on. The Châtelain was there, too. He was *en grand tralala* with his auto and chauffeur." She narrated in order not to be forced to narrate. The salad was ready, and Simone placed the wooden bowl on the table.

"Were you in the city when the explosion took place?" Madame asked straight out.

Simone did not blush. Simone said in a completely natural voice: "I was already on the way home."

Madame was silent for a fraction of a second. Then she asked: "Were you wearing the green striped dress?"

"No," said Simone. She looked straight at Madame and added resolutely: "I was wearing my slacks."

Madame raised the fork to her mouth. Then she said: "If you could not refrain from going to town without asking permission, you could at least have dressed decently. You yourself have remarked that the gentlemen at the Deputy Prefecture were in their Sunday clothes. It is a piece of impertinence to wear slacks on a day like this." Simone did not reply. "Did you hear me?"

Madame asked without raising her voice and without emphasis. "Yes, Madame," answered Simone.

She pretended submission, but her heart was filled with triumph. Uncle Prosper had always been the object of a secret struggle between her and Madame. Madame wanted to suppress and stifle in her son everything that reminded of Pierre Planchard. Now, through her action, Simone had forced an unequivocal decision. Now Uncle Prosper would prove himself as the brother of Pierre Planchard, and all the world would see that Uncle Prosper was a Planchard.

The telephone rang loudly. Both of them were startled. "You go answer it," Madame commanded.

It was Monsieur Cordelier. He wanted to speak with Madame. Madame considered. She wanted very much to go to the telephone but she was afraid that she might make an indiscreet remark. She restrained herself. "Tell him," she directed Simone, "that I have already gone to bed. You speak with him."

Simone asked the deputy prefect to give her his message for Madame. Monsieur Cordelier hesitated. "Tell Madame," his high, hollow, breaking voice came out of the receiver, "that she should not be worried. It is only on account of the general curfew order that Monsieur Planchard cannot come home tonight."

"Thank you, Monsieur le Sous-Préfet," said Simone. She could sense the anxiety in which Madame waited and she resolutely asked: "May I ask where Monsieur Planchard is now?"

"Monsieur Planchard is at my house," replied the deputy prefect and, still hesitatingly and carefully choosing his words, he added: "Tell Madame that every one has the greatest sympathy with him."

"Thank you, Monsieur le Sous-Préfet," Simone said once more. "Is there anything more that I could tell Madame?"

"Monsieur Planchard will return the very first thing in the morning," said the deputy prefect.

Madame was standing out in the hall; she had not been able to remain in the room. Simone saw how she struggled against herself, undecided whether she should come to the telephone contrary to the dictates of wisdom. Simone, at the telephone, asked: "Could Monsieur Planchard perhaps come to the telephone in person?"

Again the deputy prefect hesitated. Then, in his official voice he said: "That is not advisable," and, as though to make amends for this harshness, he quickly continued: "Good night, my dear," and hung up the receiver.

Madame pushed her massive, fleshy face forward. Simone had never seen her so completely uncontrolled; her entire frame was in quivering, anxious expectation. Simone hastened to report the content of the telephone conversation. She had to report every word exactly. Madame asked again and again: "How did he say that? 'Every one has the greatest sympathy with him.' Is that what he said? Just those words?" Simone had paid close attention; she had each word in her memory and Madame weighed each word. No matter how repugnant Madame was to Simone, nevertheless she felt pity for this woman who was worried about her son, and if it had not been too indiscreet she would gladly have said: "Don't be afraid. Nothing can happen to him. I did it and I will let no one else suffer for it."

Madame brooded over Monsieur Cordelier's message. She no longer made it a point to appear calm and superior; she was an old woman afflicted with a mortal fear for that which was the content of her life. Suddenly, circuitously, her worry and rage broke loose. "That Philippe, that idiot," she said softly but with undisguised anger. "I can understand that he is cautious; he has been a coward from birth. But he might have told me a little more. He could have expressed himself a little more plainly. 'Every one has the greatest sympathy with him.' What does that mean? That may mean everything and it may mean nothing. He did not need to ring me up to tell me that." And: "Everybody hates my son," she continued softly, pathetically, grimly. "Everybody is glad if something happens to him. Everybody is jealous of him, all those small, mean people round him. They have always been waiting to play him some sort of a dirty trick. It was probably one of the truck drivers who did it. They'll say they did it for political reasons, they did it for the fatherland, but I know them. It is nothing but hatred and envy. It is the hatred of the riff-raff, because my son is bigger than they, because he accomplished something in life. They begrudge him his success and that is why they have used the first opportunity to ruin him." She was now speaking in an almost inaudible tone but with constantly rising bitterness: "And how maliciously they figured this thing out and planned all its details! It's perfectly clear now: they were the ones who stole the key." She stared straight ahead, furiously and impotently.

Suddenly she composed herself. "I think," she said in her usual cold, polite manner to Simone, "that you had better wash the dishes and go to bed. But first give me another cigarette."

Simone gave her a light. Then she left. In the doorway she looked back at Madame with a fleeting glance. There she sat, in the very harsh, unshaded light, alone, fat, black—smoking.

VII: The First Consequences

FROM the moment of daybreak on, Simone impatiently awaited Uncle Prosper's return. "The very first thing in the morning he will come home," the deputy prefect had said. The morning advanced. Ten times she ran out into the garden to the spot from which she could overlook a part of the road. Ten times she returned disappointed.

Just as Madame had done yesterday, and as she was probably still doing, Simone, too, now weighed the words of the deputy prefect again and again, but she did not share Madame's worry over Uncle Prosper's physical fate; she was rather certain that Monsieur Cordelier's message had not been mere empty words of comfort. What disturbed her were her suppressed doubts about Uncle Prosper's inner attitude towards her action. She did not permit these doubts to take shape. She was sure that her action had been most welcome to him; the entire city—Monsieur Cordelier's hint proved it—evaluated the incident correctly and understood the motives. But the mentality of the Villa Monrepos was different from that of the city, and Madame's soft, evil words sounded constantly in Simone's ears, the grimly convinced, false accusation that only hatred of Uncle Prosper had caused the fire in the garage. Madame's words crawled like spiders over Simone's faith.

At last the telephone rang. Simone answered it at once. Yes, it was Uncle Prosper. He said good morning, he asked how everything was in the Villa Monrepos, he spoke as he always did. Simone regretted that; she had expected him to say something unusual to her. But he probably considered it inadvisable to speak freely over the telephone where the Germans would overhear him. He contented himself with a few general phrases and then asked for Madame.

Simone called Madame. Madame was already standing there. Squeezed into the corner of the corridor, Simone listened to her answers. Madame was monosyllabic and little could be gathered from her words; moreover, the conversation was brief. Simone hoped that Madame would inform her of its content. "Is Uncle well?" she finally asked since Madame remained silent. "He is well," Madame answered.

After the noon meal, as her uncle had still not returned, Simone prepared herself for her usual trip to the city. She knew perfectly well that this did not correspond with Madame's wishes, but she did not care. She put on her green striped dress, she took the basket and the bicycle.

At the entrance to the city a barrier had been erected across the road and German soldiers stood guard. The sight shocked Simone. She had known that the Boches were here and she had imagined countless times what it would be like. But now, when she saw the Boches in the flesh, she was startled as though it were something new and unexpected. And still the German soldiers were young fellows with harmless, indifferent faces. They scarcely paid any attention to Simone. A narrow gateway had been left open for pedestrians and without any interference they permitted her to pass.

Simone walked numbly through the city. German soldiers were everywhere. Her reason told her that this was tangible reality, but her whole being refused to believe it. The shocked surprise did not leave her. It was not possible that they were actually there, sitting, standing, speaking loudly in their incomprehensible, barbaric language.

Simone had had no clear conception of the character of the entering victors. Only this she had expected: the evil which was to come would be marked by an evil exterior; she had believed that the victors would be distinguished from the inhabitants by hard, cruel faces and a wild manner. But this was not at all the case. The Boche soldiers were young, loud, and cheerful, and that was all. Simone perceived this, since she was a sensible girl, and yet she found the strange soldiers unbearably insolent. Their mere presence was an impudence which filled Simone to the brim with pain and rage.

The Boches felt quite at home. They sat about in front of the hotels, in the squares, on the platforms of the cafés; they had made themselves comfortable, they had unbuttoned their shirts in the heat, they laughed and spoke loudly, they splashed each other with water from the fountain in the Place Sauvigny. And the matter-of-factness with which they seemed to feel at home here, this easy-going manner, appeared to Simone worse than the worst brutality that they could have devised.

There were more stores open than previously. The inhabitants of Saint-Martin, however, so far as they were visible at all, sneaked timidly along the walls, they spoke in undertones, they hurried across the streets to get back into their houses. They seemed strangers in their own city. As Simone walked through the familiar, winding, hilly streets she seemed doubly a stranger, a stranger to the Boches and a stranger to the people of Saint-Martin on account of her action, on account of her secret. Indeed, it seemed to her as though the inhabitants also regarded her as something strange, something extraordinary.

She passed Etienne's house. Since her deed she had not spoken with any one who was near and dear to her. She had to see Etienne. She whistled their signal. She hoped that he had stayed; she hoped that he was here. She waited for his coming as for a vital verdict. He came.

On his honest, broad-browed, pointed face, all his emotions were unmistakably reflected, and Simone saw at once that he knew everything. Of course, that was to be expected, after she had so rashly told him about her dream. She regretted having told him, but she was glad that she could now talk freely with him.

Just as the day before, as by tacit agreement, they walked to the Parc des Capucins. There were children on the playground today and two German soldiers were watching the children and were laughing. That did not prevent Simone and Etienne from sitting down on one of the low benches.

Etienne looked at Simone admiringly. "I always knew it," he said and his voice was hoarse with reverent emotion. "I knew it all the time, that you would do something really great some day."

Simone blushed deeply, she perspired, she did not know where to look in her embarrassment, she busied herself with her bicycle which was leaning against the bench. But in her heart she was full of pride and happiness. "So you really think that it was right?" she said a little awkwardly.

"Right?" he asked passionately and indignantly. "It was splendid, marvellous. I am so proud to be your friend. That was a wonderful dream that you had."

Simone blushed even more deeply. She remained silent. She did not know what to answer.

After a little, with a sly, good-natured smile, he continued: "And everybody knows that it was you."

She was startled. "But how? How could they know?" she asked.

"That's perfectly clear," he replied. "You are Pierre Planchard's daughter, aren't you?"

"And doesn't any one think," she asked, "that Uncle Prosper might have done it?"

"Monsieur Planchard?" exclaimed Etienne in surprise. "No, I guess no one thinks of that."

He noticed her embarrassment. "Why, didn't you want them to know?" he asked. "It seems to me that they should all know it; only they shouldn't know it in the presence of the Boches."

Simone reflected for a while. The children played noisily. The soldiers had gone away. Of course that was the way she had wanted it. "Listen, Etienne," she said, "you are quite right, they should know it, but it is important that they do not know it. It was not I. It can't possibly have been I. I was in town the entire time, everybody saw me. I was at the Deputy Prefecture, I left my bicycle at the Deputy Prefecture. Do you understand?"

"You thought of everything, didn't you?" Etienne said, admiringly.

They walked back to the interior of the city. Simone felt that every one was looking at her. It was embarrassing, she had a prickling sensation as though ants were crawling on her, but at the same time it was satisfying. She was glad that she was not alone and she chatted self-consciously with Etienne.

They went across the Place Saint-Lazare. On one of the benches under the elms sat Maurice, again with the overdressed Louison. "Hello, Simone," he called to her. "How's everything? Don't you want to join us today? I think we have every reason for a little chat."

"I don't know," she said hesitantly.

"But I know," he answered. "Just send your young man home. If he wants to, he can go walking with my Louison. I really have things to talk over with you."

"Monsieur," said Etienne and tried hard to put a threat into the word.

"Don't get excited, young man," said Maurice. "Nothing is going to happen to your Simone. She needs some good advice, believe me."

Simone was annoyed that Maurice was ordering her about again. On the other hand, she was pleased that here was a man who knew something and was willing to take charge of her somewhat complicated affairs. "Please let me talk with him, Etienne," she begged.

Louison had arisen and inspected her with a little, amused and insolent smile. Simone paid no attention to her. She sat down beside Maurice. "Well, at last," he said, and waited until they were alone.

"Well, my dear, you've certainly gotten yourself into a fine mess," he began. "With your flapper's enthusiasm," he added, a bit maliciously. Simone blushed deeply. "You know, I've been the first one to suffer for your patriotic impulses," he continued. "They accused me right off the bat."

"Why should they?" asked Simone, "and who are 'they'?"

"That's not quite clear," answered Maurice. "I was called up to the Deputy Prefecture," he reported, "and the District Attorney Lefèbre from Francheville, Monsieur Xavier, and a German officer were there. The German paid damn close attention, but he didn't open his trap."

"And they really suspected you, of all people?" Simone asked.

It grieved her that she had involved Maurice, too; at the same time, however, she was vaguely pleased that in this way he had become a participant in her action.

"Does that seem so incredible to you?" Maurice asked. "It's perfectly obvious, isn't it?"

"I certainly wouldn't have left you in the lurch," said Simone, eagerly and decidedly, "if they had done something to you."

"That's kind of you," Maurice commented. Simone was not offended by his sarcasm.

"How was it?" she asked.

"Well, you can bet it wasn't a picnic," Maurice answered. "I didn't know what they were driving at, and I didn't want to get anybody else into trouble. It took quite a while before I could figure out the lay of the land. The Boches wanted to know two things. In the first place, when the thing happened. Because, if it was before they moved in and fixed penalties for the destruction of war materials, then the whole affair is none of their business and technically not punishable. But most of all they want to find out the inside story; they want to know who the local patriots are and where to look for their enemies. They asked devious and tricky questions, and at first I had to do a lot of dodging. Then finally Monsieur Xavier put me on the right track."

"Was the cross-examination very bad, Maurice?" asked Simone, almost with a consciousness of guilt.

"Well, I didn't want to get anybody into a jam by a careless word," replied Maurice. "It wasn't very hard to prove my own innocence."

"I'm glad that they couldn't do anything to you, Maurice," Simone said candidly. "But, you see," she added proudly, "you lost your bet after all."

"What bet?" Maurice asked with surprise. "Oh, of course," he corrected himself. "I'll pay it all right. You can collect your liquor and cigarettes from me any time. But I'm only paying up because I'm a gentleman. In the end I was right and you were wrong."

"How come?" Simone protested. "You maintained that Uncle Prosper would never sacrifice the truck yard."

"Did he sacrifice it?" Maurice inquired in amazement. "Did you get his permission?" He grinned all over his broad, shrewd face.

Simone was angry. "How do you know," she declared defensively and foolishly, "that I did it at all?"

Maurice laughed loudly and good-naturedly. "My sweet little innocent," he said, "nobody in the whole world except you could have done such a childish job. You know, there are other means that would be less obvious. For instance, you could put sugar into the gasoline; that works pretty well for quite a long time. But I don't understand why you did it at all, if now you do not want to own up to it. What was the whole thing for, if it was not to be a signal? Or did you imagine that you would hold up the whole German army by destroying Monsieur Planchard's gasoline?"

Simone sat in pensive silence. "Was it wrong, Maurice?" she asked timidly in a childlike manner.

Maurice looked at her askance. She sat there a little awkwardly, modestly, like a diligent pupil intent upon doing the right thing. Maurice was completely disarmed. Something of human warmth came into his voice. "Wrong, my dear?" he rejoined. "No, it wasn't exactly wrong. But the danger is entirely out of proportion to the advantage."

It was the first time that Maurice had ever spoken with her cordially and as a true friend. Simone was happy. She did not mind being treated by him as a child. She believed in his greater knowledge and in his better judgment, and even though he perhaps did not completely approve of her action, no one had more understanding for it. She felt safe now that she knew of his concern for her.

Presently she took up the conversation again. "And do you really believe," she asked, "that everybody knows that I did it, even the Germans?"

"Of course," Maurice replied.

"But," Simone considered, "after the Germans have determined that it happened before they came, everything will be all right, won't it? That is what you said."

"I did not say that, Simone," answered Maurice. "In the first place, the Boches can reopen the case any time it suits them. In the second place, the chief danger does not come from the Boches."

Simone looked at him with wide-eyed surprise.

"My God, such innocence," he jeered and his voice was high and squeaky again. "Don't you understand that this case of arson will enrage our own fascists much more than the Boches? The Châtelain and Joe Blow will never forgive you for what you have done to them. You can just bet your life on that. Why do you suppose these gentlemen let the Boches into the country? Only for the purpose of thoroughly cleaning up everything that they call subversive. And then you go ahead and set fire to their house right over their heads. Patriotism? Why that is mutiny. All the more when you are the one who did it, you, the daughter of Pierre Planchard. That smells like *la Commune,* that smells like revolution. No, my dear, the war is just starting. From now on you won't have a bed of roses at the Villa Monrepos."

Behind his light mocking tone Simone felt the incisive quality of his words. She thought of Madame, sitting alone under the bright lights, black, smoking; and a chill ran over her. In her heart of hearts she told herself that Maurice was right and that the war was only starting, but she did not want to believe it. He said these things out of pure prejudice, his hatred carried him away, he had always been unjust to Uncle Prosper. "What you say there is all wrong," she declared passionately. "You have it in for Uncle Prosper. Even old Georges knows that. It is utterly out of the question that Uncle Prosper would do anything to me."

Maurice only looked at her and smiled. "Have it your way, Mademoiselle," he said and shrugged his shoulders.

Simone's attitude suddenly changed. "If they try to do something to me," she asked full of confidence, "would you help me, Maurice?"

"That is a funny question," rejoined Maurice. "How do you expect a little truck driver to help you if the whole German army moves against you?"

"But you said," Simone replied softly, "that the danger need not come from the Germans."

"Oh, that's what you mean," said Maurice with a smile. "So you are not as stupid as you pretend to be. Of course we would help you," he said. He spoke in an ordinary tone and yet it inspired confidence. "We are all back of you."

"Thanks, Maurice," said Simone. She felt very much relieved.

"But now you will have to go," he said.

"Why should I?" she asked, for it was still early. Did he want to get rid of her?

"Didn't you notice?" he replied. "It is an hour later than you think. When the Germans came they introduced their time here. Night falls an hour earlier now than it used to."

Simone gulped. So now they had German time in Saint-Martin.

She bade farewell to Maurice. As she pushed her bicycle back through the town she felt even more plainly that all the people were looking after her and were talking behind her back. She was no longer pleased about it; it embarrassed her, annoyed her.

She rode home. She was very happy that Maurice was her friend. But her relation to him was not easy. He had spoken about Uncle Prosper with great bitterness and with great scorn. He was not right. She did not want him to be right.

When she arrived at the Villa Monrepos she saw that Uncle Prosper's hat was there. So he had come home. In just a moment she would know, she would see that Maurice had done him an injustice. However, she heard Uncle Prosper in deep conversation with Madame and she did not want to see him in Madame's presence. First she would have to talk with him in private.

She changed clothes. She prepared dinner as usual. She awaited an opportunity for a talk with Uncle Prosper. Madame came into the kitchen. She examined what Simone had prepared and instructed her to toast croutons for the soup. Then, coldly and politely as always, she said: "As a result of the recent events I must prescribe some rules of conduct for you, Simone. My son does not wish you to show yourself in town in the next few days.

For the present, therefore, you will not leave the house. Moreover, my son and I will have questions of a confidential nature to discuss at meals for some time to come. Therefore, until further notice, it is better that you should take your meals here in the kitchen and not with us."

PART THREE

REALIZATION

I: Uncle Prosper's Face

SIMONE was at work in the garden. She wore coarse, faded overalls and a large straw hat. It was towards evening, but still very hot.

Since Madame had banished her from Uncle's table and had declared her to be a prisoner, a brief week had passed, a week devoid of outward events. Simone had been asked nothing, she had not been called to account, she had not been permitted to make any explanations; she was simply imprisoned and ignored. Madame restricted herself to the most necessary instructions; Uncle Prosper appeared only in Madame's presence and Simone had no opportunity to speak privately with him.

She knew nothing, nothing at all about the events in the city or in the country. She was prevented from receiving any information. She was prevented from learning what the people of Saint-Martin thought of her action. What had happened in the investigation of the destruction of the truck yard? Did the inquiry produce any consequences? Did the Boches take steps against Uncle Prosper? Did they seize his plant?

It was almost intolerable to be in the dark about all that. She brooded over what might happen to her but she could not imagine anything.

One thing was certain, Madame was her enemy. The fact that Madame did not reproach her, that she persisted in cold and evil silence, was only an indication that she was preparing dark, complex plots against her. But Uncle Prosper, what about him? He did not like to conceal his emotions; he liked to speak out freely, to give vent to his anger. The fact that he also passed her in silence, and only occasionally cast a gloomy, embarrassed glance in her direction, surely was not the result of his own impulse, but the wish of Madame. It was cruel that Uncle Prosper had gone over to Madame's side without giving Simone a hearing.

In this week of solitude, of silence, and of imprisonment, Simone had become harder and more grown up. She had taken stock of her friends and had realized to what extent she was dependent upon herself alone. Père Bastide, Monsieur Xavier, Etienne were not clever enough to help her; much as they were attached to her and great though their efforts might be, they simply could not. Maurice was not nearly so close to her, but if any one could help her, he would be the one. He knew what he wanted, he was a *débrouillard,* he was a man. Her heart warmed when she thought of that conversation with him on the bench under the elm trees. It was too bad that she had been able to talk confidentially with him only that one time.

Simone was now working at the wall in the western corner of the garden. The garden was laid out on hilly ground but in spite of its extent all parts of it could be seen from the house. Only this little spot by the westerly wall was not visible from the windows. Wherever else Simone worked in the house or in the garden, she knew that Madame's eyes were on her. This part of the garden, however, gave her freedom from surveillance, and all day long she looked forward to the hours which she could spend here without supervision.

The wall was high. But if Simone stepped up on the big rock she could see out into the road and she could even overlook a considerable part of its length. It was the narrow, neglected road to the mountain village, Noiret, and hardly any one ever appeared on it. Nevertheless Simone again and again climbed upon the rock, clung to the wall until her hands were sore, and gazed out along the road.

There she was, standing on her rock, clinging to the wall with both hands and looking into the distance. Her serious, thoughtful countenance was hard with longing. She yearned for the sight of a familiar face, for one of her friends. She had expected to pay for her action in suffering, and she bore her imprisonment with patience. But she had not imagined that she would have to bear everything all alone. Every day, as she clung to the wall, she hoped that one of her friends might find the way to her. But no one came. Madame let no one come near. Madame guarded her well.

It was also Madame who prevented Uncle Prosper from speaking with her. After all, that was a comfort for Simone and gave her hope. For if Madame had felt entirely certain of Uncle Prosper, she wouldn't have prevented her from having a talk with him. But Madame evidently feared that Uncle Prosper would understand her action in spite of everything, and that he might even approve of it. No, let Maurice say whatever he wished, Uncle Prosper was not her enemy.

Uncle Prosper had a perplexed and furious face whenever he saw her. He avoided her. But he could do that only because she, Simone, permitted it. She was too proud; she made things too easy for him. She felt that she really ought to corner him and force him to speak with her.

Tall and slim, Simone stood on her rock. She looked lost in her faded, baggy overalls; her large deep-set eyes gazed tensely, sadly, darkly along the road that stretched out empty and white.

She would no longer allow Uncle Prosper to pass by her in this foolish, sulky way. He would finally have to give her an accounting.

She knew that Madame was upstairs just now and that Uncle was sitting in the Blue Room, moodily twisting the radio dial. Simone had instructions to stay in her mansard and nowhere else when she had no work to do. She paid no attention to this order. Just as she was, in her overalls, and with the traces of her work in the garden, she went to him.

He looked up in surprise when she entered. "I have to speak with you, Uncle Prosper," she said boldly.

He looked at her morosely. "But I don't want to speak with you, you—" he answered; he suppressed the insult which he had evidently intended to add.

"You *must* speak with me," she insisted. "I would rather go to the Germans and tell them that I did it than to go on living here in the house this way."

He was sitting in an arm-chair and he looked at her askance. Her face was filled with gloomy courage; she was capable of everything. "What do you want, anyhow?" he grumbled. "You ought to be satisfied that they haven't come after you. You ought to be satisfied that you are getting off so easy." And with rising anger he exploded: "To steal my key, the key to my private office! Such deceitfulness! A thief! A household thief! The daughter of my brother!"

It had cost her a tremendous effort at that time to take the key. She was thoroughly honest by nature, and moreover, she had been taught that larceny was the worst of all crimes. But that Uncle Prosper should emphasize this one tiny detail above everything that pertained to her action, filled her with angry contempt. She did not reply nor did she turn aside her glance, as he had probably expected. On the contrary, she looked at him long and unflinching, and it seemed to her as if she were seeing him for the first time.

Until now, even on the rare occasions when she rebelled against him, he had always appeared to her as a man of the highest integrity, and his strong, virile face had inspired respect. Now she recognized him as something else. No, this large face with its marked features had nothing in common with the face of her father. There was the fine, strong, well-shaped mouth; there were the bright, grey-blue eyes under the heavy reddish-blond eyebrows. And yet it was not a manly face. This Uncle Prosper of hers was not capable of a great act; he could not understand great emotions; he could see nothing in her action except that she had stolen his key. Without putting the feeling into thought, Simone perceived what a miserable game of hide-and-seek this man was playing with himself. He had done many good things for her, he was fond of her, he had helped others, he was an active man with ideas, he had built up a big business. But when it came to something that really mattered, he failed. His face was a mask and she could now look behind the mask. He was a failure.

"Why do you look at me like that?" he asked. She still did not answer, but he probably sensed that she had no feeling of guilt at all; that, on the contrary, she had come to make accusations and demands. He did not pursue the matter of the key.

"You still don't seem to have any clear understanding," he said, "of the misfortune that you caused. You didn't only blow up a few trucks, but you destroyed everything that I built up in the course of a lifetime of hard work."

It was not Joe Blow speaking at this moment. Simone, however, still more calmly and with her eyes still on him, declared: "You knew perfectly well that the gasoline and the trucks were not to fall into the hands of the Germans. Monsieur Cordelier told you that again and again. You said yourself that you would do it at the right time."

Uncle Prosper only laughed. "At the right time," he mocked. "Two minutes before the surrender, I suppose that was the right time? Did you believe that you could prevent the armistice by blowing up my plant?"

"Surrender? Armistice?" asked Simone, turning pale.

"Any blind man could see," he continued, "that the armistice was only a question of days. What Philippe was saying was only a repetition of the silly phrases that his superiors, the pen-pushers, put into his mouth. He didn't take that stuff seriously himself. But Mother is right. These are bad times. People who are not dry behind the ears think they know everything and set fire to the roof over our heads."

Simone was not listening. Surrender, armistice. So everything had collapsed.

Meanwhile Uncle Prosper had risen and was walking back and forth with heavy steps. "You haven't got an ounce of sense," he scolded. "You can take my word for it, you have ruined the Planchard firm for ever." He was silent for a little while; then he complained viciously: "And at that, everything might have turned out well. The armistice is bad, true enough, but the Marshal is a great man, the Germans respect him, he is maintaining order. 'Work, fatherland, family'—that's a watchword under which one can live. As long as the Marshal remains at the head of the State, we will get along with the Germans."

He planted himself in front of Simone. "We, but not I," he continued, explaining grimly, straight at her. "With *me* they won't get along, the Boches. Even though they are willing to make certain allowances, they won't go so far as to leave concessions to a man who burned down everything right under their noses. And why should they?" he asked with quiet, furious derision. "They will merely turn over everything that I have built up to my competitors. Fouginet Brothers in Dijon have already applied for it; of course the Châtelain is back of it. If I don't transport his wines, then he will transport them himself, and everything else besides. He only needs to ask for it and the Germans will give him the concession. Then my drivers will work for him, then his trucks will run on the roads that I built. Do you think that you harmed the Germans? I am the one whom you ruined; I am the one whom you destroyed. You have given the Châtelain a welcome pretext for stealing my business away from me. That's all you accomplished."

Simone had recovered from the shock that the word "surrender" had produced in her. Attentively she listened to her uncle's lament about the fate of his establishment. She understood it fully. She grasped the fact that it had been a hard blow for him. And yet it was a good thing that she had acted as she did. It was a good thing that the Boches did not get the trucks. It was a good thing that her action had taken place. She said: "I did accomplish something. You know that perfectly well."

"Certainly," he mocked. "You gave a signal, you lighted a beacon. And is your beacon effective? You blasted me and my business, that's what you did and nothing else. Mother is quite right. Why was I ever so crack-brained as to take you into my house?"

Simone's eyes calmly followed him up and down. "I thought you did it for my father's sake," she said.

He was about to make a violent reply, but he swallowed it. "It's no use talking with you," he answered angrily. Then, since she remained silent, he continued. "Don't you understand," he said, "that I can't live without my business? I am a business man. I can't help that." He talked himself into a new state of excitement. "Some people are born to be artists, others to be engineers; I was born to be a business man, a promoter. That's what I was made to be, that's my place in life; I am a business man from head to foot. I can't imagine an existence without my business."

That was not empty talk, that was a confession, and Simone recognized it as such. She recognized how inextricably Uncle Prosper was tied up in his business. The loading yard, his private office, his bank account, Monsieur Laroche of the Crédit Lyonnais, the book-keeper Monsieur Peyroux, all that belonged to Uncle Prosper, all that was part of him, that was his life and his blood, that could not be taken away from him; without that he could not live. He had uttered his most intimate truth; he could not exist without his business.

Simone had seen that fact before, but today for the first time her inner eye saw it. She considered it in silence. "Some day the Boches will leave again," she said. "Maybe very soon. And then you will get your business back, Uncle Prosper. And then it will be a good thing if the Planchards have done their duty and have taken a stand against the Boches."

" 'Some day the Boches will leave again,' " jeered Uncle Prosper. "When? in two years? in three? in five? At any rate, not until the Planchard firm has gone into other hands. And how shall I rebuild it then? For an undertaking like mine, connexions of all sorts are necessary. You have to have your fingers in many pies. It takes more than a good patriotic name to organize bus lines."

"Did you want to do business with the Germans?" asked Simone. "Would you have given your trucks to the Germans for the transport of their war material and your gasoline for their tanks?" And since he remained grimly silent, she said: "You see. You are a big business man, but you are also a Frenchman." And quietly she added: "I don't know what I would have done if the Germans had hauled their munitions with our trucks and had filled their tanks with our gasoline. I would have had to take my father's picture down from the wall."

Uncle Prosper gulped. "It's no use talking with you," he repeated and left the room.

II: The Bitter Waiting

THAT night, in bed, in the solitude of her mansard, Simone thought about this conversation.

She had been the victor. Uncle Prosper had left the Blue Room, seeking refuge in flight. But it had been a sad victory. She had seen his face. She had been forced to recognize that she had not succeeded in raising him by her deed to the place which he should have occupied as Pierre Planchard's brother.

Now he would probably comfort himself with fine words, Joe Blow to the end. Presumably Madame Mimerelles had returned and he would seek consolation at her side. Scornfully she pictured them clinging to each other, Uncle Prosper and the blonde, plump, white-skinned Madame Mimerelles.

And yet the silent, bitter war between Simone and Madame, with Uncle Prosper as its object, was far from ended. Madame had locked her up, Madame had tried to prevent the discussion between her and Uncle Prosper, Madame had filled Uncle Prosper with evil prejudice against her. But Madame, with all her talk, had not been able to rob her action of its meaning. No matter how incensed Uncle Prosper had been over the outward consequences, he had made no reply when she raised the true issues. He had swallowed the insult which he had been about to hurl at her. Perhaps he was not the great man that he had been until now in Simone's estimation, but he was far from being as mean as Maurice believed him to be.

Madame held Uncle Prosper by many strings. The firm, the social position, the bank account—all that was in Madame's hand, and Simone had nothing on her side except the name and the memory of her father. But Madame had made one mistake; she had overdrawn her bow. Because Madame treated her like a scullery maid and abused her and pushed her round, for that very reason Simone's mere presence remained a constant reproach to Uncle Prosper. Simone never thought of giving up the battle.

She lay in the dark, the crickets chirped and the frogs croaked; she told herself that it was useless to mull over the same thoughts again and again, that she ought to sleep. She told herself sensibly that hard days lay before her and that she needed rest. But she continued to torture herself with the attempt to patch up her torn confidence in Uncle Prosper, and she could not sleep.

Finally she turned on the light again and resolutely picked up the books of Joan of Arc, the red, exciting one with the many pictures, and the black, large, scientific one, and the golden, worn, old-fashioned one with the pretty legends and anecdotes. She had been deprived of her friends but in her books she felt a connecting link with them. In these hard days she had often read in her books and they had become a reminder and a symbol, an incentive, a consolation, and a source of understanding.

Again she lay there prone and read. And about her were the dead Napoleon and his grenadiers, and Saint Martin and her father.

Simone read about that brief year, about those ten months following Joan's greatest triumph, the crowning of her Dauphin in Rheims, a year that ended with her capture before Compiègne. It was a year of inactivity, of trivial successes and trivial failures; a year in which she was surrounded by enemies who pretended to be friends, and by friends who were either not willing enough or not strong enough; a year of twilight and of wasted effort.

There they were in Rheims; they had gained their first tremendous success. The Dauphin Charles had been crowned King. But now he wanted to be left in peace, he wanted to enjoy his success. What was the use of being King if he did not have the privilege of being idle when it suited him? But Joan wanted to go on, she wanted to go on at once, she wanted to take Paris without delay. He did not oppose her directly, but he sabotaged her efforts, he made excuses, he no longer wanted to wage war.

That was the man whom Joan had crowned King, the man who owed her everything. He was by no means her enemy, but neither was he her friend; he was a colourless fellow of half-measures and half-deeds. To such a man Joan must have been most annoying, even repugnant, with her constant urging for decisions and for the command to attack. He avoided her, he declared this and that, he declared that the right time had not yet come and that at the right time he would act. Alas, Simone knew all about that.

She studied the picture of the Dauphin. He had a long, soft face under the flat, ostentatious feather hat; his nose was large, thick, and bulbous; his strangely vacant, evasive, dreamy eyes, beneath very high, foolish eyebrows, were turned within him; his mouth was wide, epicurean, and sensuous; his large ears were pointed at the top. Simone read that Charles had been pampered and spoiled from early childhood. Three sets of curtains had protected his cradle against draught; his nursery was carpeted with felt; harps and all sorts of musical toys were used to disperse the ill humours of the infant. According to the accounts of his contemporaries Charles the Seventh was a small and miserable creature. He liked to go about in a short, green cloth-coat, and the men who had only seen him in his proud coronation robes were surprised at his scrawny and pitiful figure when he appeared without these robes, with his thin bowlegs and his thick, unsightly knees.

Simone read how this King began negotiations with his enemies immediately after his coronation, much to Joan's sorrow and indignation. He wanted peace, a negotiated peace. He parleyed with his most violent opponent, the Duke of Burgundy. Joan pleaded and warned; Charles negotiated. The Duke of Burgundy treated him with contempt; Charles continued to negotiate. And many great French lords imitated their King; they too negotiated with the enemy. No matter how promising the war appeared, the Two Hundred Families preferred a negotiated peace to a victory. Joan, and Simone with her, did not understand that these Frenchmen were not intent upon the welfare of France but only upon their own.

And Simone read how Joan nevertheless prevailed upon the King to make preparations for an attack upon Paris. However, they had discharged the bulk of her army, they made half-hearted preparations, they sabotaged the attack before it had even begun. And yet Joan succeeded in taking the field against Paris and in beginning the siege. The King, however, continued to negotiate with the foe even during the siege and made strange treaties with him. He conceded the right to the Duke of Burgundy to send auxiliary troops to the English in the besieged city of Paris. King Charles even went so far as to offer the City of Compiègne, which Joan had won for him, to the Burgundian as a pledge. And when, in spite of these intrigues, Joan did not give up the investment of Paris, the King recalled her. And when she still did not give up, he made use of a particularly insidious trick. Joan and her troops had built a bridge across the Seine; the final attack upon Paris could only be made across this bridge. King Charles gave orders over Joan's head to destroy the bridge secretly at night.

Simone lowered her book. Was this King of France no Frenchman? "You are a big business man, but you are a Frenchman," she had said to Uncle Prosper. Would Uncle Prosper have destroyed the bridge if he had been in King Charles' place? No, that was impossible. To be sure, he neglected to perform an act for France which would have cost him some sacrifice; but it was out of the question that he would commit an act against France.

She took up her books again. She read how Joan was kept at the court of the King, honoured as the saviour of the country, charged with the conduct of the war, and in reality a prisoner.

What agonies Joan must have suffered, she who always acted out of the fullness of her heart, in such a life of intentional procrastination, of intentional half-measures. Full of sorrow Simone read how she was forced to spend a large part of her brief allotted time in reluctant idleness and how she had to dissipate her strength in silly trivial affairs.

She made it her business, for instance, to unmask the fortune-teller Cathérine de Rochelle, who, on the ground of her alleged visions, advised a negotiated peace with the Duke of Burgundy. Cathérine received her messages from a white and gold lady who appeared to her at night. Joan watched with her in order to see this vision. After midnight, however, she fell asleep and, of course, the white and gold one did not appear before Joan was sleeping. The next time Joan was cleverer; she slept through the day in order to be able to remain awake until the white and gold one's arrival. But the white and gold lady did not appear. Thereupon Cathérine, the prophetess of the negotiated peace, was sent home in disgrace.

Another large part of the time, which Joan wanted so much to use in driving the enemy out of the country, she wasted, for want of a worthier occupation, in trying to secure a dowry for a friend. Simone was almost ashamed to read of the strenuous efforts on the part of Joan to get a dowry from the City of Tours, which she had liberated, for a certain Héliote Power at the occasion of her marriage. This Héliote was the daughter of the Scotch painter, Hamish Power, who had painted Joan's banner. There were long sessions of the City Council of Tours in this affair, but they led to no real result. The city did not grant the dowry, but they decided, in honour of the Maid, to offer up prayers for her friend on her wedding day, and to make her a solemn presentation of bread and wine. Simone sighed a little. How hard it was to get anything more than honour and affection out of people.

In these months of idleness and futility Joan was very much alone. Her friends were far away and she saw and heard nothing of them. There was Iolanthe of Anjou, Queen of Sicily, her powerful patroness who, according to the opinion of the big, black, scholarly book, had been the one who from the very beginning, secretly and without Joan's knowledge, had guided her destinies. It had been Iolanthe's plan that a messenger from heaven should arise and strengthen the faith of the doubting Dauphin and his people in his legitimacy. Before Joan had brought about the coronation of the Dauphin, the Queen had sent her many friendly messages in various ways. Now that she no longer had any need for the favoured girl, she had lost interest in her. Other friends of Joan, Gilles de Rais and several others of the young generals, had been given commands far away from her. In their stead a certain Sire d'Albret had been assigned to her; he accompanied and watched her wherever she was. He was a stepbrother of her stubborn enemy, La Trémoille.

She had many enemies. Avidly Simone read the reports in her books about Isabeau, the mother of the King, his and Joan's grimmest opponent. There was a picture of her as she appeared on her tombstone in the Cathedral of Saint Denis. So that was how she looked, Isabeau, Princess of Bavaria, Queen of France, this lusty, gifted and dangerous woman, mother of many children, mistress of many men, who all her life thirsted for more power, more pleasure, more money. It was a broad face, a smooth forehead, wide-set eyes, a generous mouth, a strong, straight nose, a forceful chin. Simone read that this woman loved her husband, the father of Joan's Dauphin, and that she bore him many children; that when he became insane she stayed with him and did everything to take care of him. Simone read that Isabeau became infatuated with her husband's brother, to whom all the women were attracted; that Isabeau could not live without the greatest luxuries and without all the wealth in the world; and that she went over to the enemies of her husband and of her lover out of greed. She read that, when she demanded the return of her son from the care of her adversary, the very same Iolanthe of Anjou, she received the following answer from her: "We have not raised your son with love and affection only to have you kill him, like his brothers, or drive him insane, like his father, or, at best, make him English, like yourself. I shall keep him. A woman who has a lover needs no son. Come and get him if you have the courage." And later she declared with magnificent shamelessness in an official document that her son, the so-called Dauphin, was not born in wedlock; for the rest of her life, the book went on, she fought like a fury against this son of hers, the Dauphin; with increasing age she became more and more greedy and more and more possessed of hatred for her son. And Simone read that this once radiantly beautiful woman became fatter and fatter and her flesh became bloated. And Simone could not help but think of Madame, enthroned in her wing chair, ruminating over the life of her husband and her stepson, suffering from the impertinence of these two whom she had been unable to tame.

But Joan was ruined not so much by the power and malice of
her declared enemies as by the secret machinations of men in
her own camp and by the lukewarmness and half-heartedness
of her friends. Simone frowned when she realized how indifferent these friends were, how they had to be thrust forward
again and again before they undertook even the smallest positive action, and how glad they were finally to be rid of this
troublesome girl who constantly pushed them.

There was the Archbishop of Rheims, instructed by the King
to protect and conduct Joan, but plotting behind her back wherever he could. There was the royal commandant of the City of
Soissons, who refused Joan entrance into the city; the fact was
that he had sold the city secretly to the Duke of Burgundy and
had already received an advance of four thousand gold pieces.

And there was, most prominent of all, the commandant of the
City of Compiègne.

Simone read about him in her anecdotes. The Maid was informed, so she read, that the Duke of Burgundy was threatening
the City of Compiègne, and she set out with a body of warriors
to help this city. Under the noses of the besieging army she entered Compiègne to the great joy of the inhabitants, and they
gave the Maid a gift of four kegs of wine.

Appointed as commandant of the City of Compiègne by the
King of France was Sire Guillaume de Flavy. He was a brave
soldier but the hardest and most cruel man of this cruel time.
Without pity, day after day, he ordered people tortured and
executed.

And the Maid attended mass in the church of Saint Jacques,
and she was overcome by great sorrow, and about her were the
people of Compiègne and very many children; and she leaned
against a pillar in the church and said: "Dear friends, dear children, I tell you that I have been sold and betrayed. After a little
time they will put me to death. Pray to God for me, I beg of
you. For I can no longer serve the gracious King Charles and
sweet France."

And Simone read that Joan was captured on that very day. It
was not a real battle in which that took place; it was a silly,

trivial skirmish such as Joan had frequently encountered successfully.

Simone read some exact details. It was the twenty-third of March 1430, at five o'clock in the afternoon. Joan had ridden forth with a small troop in order to ambush a Burgundian division that had been reported; she was riding her dapple-grey horse; she was wearing a red and gold cloak. The Burgundians were taken by surprise, according to plan, and it appeared that the ambush would succeed. But then superior forces came to the aid of the Burgundians, and Joan and her men were outnumbered.

Joan's soldiers withdrew but Joan did not want to give up the undertaking. "Forward," she cried. "Every man for himself," cried her soldiers and fled. Now there was a river separating the City of Compiègne from the scene of the skirmish, the river Oise, and a bridge led across this river to the city. The greater number of the fleeing soldiers reached the bridge; others leapt full-armed into the river; the majority succeeded in finding refuge within the city walls. When all were inside, the commandant, Guillaume de Flavy, had the drawbridge raised and the gates closed. Joan, however, was still outside the walls. She was practically alone. She was cut off.

Simone considered what she had been reading. "Forward," cried Joan. "Every man for himself," cried the others. Simone drew her shoulders a little higher with a shiver. What good was it to know what is right and to do what is right, what good was it to cry: "Forward," and to advance when no one followed? "Every man for himself," they cried and raised the bridge and closed the gate and left Joan alone.

In her three books Simone read three different opinions of the reasons for which Commandant de Flavy might have closed the gates and raised the bridge. It was quite possible, stated the first of the books, that De Flavy acted upon practical, military motives, because he saw that his troops were hard pressed and there was danger that the enemy might penetrate into the city. The second book said that more probably De Flavy gave his orders for the very purpose of destroying the Maid, and that there was good reason to suspect that higher authority had directed him to get rid of her at the first opportunity. The old-fashioned, worn, gold anecdote book, however, stated simply: "Thanks to her courage the Maid reached the bridge. But the cruel Captain Guillaume de Flavy, jealous of her fame, had the bridge raised."

No matter for what reason, Joan was outside the walls; she had a scant dozen of her men about her, and from all sides English and Burgundians rushed upon her and encircled her. One of them seized her coat, another pulled her from her horse. There was no longer any hope, but she continued to fight on foot until she was overpowered and captured.

III: The Call of Liberty

SIMONE, soiled from work in the garden, in her worn overalls and her large straw hat, stood on the rock by the wall and gazed along the road. In these last few days she was doing this only so as not to miss anything, as from a sense of duty; she had scarcely any more hope that one of her friends might come.

Far away, from the direction of the city, something approached; a bicyclist, so it seemed. At once her small spark of hope grew large again. She wished with all her heart that it might at last, at last, be one of her people. The cyclist came nearer; she could not yet distinguish anything, but she already knew, she was perfectly certain, that it was a friend; she had willed it so stoutly that it could not be otherwise.

The bicyclist approached rapidly; road and time disappeared before the speed of his motion; he wore a windbreaker; near the wall he leaped from his wheel, he came diagonally across the road, he grinned all over his large face. With one hand he held the bicycle, the other was propped on his hip. He said: "Well, here I am."

Simone, beside herself with happiness and excitement, tried to answer but she produced only a hoarse, vague sound. She stood on her rock, her arms extended and clinging to the edge of the wall. It was a high wall and only her face projected above it. It was a vivacious face, it showed the strength of her emotion.

He looked up at her. Then he said: "That's uncomfortable, isn't it? Don't you want me to come over to you? Or can you climb over here? Is it very dangerous if we are caught here together?"

She hesitated. Of course it was dangerous, but she had to speak with him and time was so very short; otherwise they really would be caught, and she had so terribly much to ask, and where

would she begin? And she also had to tell him how grateful she
was to him and how glad that he came. And she really could not
speak with him in this position, from the top of the wall, with
only her face showing over its edge, and it was hard to hang on
for such a long time, and her hands were already numb.

But before she had completed these deliberations he had
climbed up on the wall. And now he was sitting on the wall,
his legs dangling on the outside, so that he could jump down
at any moment and make his get-away; and now his laughing
face was above hers and now they would be able to talk.

She was well aware that the loose, baggy overalls and the straw
hat were not becoming to her, and that she looked dirty, perspiring, and unlovely. The last time she saw him, in Saint-Martin,
just before her action and soon afterwards, she had looked pret-
tier, more lively. Whenever she looked into the mirror now she
was startled at the hard and careworn appearance of her face;
it had become much more adult but much uglier.

He smiled. He was sitting on the wall, smiling, and looking
down at her, and she, standing awkwardly on her rock, looked
up at him, and everything was very queer.

"Well, you silly cluck," he began, but he really sounded quite
friendly, "didn't I tell you right away that you had gotten yourself into a fine mess? Now you're in a sweet jam, and who is
going to get you out of it? Nobody but good old Maurice." And
then he began to relate. Things were getting a little hot for him
in Saint-Martin, the Boches were making preparations for a long
stay, and there would be no peace for some time. "I am sorry to
say that I was right again," he said and grinned cheerfully. "The
Holy Alliance between the Nazis and our fascists is very strong;
the wolves didn't devour each other but are howling in unison,
and I am willing to bet three more bottles of Pernod that this
damned armistice will last for years. As far as I am concerned,
the matter is settled," he summarized in his sharp, positive tone.
"I haven't any more business here; I'm going to scram. I'm going
into the Unoccupied Territory and from there to Algiers. There
seems to be the possibility of keeping up the battle from there."

She listened to his voice and, although it was not a beautiful voice, its sound cheered her spirit. Of course what he said was a blow for her. He was going away, he was going to Algiers, he was going to war, and she would remain all alone. She felt so weak that she had to cling still more firmly to the wall in order not to fall from her rock.

Maurice saw it. Briskly he said: "Just make yourself comfortable, Mademoiselle. What can those people in there do to you that they haven't already done?" And he pointed to the house. He swung himself over into the garden and squatted on a tree stump. "Allez oop," he said, "get down, sit down here. I have things to say to you." Obediently she detached her hands from the wall, stepped down, and seated herself on the rock.

He took off the straw hat which covered her wide, strong forehead. "Now," he said, laughing.

"Why do you want to fight now, all at once," she asked and her voice did not sound as firm and sure as usual, "when everything is already settled? At first you didn't want anything to do with it and now suddenly you are all for it."

"Well, that's as clear as crystal," he declared a little impatiently. "At first it wasn't our war. We knew perfectly well that our fascists only intended to deliver us and our material to the Nazis. Now everything is changed. Now the fronts are plain; now the biggest idiot in France knows who the enemies are. Work, Family, Fatherland, the Nazis, Pétain, the Defeatist of Verdun, and all the French fascists on the one side; Liberty, Equality, Fraternity, and the anti-fascists of the whole world on the other."

She heard what he said, she took it all in, but she did not feel it. She felt only one thing: he was leaving. "When are you going away, Maurice?" she asked, and she spoke very softly.

"Tomorrow," he replied, "tomorrow night. That's why I am here. I would like to straighten out your affairs before I pull out."

Tomorrow. That was terrible. She was completely stunned. Tomorrow, and then she would be all alone. "Have you seen the others?" she asked with an effort.

"You mean your little friend, Etienne?" he returned, leering pleasantly. "He is over in Chatillon again, they ordered him back. There is strict discipline in the country now. The slave drivers are cracking their whips again with a vengeance; the tanks of the Boches have made them bold. Oh yes, and then of course there's that devoted admirer of yours, the bookbinder, the old crackpot. Naturally, he tried to contact you. He came out here as big as life and he thought he had it all figured out; he asked for you and said he wanted to get back some books that he claimed to have loaned you. But they were very sorry, they said that you weren't here, and they didn't let him in. Your friend from the Deputy Prefecture didn't have any better luck. And then, of course, I had to try my hand at it. I figured out that at the time when Mademoiselle is at work in the garden it would be fairly easy to find her without being blown at by Joe Blow."

Simone laughed happily. Such a *débrouillard*. He always hit on the right thing. She was deeply moved. She was moved at the thought that she had friends who racked their brains how to help her, and most of all she was moved because Maurice did not want to leave without helping her.

He lighted a cigarette. "I am telling you how things are," he explained to her. "I think your affairs are getting a little hot, too; incidentally your friend at the Deputy Prefecture is of the same opinion." In his cool, direct manner, covering all details, he analysed the situation as he saw it. The civilian transportation system of the Département had almost completely broken down. Saint-Martin was being served by only two autobuses, one of which he, Maurice, was driving. Now the Deputy Prefecture was making great efforts to delegate the reorganization of traffic to the Planchard firm. The Boches were convinced of Monsieur Planchard's ability to get things moving, but they mistrusted him and they upheld the confiscation of the establishment. If anything could be done for Monsieur Planchard, it would have to be through the Châtelain. He was the only one who had any influence with the Boches. All this Maurice had learned from Monsieur Xavier.

Simone listened attentively. Now, Maurice continued, he had figured out what Joe Blow's attitude towards Simone would be under these circumstances, and he had concluded it would be as follows. So far, the Châtelain was the only one who was playing ball with the Boches, and in the long run he would not like to be the only one. He was a slick customer, and he would therefore try to force others to compromise themselves beyond repair. That meant that he would, for instance, not let Joe Blow have his business back before the latter had clearly proved in the eyes of every one his willingness to collaborate with the Boches. "Do you get that," asked Maurice, "or is it over your head?" Simone nodded. "Well," Maurice resumed, "how can Joe Blow demonstrate such willingness? Best of all, by ostentatiously disavowing the daughter of Pierre Planchard, the *pétroleuse,* the silly, little arsonist, the patriot girl. If he puts her out of the way, if he turns her over to the fascists, then he will have proved his good, collaborationist intentions. Therefore he will turn you over to them."

As long as Maurice was analysing in theory the situation regarding the firm and the Marquis, Simone had listened calmly and had weighed his arguments impartially. But now, when he drew this vile conclusion, her resentment completely upset her logic, and she forgot that she herself had doubted Uncle Prosper. Uncle Prosper was changed back for her into the man he had been, the brother of Pierre Planchard, and Maurice became again the Maurice of the loading yard, the wicked, malicious fellow, who ran down everybody and everything. This stuff that he had cooked up in order to besmirch Uncle Prosper was nothing but poisonous nonsense.

"I will admit," she replied with an effort to control herself, "that appearances are against Uncle Prosper because he did not destroy the trucks himself. Maybe he actually failed. But that's no reason for thinking him capable of such vile treachery, such abominable treachery." And now her emotions broke loose. She flew into a passion: "He would never, never, do anything to harm me," she said. "Never," she repeated excitedly in her fine, dark voice.

Maurice made no reply but continued to smoke, surveying her with a little, ironic smile. "Wipe that nasty grin off your face," she let fly at him, stubbornly and angrily. "You are usually so smart, Maurice, but what you say about Uncle Prosper is simply idiotic. You have only seen him at the plant. You don't know him at all. But I have seen him in these ten years. He has always racked his brain to do nice things for me. Every time he takes a trip he brings me something, not a *souvenir,* but something personal that he thought over carefully. He took me along to Paris, and what a nuisance that must have been for a man like him. And when I had scarlet fever he worried so much about me that his face actually got thin. What you say is nonsense, Maurice. It is out of the question that he will ever harm me."

"Maybe he does like you," Maurice answered and continued to smile. "But he likes his business, too. He hangs on to his business like a dog to his bone. He won't let anybody take that from him. The Two Hundred Families sent their sons to the front in this war and the last. They sacrificed their sons, but not their sous." He made this statement with grim matter-of-factness.

"He hangs on to his business like a dog to his bone"; it rang in Simone's ears. And at the same time Uncle Prosper's words resounded: "I am a business man, that's what I was made to be, that's my place in life; I can't imagine any existence without my business."

Meanwhile Maurice had continued. "If he is not planning anything against you," he said, "why do they keep you locked up here?" He was not speaking loudly, but now his incisive, cutting voice was hurting her ears. "Why do they keep everybody away from you? You have to see that yourself; that smells like a dead rat."

Simone considered for a moment. "Madame was terribly angry with me," she admitted. "Madame can't stand me. But that doesn't prove that Uncle Prosper is planning a piece of treachery against me. Didn't you say yourself," she continued, illogically and triumphantly, "that there's no danger whatever from the Boches, because I did it before they arrived? Did you say that or didn't you?"

"Don't pretend to be more stupid than you are," said Maurice, forcing himself to be calm. "You know very well, that has nothing to do with the matter. We have no time," he cut off all further argument. "I don't know how much longer they'll leave you in peace; maybe they'll strike today. Besides, I can't come a second time, before I pull out. You'll just have to believe me: things are getting pretty risky for you and something's going to happen before long. We have to come to a decision, today, right now. I'll make you a proposition: I'll take you along to the Unoccupied Territory." He spoke as indifferently as possible; he did not look at her.

Simone rode the crest of a wave of pride and happiness. He was not taking any Louison with him, not any of the girls who went with him. Surely everything would be harder for him if he were burdened with her. The point was that she had convinced him that she was worth trouble and danger.

"It's wonderful that you want to do that for me," she said. She was sitting on her rock, looking straight ahead, a tiny smile about her lips. She imagined herself riding through France with him, trustfully, through the night. In order to get into the Unoccupied Territory they would probably have to cross the Loire somewhere. She imagined herself in a boat, crossing the river, secretly, with him, being shot at, but there would be no danger as long as he was with her. Or perhaps they would swim across the river; it was a good thing that she was a strong swimmer. How wonderful all that would be.

But what would happen here, if she left? Maurice himself had said that the Châtelain and the other fascists would try to get the better of Uncle Prosper at all costs. If she ran away, they would surely say that Uncle Prosper had instigated the arson plot and had then helped her to escape. And they would certainly do something to him; at the very least they would ruin his business for ever. No, she could not let another one suffer for her deed. She would have to take the consequences herself. It would be vile ingratitude to run away and to cast suspicion on Uncle Prosper. In her mind she could plainly hear Madame's low, scornful voice: "So she ran away, she pulled out; I knew it all the time."

Maurice had meanwhile continued. He would call for her the following night with the motorcycle of the Deputy Prefecture. He already had a licence for a motorcycle. Then they would have a head start of a good twenty-four hours, and they would easily manage to get away. Beyond the Loire he would turn her over to reliable friends. And then he would see about getting himself across the water.

Simone was only half listening. On a motorcycle. He would wear the leather jacket and she would cling firmly to him as they rode through the night, and she would not be afraid. It was all very attractive. But she couldn't go. She simply could not. She mustn't regard Uncle Prosper as a villain just because it suited her purpose, just because it would be so much fun to run off with Maurice. She could not let Uncle Prosper pay for her acts.

She would have to say no to Maurice. But not yet. For only two minutes, for one minute, she wanted to revel in the joy of his proposition, in the dream of riding with him through the night into a great freedom.

"Why are you interested in saving me, Maurice?" she asked. She spoke as though to herself, softly, smiling, as out of her reverie, so softly that he had to ask: "What? How?" She looked at him, still with a smile. "Why are you interested in saving me?" she repeated more loudly. "After all, you regard what I did as nonsense, and all wrong, don't you?"

"Of course it was wrong," Maurice promptly replied. "But you can still be educated. You have had a chance to learn, now. You might still develop into something worth while." He arose. "Well, then, I'll expect you tomorrow night at half-past twelve, right here at the wall. But you can only take along the barest necessities. In a knapsack or a very small hand-bag. Is that clear?"

Now she would have to answer, now she could no longer hesitate, now she had to tell him. "You explained to me, didn't you," she once more queried, and remained seated while he already stood, "you explained to me that the Châtelain and the other fascists would take it out on Uncle Prosper if he lets me get away?"

"Of course I didn't say that," Maurice replied, annoyed. "Didn't you understand anything?" His scornful question irritated Simone, especially as it was costing her great self-denial to say no to him.

"Yes, you did," she reiterated stubbornly. "That's what you said."

"Don't chew that same nonsense over and over again," Maurice answered impatiently. But he controlled himself at once. "We haven't any time to quarrel," he said, "and that isn't what I came here for. Tomorrow, then, here, at half-past twelve," he repeated, almost pleadingly.

But: "I can't let Uncle Prosper suffer for what I have done," she persisted. And, resolutely she announced: "It was grand of you, Maurice, to come here and offer to do this for me. I thank you as I have never thanked any one. But I am not coming with you. I can't. I mustn't."

As she spoke she was torn with grief that she would have to let him go alone, and at the same time she was happy; she had brought Maurice, who was her enemy, to a point where he urged his help upon her.

Maurice shrugged his shoulders. "Very well," he said. "If you insist on ruining yourself with your naïve faith in Monsieur Uncle, every one to his taste. I must say that Joe Blow has put it over on you. Pardon me, Mademoiselle," he concluded with grim politeness, "for having annoyed you." But then he added urgently: "I am asking you for the last time. Shall I come tomorrow night at half-past twelve and await you here? Yes or no?"

Simone was torn with indecision. She knew that in this moment she was making a choice for her entire future life, and that that which she was about to refuse was Happiness. But it would have been the height of cowardice and of treachery if she had shown distrust of her father's brother at this very time and brought him into danger.

She stood up. Tall, slim, brave and determined, she stood there in her worn, dirty overalls. "No, Maurice," she said.

What a tremendous effort this No cost her. How much it hurt her. It cut and burned; she felt battered and bruised.

She had to say something to Maurice. He was prepared to assume a great risk on her account. He probably regarded her conduct as overwrought and miserable. "Thank you, Maurice. Thank you, dear Maurice," she said softly and pulled herself together to keep from crying.

He took two steps towards the wall, a little awkwardly. "Well, all right, then you won't go," he said and shrugged his shoulders. He turned once more and came very close to her; he took hold of her shoulders with both hands. "You really won't come along, you goose?" he asked and shook her; he shook her quite hard but it did not hurt.

"I can't, Maurice," she said and now she had to gulp after all and could not keep her eyes dry. And: "The very best of luck."

He stepped up on the rock and swung himself on the wall. There he sat astride. "Good-bye, you little fool," he said. "I guess nobody can help you," he added briskly after a tiny moment, and then he repeated, but this time sadly and surprisingly gently: "Good-bye, Simone," and he jumped down into the road.

She was standing on the rock again; she did not know how she had gotten there. Now he mounted his bicycle, now he rode away. She looked after him; she saw his broad back in the windbreaker. Of course she would have to go with him; it was her only chance; he was right, a hundred times right. "Maurice," she wanted to shout, "it is all nonsense. Of course I will go with you." If she called now, he would still hear her. Even now. And now. Now probably no longer. But there, where he had to begin to push his wheel, he would surely turn round once more, and if she climbed on the wall and gave him a sign and then jumped down, he would certainly wait, and then she could tell him that she wanted to go along.

Now he had reached the little rise; now he dismounted to push the wheel. And now he turned round. Now she would have to climb over the wall. This instant she still had the choice, only this instant. He waved, he waited. This was the last moment. But she did not climb on the wall; she remained standing, clinging with her hands that had no more feeling. She could not move a muscle.

Now he turned away. There he went, pushing his bicycle, he went away, and everything that seemed worth while to her in the world went with him. And now, presently, he would be at the crest of the little rise and then beyond it, and she would see nothing of him any more, never, not even his back.

It took an eternity until he reached the top of the rise, the bicycle at his right side. It took only a brief moment. Now he was at the top. And now he was gone, and now the decision had been made, and now everything was finished, and now she was a heroine, and now she was the greatest fool in France.

She stepped down from her rock very slowly. Behind her was the wall, and the wall barred her for ever from Maurice and from the world. She could have climbed over it, she could have found liberty, but she had said no. There she stood with a loose, vacant face. No human being could be as sad as she. Everything she had done was wrong and foolish. She was a very poor heroine.

She picked up the big straw hat that Maurice had taken from her and hung it over her arm. Mechanically, neatly, she carried her garden tools into the little shed. She walked into the house, into her room; she washed herself and changed clothes, everything neatly, mechanically. She went into the kitchen to prepare the evening meal.

Madame came into the kitchen. "You need only prepare food for the two of us today," she said in her low, cold tone. "Also tomorrow. My son has gone to Francheville. On your account."

IV: The Great Betrayal

AND the night came, and the next day, and another night. Through this entire time Simone brooded without end over Uncle Prosper's attitude. What did his trip to Francheville mean? It was probably true that the Boches were preparing to take action against her and that Uncle Prosper had gone to the Prefecture and to the Boche Headquarters to intercede for her. It could not be otherwise. With all her strength she resisted the suspicion that it might be otherwise.

But the doubt was fixed in her brain like a splinter.

If she was in danger, what could Uncle Prosper do for her? If he interceded for her, he only increased her danger and his own. Would it not have been better to follow Maurice? But if she had followed Maurice, that very act would have imperilled Uncle Prosper.

She lay in her bed, in her dark mansard; it was the second night and her thoughts continued to revolve in the same painful circle.

She imagined how it would be if she had said yes to Maurice. Now it might be about half-past eleven. Now the time had come. Now she would be getting up, very quietly, and preparing her things. She would take the little bag which she sometimes used to carry supplies.

Why had Uncle Prosper gone to Francheville? Should she have said yes to Maurice after all? It seemed to her as if the night became darker and darker, hotter and hotter. She could no longer bear it, neither the heat nor the darkness.

Nor the regret. For no matter what the purpose of Uncle Prosper's trip might be, she regretted, she regretted bitterly that she had permitted Maurice to leave.

It was probably about midnight now. The alarm clock was

ticking and it seemed to her as if the clock were in her own heart. A great, scarcely bearable agitation came over her. She turned on the light. It was three minutes after twelve. The time had come. Now Maurice was leaving. For the Unoccupied Territory. And then for the Unknown.

Perhaps he had not believed her refusal. Perhaps he would come here and would stop at the wall below and make certain whether she was not there after all.

Quietly she arose. She dressed quickly; she put on the dark green slacks and a blouse. She packed up a change of clothing, the barest essentials. She took a pair of stout shoes but she did not put them on. She sneaked down the stairs in her bare feet; her heart pounded so loudly that she feared Madame might hear it. From the pantry she fetched the little shopping bag and stuffed it full of the things that she had picked up. Carefully she crept towards the door; she should have oiled the hinges, but that could only have been done with Uncle Prosper's help. Cautiously she pressed the latch; the door creaked only a very little.

Now she was in the garden. It was cool and very dark. She had to traverse the entire width of the large garden in order to reach the wall. The soil and the grass on which she walked felt damp and pleasant to her feet. Rapidly, on soft cool soles, she walked through the garden. Now she had reached the wall.

She climbed over the wall, sat down on the edge of the road, pulled on her socks and her stout shoes. There would not be a moment to spare when he came. How wonderful it would be to sit behind him, her hands firmly about his shoulders, riding with him through the dark cool night.

There she sat, crouched at the edge of the road, her bundle beside her, and waited. Now, at any moment, Maurice might come. At any moment Maurice would come. She listened into the darkness so that she would not miss the very first sound of his motorcycle. She sat and listened and waited.

A long minute passed, a second, a third. The crickets chirped and the frogs croaked. The night was very dark, the stars glittered and gave only a little light; the white road was only faintly visible, but it was very still and his coming would be audible from afar.

He would be a fool to come. He had offered so urgently to take her with him and she had definitely rejected his offer. She sat and waited.

Fifteen minutes passed, a half-hour passed; she began to feel chilly and a boundless misery overcame her. It was her own fault; her stupidity and her pride were to blame. And now Maurice had left for a free world and he had offered to take her with him, and Uncle Prosper had gone to Francheville in order to destroy her, and she had permitted all this to happen, although she had been warned, and she could have saved herself, and she had not done it out of mere pride and stupidity.

She sat motionless, rigid, she did not know how long, in the cool dark night, under the distant, glittering, rayless stars.

Then she walked back into the house, slowly. Her soles did not feel the dew nor her hands the bushes and trees as she groped through them. Mechanically, cautiously, she opened and closed the door. She went up the softly creaking steps to her mansard; she undressed and went back to bed.

Now the decision had been made. Now she could do nothing but wait for Uncle Prosper's return from his ambiguous trip, and for the fate which he would bring with him. Now she could do nothing but submit to that which was to come.

She was deathly tired, but her head ached, her eyes ached, her limbs ached, she could not sleep. She tried to lure sleep, to force it. She turned over on her side and drew her legs far up; that sometimes helped. She commanded herself to sleep. She counted to nine hundred; that took fifteen minutes.

No sleep came to her, only bitter thoughts.

She turned on the light; no matter now if Madame noticed it. She reached for her books.

At first she read carelessly. But then the books began to perform the service that she expected of them: they distracted her. The accounts absorbed her more and more and transported her into the life of the Maid.

She read about Joan's imprisonment. She read that a sharp dispute ensued over the question to whom the prisoner was to belong. Five individuals laid claim to her. There was the soldier who had captured her. There was his captain, the Captain of Vendôme. There was the latter's feudal lord, Count John of Luxembourg. There was the King of England, who laid claim to all French prisoners. There was the Bishop of Beauvais who, in the name of the Church, asserted his right to bring Joan to trial since she had been captured in his diocese.

Simone read how Joan's enemies bargained back and forth. It was a matter of money, and it seemed to Simone that it was not even a matter of very much money: six thousand livres of gold for the Count of Luxembourg and three hundred livres for the Captain of Vendôme. Simone tried to figure out how much that might have been. She reached the sum of about twenty million francs; that was hardly more than the wealth of the Châtelain. But it seemed a great deal to the English gentlemen who were to pay it, and they levied a special tax on the French cities for the purchase of Joan of Arc, called the Maid.

In her old-fashioned, pale gold anecdote book Simone read how this bargaining for the prisoner appeared in the eyes of the people.

To the castle of Beaurevoir, read Simone, where Joan was under the care of the ladies of the House of Luxembourg, the old Countess and her daughter, came the Bishop of Beauvais, Pierre Cauchon, and he had been commissioned to buy the Maid for the English. The old Countess of Luxembourg, however, threw herself at her son's feet and implored him not to sell Joan. But the Count had no money, and the Bishop knew that he had no money, and he came again and again. And he bargained with him, and at first he offered him 37,000 francs, but John of Luxembourg said: "That is not enough for such a Maid." And the Bishop offered more and finally he offered 61,000 francs. And then John of Luxembourg said: *"Tope, compère.* It's a deal, Cousin."

Simone wondered why only Joan's enemies tried to buy her. She read that, according to custom, prisoners were ransomed by their friends. Simone imagined how Joan sat in her prison and waited for someone to release her. Where were all her friends? Didn't the King whom Joan had crowned make any attempt to redeem her? He could have offered money for her, cities, English prisoners; he had great English lords among his captives, General Talbot, for instance. Perhaps the English would not have given Joan up. But didn't he at least make an attempt? No, he made no attempt. None of Joan's friends made an attempt.

What sort of a man was this Charles the Seventh? Simone did not understand him. Could any one be so low? Could this King breathe the air of the country that Joan had reconquered for him, and leave her in prison, and make no move, and be so low?

And Simone read how Joan was dragged from one prison to another. With bated breath she read that Joan's custody became more and more bitter, more and more painful, more and more disgraceful. Her legs were fettered, and at night, when she slept, she was chained to her bed. Her guards were five English mercenaries, selected brutal men, and they often jested rudely with her. They awakened her at night and said to her: "Rise and go. You are free," or they said to her: "Get up, witch, the time has come. Now you are going to be burned." And they laughed loudly when she believed it.

Until now Simone had never been particularly interested in the procedure of the trial and its details. She merely knew that it had been the hereditary enemies, the English, who brought Joan to trial and convicted her. Now she was shocked and horrified to discover that they were not English at all. The Clerical Court which Joan faced consisted only of Frenchmen. There were seventy-two judges on the benches, learned men with great titles, among them the authorities of the University of Paris almost without exception. Among the participants in the trial were one Cardinal, six Bishops, thirty-two Doctors of Theology, sixteen Bachelors of Theology, seven Doctors of Medicine, and one hundred and three Assistants. In the black, scholarly book the names and titles of all the participants were enumerated. With the exception of six or seven they were all French names.

Inquisition and University, Church and Science, representatives of God and representatives of the State, combined to excogitate more and more paper crimes that Joan was said to have committed. With growing interest Simone read of the magnificent, cunning machinery that the pompous, awe-inspiring judges arranged in order to frighten and convict this peasant girl of less than twenty years. Angrily Simone imagined the peasant girl Joan standing before these well-rested, well-groomed gentlemen, Joan, alone, not yet twenty years old, not knowing what they wanted of her, exhausted from long, painful imprisonment, in shabby, faded men's clothing, with short, neglected hair, in fetters.

And angrily Simone read of the insidious means which the host of judges used to defeat the defenceless prisoner. They dragged out the cross-examination beyond reason in order to tire the accused. They stormed upon her with questions the content of which Joan could not possibly understand. They jumped from one point to another, their questions overlapped each other, they interrupted one query with another. They addressed Joan so rapidly and so confusingly that she had to request: "Dear gentlemen, speak ye one after another."

The political meaning and purpose of the trial were carefully concealed. There was no mention of the war between France and England, no mention of the quarrel about the legitimacy of King Charles. It was a non-partisan, clerical court; they spoke only of clerical affairs, of Joan's belief and unbelief, of her heresy.

They tried hard to entice Joan to make statements about her saints; such statements could easily be interpreted in an insidious manner. Joan, however, remained silent about her saints. So they tried to catch her by means of trickery. In her anecdote book Simone read: At the order of the Bishop of Beauvais several of the judges, disguised as laymen, went into the Maid's prison. They said to Joan: "We are prisoners of war, we are of your party and we come from your county." And they said more such things and wormed themselves into her confidence, and they told her their stories, and they asked her to tell them her story. And they asked about the voices she had heard. But a hole had been drilled into the wall and two notaries were listening in the next room. And the Maid spoke freely and honestly with these Judases and the notaries wrote down everything, and the judges tried to catch her.

The men whom Joan faced were all trained jurists, experienced in all the tricks of the trade, and they made use of all the juristic and theological pettifoggery in the world. It was impossible for Joan to win this battle; but with joy and admiration Simone read how boldly, cleverly, and at times with striking wit Joan defended herself.

All the questions were sly and complicated, all of them held concealed traps.

Joan was asked whether she believed herself to be in the grace of God. If she said yes, that was sin and presumption. If she said no, then she had accomplished her deeds in self-confident arrogance and not upon the mandate of God. Tensely the judges waited for Joan's answer; tensely Simone waited with them. And happily, with a little smirk, Simone read with what naïve cleverness Joan escaped from the shyster finesses of her tormentors. "If I am not in the grace of God," she answered, "may God grant it to me; if I am, may God preserve me in it. I would be the saddest creature on earth if I were to hear that I am not in the grace of God."

Then there were questions about Joan's visions, apparently foolish questions, but still very dangerous, and for almost every question Joan had an intelligent, brave answer.

"Was Saint Michael naked?" the judges asked. And: "Do you believe that our Lord has not the means to clothe his angels?" she answered.

"Did you embrace Mesdames Sainte Cathérine and Sainte Marguérite?" they asked; and: "How did the saints smell?" and: "If your saints have no real body, how can they speak?" And: "I will have to let that be God's worry," Joan replied.

"Does Sainte Marguérite speak English?" they asked. And: "Why should she speak English," answered Joan, "since she is not on the side of the English?"

"Does God hate the English?" they asked. Joan answered: "Whether He loves them or hates them, or what He intends to do with their souls, about that I know nothing. But this I do know, that they are destined to be driven out of France, with the exception of those whom we slay here."

They asked: "At the coronation in the cathedral of Rheims, why was your flag alone carried in, and not the flags of the other generals?" And proudly Joan answered: "My flag had done good work. It was only just that it should be honoured."

They asked: "By what magic and what witchcraft did you influence the soldiers in battle?" Joan answered: "I said to them: Forward, let's thrash the English, and I showed them how."

And they asked her: "Why did you permit the poor people to come to you and to honour you as a saint?" And she replied: "The poor people came to me of their own accord because I was friendly to them and helped them as best I could."

But no matter what she answered, the verdict was settled.

Her accusers declared: By obeying her visions, she had permitted herself to be led by evil and satanic spirits. By wearing men's clothing, she had offended against the commands of the scriptures and against canonical law. By declaring that Mesdames Sainte Cathérine and Sainte Marguérite had spoken French and not English for reasons of partisanship, she had blasphemed against these saints and had broken the command of Christian charity. By threatening death to the English, she had proven herself cruel and bloodthirsty. By leaving her parents and going to the false Dauphin, she had transgressed the divine command to honour father and mother. By claiming that she had received her commission directly from God, she denied the authority of the Church and proved herself a heretic.

Simone pondered. It was evident that Joan regarded the judgment of her own heart, the judgment of her voices, more highly than the judgment of the Church, the judgment of God's appointed representatives on earth. Obviously Joan's judges found her guilty of the worst, the most heinous of all crimes: impertinence.

And Simone read of the great and miserable spectacle with which the court celebrated the announcement of the verdict.

In the hangman's tumbril Joan was carted out to the great, walled cemetery of the Abbey of Saint-Ouen. Two platforms had been

erected there; on the one sat the judges and dignitaries, on the
other stood Joan, in men's clothing and chains, alone but for a
cleric named Guillaume Erard. Round about both platforms the
field was black with people and the walls were crowded with
spectators. And the cleric Guillaume Erard rebuked the heretic
Joan for her sins and reviled her. "The Maid, however," the
anecdote book reported, "after her long imprisonment in the
musty dungeon, was dizzy from the fresh air; moreover she had
been shown the instruments of torture three times, and had been
threatened. And she stood there and listened in patience, silence,
and prayer to the diatribe of the cleric. And he reviled her and
her king, King Charles. He pointed his finger at Joan and said:
'I am speaking of you, Joan, and I name you heretic, and I say
that your king, too, is a heretic, and an apostate.' Then, however,
in the midst of the hostile throng, and in the presence of all the
great lords and prelates, the Maid interrupted him and cried
loudly: 'Now it is enough. I tell you, sir, and I swear it to you,
even if I had to die for it: My King Charles is the most noble
Christian in all Christendom, and the most faithful. And he is
not at all what you charge'; and only with difficulty could she
be silenced."

Simone lowered her book. For months this Joan had been tormented and had been dragged from dungeon to dungeon and
had been beset by hostile judges; and her king, the man who
owed her everything, had not raised a finger for her; he had
sent her no message, he had vanished, he and all his lords, he
had simply left her and sacrificed her. But she still believed in
him, even now, in the hour of her greatest need and danger, and
she opened her mouth, even now, and defended him when he
was being reviled.

And Simone read what else took place in the walled cemetery
of the Abbey.

The Bishop of Beauvais had prepared two versions of the sentence. The one version was intended for the heretic who persisted in heresy and condemned her to death by fire. The other
version was intended for the heretic who repented; this verdict
pardoned her and spared her life.

Three times, in due form the prelates called upon the Maid to repent and to recant her voices and renounce her king. Three times the Maid refused.

After she had refused the third time, the Bishop began to read aloud the verdict that excommunicated the unrepentant heretic from the Church and condemned her to death.

But while the Bishop was reading, other clerics had climbed on Joan's platform and continued to press her to repent. They read her a document, an announcement of recantation, and they urged her: "Recant, sign or you will be burned," and they pointed at the hangman and at the tumbril that was ready to carry her to the stake.

The crowd below saw that they were debating with Joan and they became impatient. The English soldiers grumbled loudly that they would not let themselves be cheated of seeing the witch burn; and some of the great English lords who were sitting on the platform grumbled that they should have spent such a lot of money to purchase the Maid, if she were not even to be executed. The crowd became louder and more threatening, so loud that they drowned out the loud voice of the Bishop who was reading the death sentence.

In her mind's eye Simone saw Joan standing on the platform. In front of her was the hangman's cart, on the platform opposite the inimical man was reading the terrible verdict, and below her were thousands of infuriated faces and screaming mouths, demanding her death; and around her were a few, who seemed to be friends, who argued with her that she only needed to sign to be rid of her English guards and to be for ever in the tender hand and custody of the Church.

Simone comprehended Joan's weakening. The Bishop reading the verdict had just reached the place: "for these reasons we do declare you excommunicated and a heretic and we do decree that you shall be handed over to the secular jurisdiction as a limb of Satan, severed from the Church, . . ." when Joan interrupted him and declared that she was ready to recant, that she did not persist in the belief in her visions and apparitions, and that she was willing from now on to obey her judges and the Church in

each and every regard. They gave her the document and they
gave her a quill and she signed with a big twisted curlicue, and
they said that would not do, and she signed with a cross.

Simone imagined Joan's shame and despair as she crouched in
her cell later on. Believing the words of the priests, she had expected to be transferred to the gentler custody of the Church.
Instead of that she was dragged back to her dungeon, chained
as before, and the brutal English mercenaries were still with
her, even at night, two in her room and three outside her door.
The only difference was that she now wore women's clothing.
Her clerical judges had demanded that of her and had forced
her to do it on the strength of the declaration that she had signed.
They had impressed upon her that the slightest transgression of
an ecclesiastical law would make her a recidivist heretic and
would bring about her immediate execution.

With bitter pleasure Simone read of the ensuing events. On a
Thursday Joan had recanted and had promised strict obedience
to the laws of the Church. Only three days passed before she
put on her male attire again and withdrew the recantation.

That came about as follows: On the Sunday morning, when
she awoke, Joan asked her guards to take off her chains so that
she could get up and relieve the needs of her nature. The mercenaries, however, did not give her the women's clothing, but
threw the male attire before her. They carried the dress away so
that she could not reach it. Joan said: "Messieurs, do you not
know that I am forbidden to wear that? If I do it, I will fall
into sin. Give me my dress I pray." They laughed and refused
her. And this begging and refusing continued until noon. Finally,
because of the need of her body, Joan had to get up from the bed
and take the male clothing. The soldiers in the cell, however,
shouted at those outside: "Hurrah, now we have her."

Simone read that on the following day, on Monday, the twenty-
eighth of May 1431, the Bishop of Beauvais himself came into
Joan's prison, accompanied by two ecclesiastical secretaries. He
asked Joan point-blank why she had put on male clothing again.
Joan, however—and it made Simone's heart beat higher—did
not defend herself, said nothing of the pitiful circumstances, but

declared: "I put it on of my own free will. I did it because you did not keep your word that I could attend mass and would not have to remain in chains. If you let me go to mass and take off my chains and give me female guards, as you promised, I will do as you wish."

The Bishop made no reply to that; instead, when he noticed that Joan was in a rebellious, challenging mood, he at once continued to ask: "Since the day of your recantation, last Thursday, did you hear the voices of Sainte Cathérine and Sainte Marguérite?"

To answer that question was very dangerous, for Joan had declared and signed that she did not persist in the belief in her visions and voices. But she did not fear the danger. Without regard to her renunciation she answered: "Yes. I have heard my voices."

That probably pleased the Bishop. But it also pleased Simone. And with pride and joy she read how Joan boldly replied to the Bishop's question: "And what did your voices say?" with the words: "They told me that it displeased God that I, in order to save my life, permitted myself to be persuaded to renounce and recant. They told me that, by saving my life, I denied God and that I condemned myself. They told me that, when I was standing on the platform, I should have answered the priest boldly; for he is a lying priest and his accusations were all lies. When I said that it was not God who sent me, I condemned myself. For the truth is that God did send me. My voices told me that I did wrong when I recanted. It was the fear of the fire that made me say what I said."

And the priest who recorded this reply made a note in the margin: *Responsio mortifera,* the fatal answer.

The occurrences which followed now, Simone had often read before. But in this night it seemed to her she was reading them for the first time.

On Wednesday morning Joan was excommunicated, declared a recidivist heretic, and turned over to secular jurisdiction. In the hangman's tumbril she was taken to the old market place in the City of Rouen, which was black with people. On one platform sat the judges, on a second one the other prelates. In the middle was the funeral pyre, and on it a great plaque with the inscription: "Joan, who called herself the Maid, Impostor, Witch, Impudent Blasphemer, Blood Drinker, Devil Worshipper, Heretic."

She was conducted to the pyre; the billets had been piled very high and on an elevated pedestal of stucco so that all could see Joan. A priest preached a long sermon; she knelt and prayed. The Bishop of Beauvais read the verdict. The formalities lasted long and the English soldiers shouted: "Priest, shall we eat supper here?" She asked for a crucifix and one of the soldiers had pity on her, and gave her a little, crude cross of two chips of wood, and she kissed it, and put it on her bosom, between her skin and her dress. And then they put a tall paper cap on her head, with the inscription: "Recidivist Heretic, Renegade, Idolatress." Then they tied her to the stake, and the hangman set fire to the funeral pyre. She cried: "Jesus," and again: "Jesus," and as she cried "Jesus" for the seventh time, her head drooped, and she died.

But the English feared that people might say she had escaped. Upon their command, therefore, the hangman had to push back the flaming billets, and to show the dead body of the witch before it was completely consumed, to the multitude. A citizen of Paris, who was present at the execution, described the event as follows: "She was bound to a stake, and the stake stood on a scaffold of stucco, and on it was the fire. Her dress, however, burned very speedily, and then the billets were drawn away, so that the throng might have no doubts. And all the crowd saw her dead, and naked, and they all saw her female, secret parts. And after they had looked at her long enough, hanging there dead on the stake, the hangman raked the fire and the billets over the remains, so that everything was consumed, and her bone and flesh became ashes."

But in her gold anecdote book Simone read: "Despite the oil, and the sulphur, and the coal which were used at the behest of the English in order to destroy the body of the Maid, the hangman found the said Joan's heart whole and gleaming. And in vain he tried to destroy it. And it continued to glow and to beat in the ashes. The Cardinal of England, however, dismayed by this miracle and fearing the agitation of the people, gave orders to throw the bones, the heart, and the ashes into the River Seine. And the hangman said: "I am in great fear that I shall be condemned to hell, for I have burned a saint." And many Englishmen said: "That was a good woman." And a Canon of Rouen struck his breast, broke into tears, and said: "May my soul attain the place where the soul of this Maid has gone." Another of the clerical judges remained deranged for a whole month and could not satisfy his penitence, and he took a part of the money he had received for his participation in the trial, and bought a prayer book, and used it to pray for the Maid.

And the Secretary of the King of England had gone to the execution full of pride and joy. But when he returned, he was filled with pain and grief, and he lamented: "We are all lost, for we have burned a saint."

V: The Vile Reward

SIMONE is standing on her rock by the garden wall and is watching the road. She is waiting for the ransom money. Plainly she will have to wait quite a while, for the ransom demanded is high. But she hasn't the slightest doubt that her friends will raise the money. At any moment now Monsieur Reynault, the mailman, will be coming with the big check.

Perhaps she had better go to the kitchen. The negotiations about the ransom are taking place in the Blue Room, and in the kitchen she can hear what is being said inside, even though the doors are closed. Moreover, they are having string beans with the sweetbreads today and she still has to cut the beans. So it will seem perfectly natural for her to be in the kitchen, and Madame cannot object.

She is sitting on her low stool, the pan of beans in her lap. For a time she hears nothing. Then the high, crackling voice of Monsieur Cordelier comes to her quite plainly: "Naturally I would be very glad to ransom the Maid from the captivity of Madame and of the Two Hundred Families. All my people are grumbling because it wasn't done long ago. They are taking up collections for her, just as they used to do for Spain. But that doesn't get us far. They're all poor devils and they can only give a few francs each, because they are being scalped by the Two Hundred Families. What do you think we should do, gentlemen?" the deputy prefect is speaking Latin, but Simone understands every word.

Now she hears the high squeaking voice of Gilles de Rais: "I will subscribe ten thousand francs right off. Goodness knows, that is shabby enough, when Madame is demanding twenty million. But my women and my actors are eating up my whole fortune, especially that fat, brazen Louison. Besides, I still have to contribute a battleship for our navy in Algiers, since the Defeatist of Verdun and the generals have betrayed us. I have poked around in the pockets of all my clothes without finding a single red sou." And King Charles says sadly: "My pockets are empty, too. But you, Monsieur Planchard, you are a rich man with your transfer business, and it's your niece who is in a jam. You ought to subscribe a large sum, at least half a million."

Simone stops cutting beans; tensely she awaits Uncle Prosper's answer. He clears his throat and says: "I don't need to assure you, Sire, that my heart is bleeding at the thought of my dear niece, the daughter of my brother Pierre, in captivity. She is a good girl and a great patriot, even if she is skinny as a hound. But it is not up to me, as a close relative, to interfere. People would take that amiss, and my business relations would suffer. And I am a business man from head to foot. It's a shame that these considerations, and my blood relationship prevent me from helping her. Otherwise I would raise the twenty million with my little finger."

"Joe Blow," Gilles de Rais says scornfully.

"In that case only our Châtelain can help," King Charles the Seventh remarks with a sigh, and: "How about it, Monsieur le Marquis de la Trémoille?" he says. There is a brief silence. Then Simone hears the Châtelain answer: "The Banque de France is opposed to it. In our present critical financial state the Banque de France regards it as frivolous, even criminal, to use money for the liberation of impertinent young girls."

Madame comes into the kitchen. "You've been listening, of course," she says. "That's what I thought. Well, now you know it. Eavesdroppers never hear anything good about themselves. Not a penny for impertinent young girls. And since you are not only a household thief, but are spying on me besides, I have informed my son that I am tired of sharing house and board with you. I've had enough trouble with you. Let the Two Hundred Families see about some other prison for you."

Simone is in a closed car. She is tied hand and foot and is scared to death. The inside of the car is pitch dark, the car is rattling, the motor is roaring, she bounces up and down on the cobblestones. Where are they taking her? Probably to the

Saint Michel prison where the murderer Guitriaux had been confined.

The gendarmes—one of them is Monsieur Grandlouis—open the barred car door and tell her to get out; that is hard to do with her feet tied up. Monsieur Grandlouis leads her by a chain and they walk through a big door into the interior. The prisoners are standing at long tables; each one is eating from a tin plate that is welded to the table; each one is wearing a tall cap with his number, name, and crime written on it. Quickly she looks to see whether the murderer Guitriaux is there. And he is. "No. 617, Théophile Guitriaux, habitual murderer."

All look up as she is led in, and one of them says viciously: "We are ordinary, decent criminals, working for our daily bread. But that girl set fire to France just for fun, just to spite the Two Hundred Families." And a toothless old man, with a face that is partly eaten away, says: "And the main reason why our food is so bad is because she embezzled the Roblechon cheese." And the murderer Guitriaux says: "Compared to her I'm an angel." And they put their heads together and consult with each other and finally decide spitefully: "We won't eat at the same table with her. We'll strike."

Simone is terribly ashamed. Very softly she says to the gendarme who holds her by her handcuffs: "I should rather not eat, Monsieur Grandlouis." Monsieur Grandlouis nods and leads her out.

She walks round in the yard; it is the loading yard and it is exercising time. All the others walk in pairs, but she is alone and she walks at a distance from the rest. They keep walking round and round the yard; she can only take very small steps with her bound feet; the man who is now holding her chain is Arsène, the concierge of the loading yard. The others are grumbling again about her presence, and the old man whose face is eaten away spits on the ground every time she passes him.

In one corner are all the employees of the firm, and they are all looking at her critically. The old driver, Richard, says: "It's really very bad; she has robbed all the drivers of their daily bread." And Monsieur Peyroux says: "She stole the key and she broke open the drawer. She is a household thief. Just imagine, the niece of the firm."

On the wall sits the Marshal Gilles de Rais with his blue moustache and his leather jacket. As Simone comes near him he bends forward and whispers to her: "Here I am, and I will save you. Tonight at half-past twelve I will stop here in front of the wall with my horse, Hurricane, and you can get on behind me and hang on." Then he turns away, twirls his blue moustache, acts as though nothing had happened, jumps down from the wall, and disappears. He is a real *débrouillard*.

The walking continues; the yard is very dusty, it is terribly hot, and she is thirsty. She has to walk round and round in a circle; her tongue hangs out and when she stops, the concierge, Arsène, who never liked her, drags at her chain.

Then she is standing by the red pump, and the yard is full of people, and they are all looking at her. And on the roof of the office building are the lawyers with their birds' heads and they whisper and write, and suddenly Simone knows: this is the court of law.

But she has no idea what sort of a court it is, and how can she defend herself if she doesn't know what sort of a court she is facing? "What sort of a court is this?" she asks fearfully. And Mademoiselle Rousseil, the schoolteacher, replies: "This is the very highest court in existence. If you had paid attention and had not been lacking in the required application to your studies, you would know that this court was appointed by Work, Fatherland, Family. In this court there are only two alternatives: death or acquittal; and so far there has never been an acquittal. There's no trifling with the gentlemen of Work, Fatherland, Family. Their sentence is always: to be shot at the stake. You must have done something terrible," she concludes sadly.

"I counted on that," Simone answers defiantly. "I expected the Boches might shoot me."

"Yes," the deputy prefect acknowledges, "you're a brave girl; we all know that."

"It is a Boche court, isn't it?" Simone inquires once more, just to be on the safe side.

"Well, yes," Monsieur Cordelier informs her, "in a way it's a hostile court, so to speak," and now his eyes are helpless and evasive again.

But Simone must have a straightforward answer; her entire conduct before the court depends upon it. "So the judges are all Boches?" she insists once again.

The deputy prefect twiddles his rosette. "Well, probably," he replies, "perhaps, maybe, I assume so; really, frankly, I wouldn't know about that."

At once the door opens; the judges enter. Simone cranes her neck to see them. In a moment she will find out what sort of judges they are.

But no, she doesn't find out. Hoods cover their faces; only their eyes show. They must be the cowl-wearers, the *Cagoulards,* of whom Maurice used to speak. There are very many of them, they all wear red robes, and on their hoods are white swastikas. They sit on many rows of benches that rise in the form of an amphitheatre. It really must be a very high court.

Maître Levautour rises to make the formal accusation. He has taken off his bird's head and is disguised as an ordinary lawyer. He waves his fat, white hands in the air and points at Simone with his beringed index finger. "That," he declares, "is the Spirit of Insubordination which has destroyed our fatherland, France. That is the Spirit of the Strikes and of Greed, that Spirit which refuses to subordinate itself to the wisdom of experienced business men. She inherited it from her father, the rebel. And she dragged her uncle into it, Monsieur Planchard, head of the firm of the same name, who wasn't at all originally inclined in that direction. But she suborned him to mutiny against Madame, that great woman, his mother. Probably he isn't even the son of his mother, but only the brother of Pierre Planchard, and that's why he and the accused are accomplices, and you, honourable judges and fascists, were quite right to take his business away from him."

Simone listens patiently while Maître Levautour abuses her. But when he tries to drag in Uncle Prosper, she becomes furious. "You are a liar, Maître Levautour," she shouts at the top of her voice. "I did it all alone. Uncle Prosper is a good Frenchman, to be sure, but he knew nothing of my action. You mustn't take his transfer business away from him. He was made to be a business man, that's his place in life, he is a business man from head to foot. And you, Maître Levautour, you don't belong here at all. You have only disguised yourself. You belong on the roof of Notre Dame along with the other monsters."

The judges in their red robes sit motionless; they do not take off their hoods. It is tough luck that Simone still does not know who these judges really are, not even now, as they begin to cross-examine. And they ask her many questions, pell-mell and confusingly.

"Why," they ask, "did you obey the deputy prefect when you undertook your action, and not Monsieur Planchard, knowing very well that Monsieur Planchard is a big business man and your uncle? Didn't you know Work and Family decide what is right and wrong? And when you were standing by the red pump, didn't you have mutinous thoughts in your heart, and didn't you bristle up because Monsieur Planchard was making money on the gasoline that he hoarded with so much trouble? And didn't you put too much nutmeg in the cream gravy? And didn't you run to Monsieur Xavier and speak up for the riff-raff, when you are a niece of Monsieur Planchard and so to speak belong to the Two Hundred Families? And wasn't it impertinent of you to try to save France in your dark green slacks, when Madame had expressly told you that it is indecent to wear men's clothing?"

Simone is shocked to notice that even now, in court, she is wearing the dark green slacks. They are all looking at her, and the blood stains are there again. They are all whispering. The Two Hundred Families on the platform grumble openly, especially Family 97.

And the judges persist in their questions which follow in rapid order; they simply hail down on Simone. And to top it all she discovers that she has suddenly become deaf. She can see that the judges are speaking. She can see their mouths moving in the openings of their hoods; she can see their lips parting and closing; but she hears only occasional sounds, and finally nothing at all. Not a whisper enters her ear. She sees that every one in the court room is waiting for her answer, and a pendulum swings back and forth, and when it has swung back and forth for a certain length of time—Simone can't figure out how long that time is—then all the lawyers state in unison: "The accused is silent," and the judges repeat: "The accused is silent." And that is the only thing that Simone can hear.

She feels very small and lonely. Countless people are there, almost all the citizens of Saint-Martin—Monsieur Amiot and Monsieur Raimu and Monsieur Laroche—and they are all against her; they crane their necks to see her; they are glad that she can't answer. Monsieur Peyroux looks especially inquisitive and gloating. But also Messieurs L'Agréable and L'Utile stare at her with evil eyes, and she can't understand it, because these two gentlemen always chatted with her most pleasantly, and now Monsieur L'Agréable is evidently ridiculing her muteness and Monsieur L'Utile is nodding and grinning spitefully. They are all hostile to her and not a single one of her friends is there.

It is clear that she is convicted. She is full of fear and bitterness. Why did the Mandator pick her out? There are forty million people in France, and if none of them succeeded in saving the country, why was it demanded of her? The commission means sure death. Her father is dead; Jaurès is dead; they kill everybody who is sent to comfort the poor and humble. It is unfair to choose her, of all people; she is still so young.

The presiding judge rises; all the judges rise with him. Their red robes rustle. They stand in the great semicircle of the amphitheatre like a huge red mountain. And they have all drawn their red hoods over their faces and on the hoods are the white swastikas, and Simone stands there, opposite this huge red mountain, tiny, alone, and shabby in her stained green slacks.

Now, with a heroic gesture, the presiding judge takes off his hood, and after him all the others take off their hoods. And lo, they are all Frenchmen.

Her heart stands still. There are no Germans at all among the judges; they are all Frenchmen.

She sees it. She doesn't believe it. Cold with terror she stares at the faces. She sees it.

The presiding judge, it is the Châtelain, begins the new cross-examination. "Now since it has been proven," he says with his creaking voice, "that you, Simone Planchard, have committed these serious crimes, I ask you: who instigated you? who is your Mandator?"

Simone wants to answer. She wants to tell the truth. She wants to testify for herself and for her country. But not a sound comes out of her throat; her tongue fails her. Her terror becomes greater; it stuns her. If she does not speak now, then her action has been robbed of its meaning. And she cannot speak; she is struck dumb.

She turns her head, looking for help.

And there is help. Someone is standing next to her: Henriette. She stands there, gracefully and lovely; there is no mockery in her face any more; she nods to her and with a gentle, sweet voice she invites her: "Answer boldly." Simone's spell is broken; her muteness has left her. "Joan," she says to Henriette with deep emotion. "Thank you, Joan. Thank you, my dear sister."

The others have seen nothing and heard nothing. The presiding judge repeats his question: "Who is it, then, who gave you the commission?" Judges and lawyers are just about to announce in unison: "The accused is silent," when Simone begins to speak. She smiles radiantly and, with her fine, dark voice, she states: "It was my dead father, Pierre Planchard, who gave me the commission."

Perfect silence fills the great Church of Notre Dame. Simone feels the hostility of the audience melting away. Monsieur L'Agréable nudges Monsieur L'Utile; both of them nod appreciatively and smile at her. A great warm wave of understanding flows from the audience to Simone.

The judges, however, sit up straighter. The Two Hundred Families on the platform become tense with enmity. And the Marquis clears his throat in a challenging manner, and with false, ironic courtesy he asks: "And how was he dressed, your father, the Mandator?"

"He was dressed modestly," Simone replies. "He never had much money because he was a fighter. Père Bastide told me my father, Pierre Planchard, bought his suits ready-made in the Lafayette Department Store."

"Didn't he have unkempt, neglected hair?" the judges ask.

And Simone answers: "He had no time to attend to his hair. He had too much to do comforting the poor and humble."

The thousands in the audience are happy. Monsieur L'Agréable shouts "Bravo," and: "Bravo," shout the others. The Châtelain, however, rises; he appears large in his red robe, although he is really small; he is wearing his gleaming riding boots. He switches the riding crop against his boots and threatens: "I will have the court room cleared."

Etienne stands there as a witness. "Was she arrogant?" they ask him. "Did she boast about her action? Was she pleased when the people stared after her? Did she talk to you about the Maid of Orléans?"

"We all like to speak of the Maid of Orléans," Etienne answers. "She is a shining example."

"Certainly," says Maître Levautour, "especially because she was burned." And the Châtelain explains: "The willingness to make sacrifices, that's what matters. She permitted *herself* to be burned, not a truck yard that belonged to someone else. That's why the Two Hundred Families honour her."

Gilles de Rais, on the witness stand, testifies: "Of course, Mademoiselle would have done better to pour sugar into the gasoline. But how could she know that? They never told her anything. She grew up in the Villa Monrepos in the midst of ignorance and prejudice."

"If you persist in abusing highly respected business men in this manner, you impudent witness," the Marquis warns him, "I will have you drowned in the river."

"You just try that, you fascist," Maurice replies. "You'll see how fast all the drivers will go on strike. Then you can cart your own wines."

Then another witness is called. Simone cannot understand her name, but when the witness answers: "Present," a shudder runs down Simone's back. Yes, this cold, high, soft voice, which nevertheless penetrates to the farthest corners of the cathedral, is Madame's voice. She has stepped down from her tombstone, the haughty Queen Isabeau, she has squeezed her enormous frame into the corset and the black silk dress, and now she stands in the chancel and disdainfully looks at Simone through her lorgnon. "Just look at her, gentlemen of the court," she says. "She is in truth the daughter of her father. You have heard that this infamous Pierre Planchard did not even have enough money to go to the barber Armand to get his hair cut; and he was dressed so shabbily that the text from the reverse side showed through his clothes. But he carried his head as high as a giraffe. And the accused is just such a Miss Penniless and High-and-Mighty. She hasn't a red sou; she would be dead and gone by now if my son hadn't offered her a home and bed and board. But she puts on airs, as though she owned the whole transfer establishment. She's just full of arrogance and impertinence. These Planchards aren't after anything except to be popular with the riff-raff. That's why Pierre Planchard went into the jungle and stirred up the poor Negroes, who had been so happy until then. And that's why she set fire to the loading yard and broke up my poor, good son's life. And that's why she put on the green slacks, too. Everything, just so the people of Saint-Martin would stare after her. And especially that driver, Maurice. And what is she, if you examine her more closely? A household thief. There," and she pulls out the key to the private office, and holds it up before Simone's eyes, and the key gets larger and larger.

"We thank you, Madame," says the Châtelain. "We are now fully informed"; and he and all the others draw the hoods with the swastikas over their faces again.

"We proceed to the verdict," the presiding hood announces. "Judicial colleagues and fascists, this Simone, who calls herself the Maid of Orléans, has blasphemed, and by word and deed has desecrated the sacredness of profitable work. What is the penalty?"

"Death," answers the red mountain with the swastikas.

"She has denied the authority of the generals, who surrendered the French Army to the Nazis for expert military and patriotic reasons. What is the penalty?"

"Death," the red mountain answers.

"She has secretly and openly revolted against the superior wisdom of Madame and thus shown disrespect for the authority of the Family. What is the penalty?"

"Death," the red mountain answers.

"We hereby declare," the Marquis summarizes and proclaims: "this Simone Planchard, also called Joan of Arc, has treasonably clung to the threadbare ideals of her poorly dressed father, 'Liberty, Equality, Fraternity,' and has impertinently disregarded the principles of the new France, symbolized by the aged Marshal, the principles, 'Work, Fatherland, Family.' We therefore condemn this impertinent and degenerate girl to public death. I ask you, Messieurs, how shall the execution be carried out?"

"She is to be burned," the red mountain declares.

"She is to be burned, yesterday, today, and tomorrow," the Marquis announces and breaks the rod, and all the monsters croak.

She is crouched in the tumbril, it is the Peugeot, which should have been scrapped long ago, and the old driver, Richard, has hitched four horses to it so that he will be sure to arrive safely. The execution is to be held in the Place du Général Gramont. There stands the guillotine.

At first Simone is driven around the big square several times so that every one can get a good look at her. The fugitives look closely at her; the child stops playing with its cat and stares at her. All the windows of the hotel are filled with people. Out of the Napoleon room Madame looks down; today is her big day.

The platform of the guillotine grows higher and higher. Simone stands there and looks up and feels very small. Beside her and a little back of her, stands Monsieur Peyroux, the bookkeeper, with his rabbit face, and whispers to her secretively: "The Planchard firm does not leave any of its employees in the lurch. The boss has spared no expense to save you, Mademoiselle. Now you only need to recant a little, then you can go home, and get a good night's sleep. Here, if you please," and he hands her his fountain pen. "Just a tiny, tiny, little signature."

She holds the fountain pen in her hand. She stares at the document, at the white spot, where her signature is to go. She does not want to sign, but she does not return the fountain pen either. It is terrible to die so young and in such a horrible manner, and only because she did something good and decent. It is an unmerciful, unjust world, and every one has deserted her.

Monsieur Peyroux pulls out his watch. "I am extremely sorry, Mademoiselle," he says, "but the hangman will only wait another minute. I will count to sixty." He stands there, polite and disapproving, and begins to count: "One, two, three, seven, twelve," and with every number Simone feels a pang. She doesn't want to die. She only needs to sign, to scribble a few letters, and she can live. "Twenty-seven, thirty-one, thirty-six," Monsieur Peyroux counts. She feels an overwhelming temptation to sign. Only a few letters. She must not, she must not betray her commission. He still holds the document in front of her; the temptation is irresistible; her hand moves closer and closer to the document. If only he would finish counting. "Fifty-four." It will not be much longer now. "Fifty-eight, fifty-nine, sixty."

Ah, now he has finished; the decision has been made. Now she is rid of the temptation. Now she must die. With a tremendous sense of relief and with crushing fear she sees Monsieur Peyroux, his document, and his fountain pen vanish.

And now she is to climb the steps. She must not show any fear. The important thing is to be brave; it is expected of her, and justly so; if she is not brave now, then everything she has done up to this time was empty boasting. Courage, up, up the steps.

The knife waits up above. It quivers gently back and forth; it is blue and glittering, and in a moment it will be red. And she will be without a head, and the blood will spurt out horribly.

She cannot climb the steps. She is paralysed. She can't put her foot on the lowest step. She can't raise her foot.

A hand reaches down to seize her and to drag her up. The hand reaches down from behind, from above; Simone cannot see it, but she feels it, coming nearer, dropping towards her, heavily, threateningly, horribly. And what a disgrace, what an unthinkable disgrace, that she will have to be dragged and shoved, because she is too cowardly. The hand comes closer, closer, with cruel deliberateness, and still closer. It is a hard hand; it will grip her hard; Simone's shoulder will be black and blue as it was that time when Uncle Prosper's hand seized her by the shoulder.

Now she feels the emanations from the hand. Her neck quivers with a sudden chill, her hair stands on end. Then a voice sounds in her ear, gentle, clear, comforting: "Don't be afraid." It is Henriette's voice. And the hand is gone. And her fear is gone.

Simone raises her foot. She climbs the steps, not pushed forward, but unaided. Ahead of her is Henriette. Henriette is not walking, nor is she floating; she is gliding up the steps in a blissful manner.

Up above the knife is still waiting, blue and glittering. It still quivers gently; it is enormous, it grows larger and larger, but there is no longer anything terrifying about it. It is only an azure expanse, a bright, friendly azure. And the azure vaults above her; it vaults higher and higher; it is no longer the knife, it is the sky. And there are no longer any steps on which Simone walks. She soars, she glides upward. And she feels: when she has reached the top, then everything that is cowardly and mean will lie far beneath her feet, and she will herself be a part of that bright, brave, blessed azure.

VI: The Trapper

ON THE morning of the second day following, fairly early, Uncle Prosper returned from his trip.

Simone was just engaged in tidying the Blue Room, the door to the hall was open, and she saw him coming. She did not move. He removed his hat and overcoat, put his suitcase into the hall closet, and went up to his room. She did not know whether he had seen her.

Intentionally or unintentionally, he had not spoken with her, he had not greeted her, he had overlooked her; that much was certain. It intensified her deep dejection, the dull resignation with which she had been filled since refusing Maurice's offer.

She observed what Uncle Prosper did during the day. He did not go out; he remained in the Villa Monrepos; he did not go to Saint-Martin. But Simone saw him face to face only at meals while she waited on the table. For the most part he spent his time in Madame's room which was remote and safe from eavesdropping. Unquestionably, they were talking about her, Simone; they were deciding her fate.

And all at once Simone's buried hopes rose anew. It was a good sign that there was still so much to be discussed about her and her fate. Perhaps, even probably, Uncle Prosper had found ways and means in Francheville to save her from the Germans. Perhaps, even probably, this deliverance was expensive. Perhaps, even probably, he was now seeking Madame's consent.

Towards evening, shortly before the meal, Madame appeared in the kitchen. She examined what Simone had prepared for dinner, tasted, and demanded a trace more onion in the soup. Then she said casually: "But before you do that, go to the Blue Room; my son wants to talk with you."

Simone had made up her mind to fear nothing more and to

hope for nothing more. In spite of that decision, her knees became weak now that the big discussion between her and Uncle Prosper was about to take place. She wanted to go up to her mansard to make herself more presentable. Madame said: "You can go just as you are."

Simone went to the Blue Room in her kitchen dress with an apron over it.

Uncle Prosper was standing at the window looking out on the garden. When she entered he turned round with a preoccupied expression, his heavy brows uneasily knitted. He was wearing a bluish grey suit and looked important; it was mean of Madame to send her in to him wearing her kitchen apron.

Contrary to his usual manner, Uncle Prosper seemed embarrassed. It took him a while to get started. He walked back and forth; then he sat down at the little table at which he usually drank his coffee. There stood a bottle of Pernod and a liqueur glass; he had taken an apéritif.

After she had politely greeted him, Simone stood there and waited. She was quite calm again but filled with a controlled tenseness. She not only clearly saw every feature of his face, she also observed with attentive senses everything else in the room. The peg which held the cord of one of the window shades had become loose; she made a mental note to hammer it down firmly tomorrow.

"Sit down," said Uncle Prosper a little nervously. He tossed off another little glass of Pernod. "It's too bad that you don't drink," he said with artificial cheerfulness. "It's so much easier to talk over an apéritif."

Simone did not answer. She sat there in her little chair, modestly, like a scullery maid.

Countless times in these last ten years she had sat like this, shabby, humble. Today all at once he found it objectionable. "This whole situation is insufferable," he began. "I find it unbearable that you cringe about the place like a despised employee. You, the daughter of my brother. But Mother has her good reasons and I have to defer to them."

So it was as she had assumed. It had been Madame's idea to banish her from the table and to keep her a prisoner.

"That was a good idea of yours a few days ago," he resumed, "that you wanted to talk frankly with me. But it's too bad that you started right in with a harangue and cut me off short, so that we couldn't possibly have a sensible discussion. My brother's daughter a thief, a household thief, and then she stands up in front of me and acts as if she had the right to demand an accounting from me. I am a very patient person, I make a great effort to be fair to every one, but patience has its limits."

Simone was silent. "What I can't understand to this day," he began again after a while, "what I simply can't get through my head, is why you didn't come to me before you caused this disaster, and that you didn't try to talk things over with me. You've been living in my house for ten years now. You've had every chance to know me well. You certainly know that I'm not hard to talk to. Why didn't you simply come to me and say: 'I think that it is time for us to destroy the loading yard now'? Then we could have discussed it, and I would have explained to you why I didn't consider it right. I would have told you my reasons, and I'm sure you would have understood them; after all, you are a sensible girl. I could certainly have talked you out of this piece of folly. Instead of that you go and steal the key from behind my back and you ruin all of us."

He spoke to her cordially, frankly, companionably, paternally. Only a week ago Simone would have let herself be persuaded by him. Today, however, she saw in him only a man who turned and twisted everything to suit his convenience. She replied obstinately: "You know exactly why I did it." That answer was all-inclusive, and with it all his fine arguments were obliterated.

He dropped the subject. Acrimoniously he retorted: "When I hear you talking like that, I can't imagine why I have been racking my brains all these days to find a way of helping you."

"I don't believe I need any help," said Simone. "I don't believe I am in any danger." She had pondered over Maurice's explanation again and again; now she could show Uncle Prosper that he couldn't make a fool of her so easily. "I did it before the Germans were here," she set forth. "I carried out an instruction which had been issued by the Deputy Prefecture. I only did a thing that every French soldier did, or should have done. If I am punishable, then every French soldier is punishable. You don't need to rack your brains, Uncle Prosper," she concluded with the slightest trace of irony. "I can't imagine that the Boches will do anything to me."

Uncle Prosper, a little confused by the logical consistency of her arguments, drank some Pernod. "I should like to know," he grumbled, "who put those ideas into your head. You don't really believe that if the Boches want to do something to you, they will be embarrassed by fine points of law. They don't stand on ceremony, my dear, you can bet your life on that. If they didn't arrest you right away, you owe your good luck to a fortunate combination of circumstances. Just now they're merely adapting themselves to us; they are playing a game of appeasement. But that won't last for ever. They're going to switch back and forth between honey and the whip; one of their own officers told me that the other day in Francheville. It may be that by tomorrow it will serve their purpose to claim that we have incited even children in their teens against them; and then they will grab you, and in order to set a horrible example, they'll shoot you or send you to a penitentiary in Germany. They're the masters; they can do what they please. And you stand there and say: 'I am not in danger. I can't imagine that the Boches will do anything to me.' "

What Uncle Prosper said was reasonable; it even corresponded in part with what Maurice had set forth. Simone's heart contracted with fear at the thought of the nearness of danger. But at the same time she breathed a sigh of relief. The danger did not come from Uncle Prosper; it came from the Boches.

And now Uncle Prosper even began to smile. He smiled all over his face, that beaming smile which always touched Simone's heart. "But you are right, nevertheless," he said. "Without knowing how or why, you are still right. You are really no longer in danger, or, at least, not for much longer. You see, I had an idea, a practical idea, and I didn't take it first to that idiot Philippe;

I took it straight to Francheville, to the prefect. I expounded my idea to him and he at once put out some feelers in German Headquarters. And," Uncle Prosper breathed deeply, "I am happy to say it seems to be working. The danger is as good as past."

Simone sat on her little chair, her face thoughtful and inscrutable. Strangely enough, her doubts of his good intentions had returned, and she was much more interested to know whether or not he was being honest with her than to hear the details of the plan he had figured out.

He, disappointed by her silence, continued with less spirit. He explained to her what he had in mind.

The Boches, he declared, kept themselves carefully informed as to the reliability of the localities that they occupied. Saint-Martin had a particularly bad record on account of the burning of the loading yard; the city had been subjected to a lot of vexations that other communities did not suffer. Now, of course, the fact of the incendiarism could not be denied. It was possible, however, to argue whether it had been done from political motives. "Do you follow me?" he asked.

Simone had listened with some misgivings. Drily she answered: "Yes."

"The point is," Uncle Prosper continued, "to push this incendiarism out of the realm of the political into that of the purely criminal, in other words, to make a sort of private matter out of it. The Boches take the attitude that, in districts where acts of national fanaticism have taken place, they naturally have to take the strictest measures. But wherever the population shows its good will to co-operate with the occupation authorities in the maintenance of law and order, there the Boches are also willing to meet the people half-way. The German Staff officers have expressly told the prefect, if the incendiarism is cleared up in the manner I just indicated, then the special restrictions for Saint-Martin and vicinity will at once be lifted."

Simone inquired drily: "If a Frenchman obeys the orders of the French authorities, is that fanaticism?"

"It doesn't matter," Uncle Prosper replied impatiently, "how we answer this question. Unfortunately the only thing that counts is the opinion of those who hold our fate in their hands."

He walked back and forth without looking at her, but she followed him with her eyes and saw that his heavy reddish-blond eyebrows were quivering nervously. She was on her guard. "How could it be made plausible," she asked slowly, carefully choosing her words, "that the deed was done for private reasons, when quite obviously the motive was political?" She sensed that the answer would be decisive.

Uncle Prosper was standing at the window and drumming on it with his fingers. He walked back to the table, took a sip of Pernod, wiped his lips, and then said lightly: "At present the Boches seem to be interested in emphasizing the idea of collaboration. At any rate, they are inclined to close one eye. A stamped and sealed paper with something half-way plausible on it would satisfy them. You would only need to sign a declaration that you set fire to the garage for personal reasons. Let's say, because you had quarrelled with Mother."

Simone felt as if someone had hit her on the head. Everything turned black before her eyes; she was afraid of falling off her chair. But the spell quickly passed and she could speak again. As through a fog she heard her own voice and it sounded clear and firm: "I will never sign such a declaration. You can't seriously expect that of me."

Uncle Prosper gulped. He had probably not expected her to agree at once with his preposterous proposal. "I realize," he argued gently after a brief silence, "I fully realize that you stand behind your act, and that you don't want your motives falsified. But please consider this. Your"—he groped for the word—"action may have made sense when you committed it. At that time you were able to say to yourself: perhaps a miracle will still take place, perhaps the army will hold out after all. But now, after the armistice has been signed and the war is over, I don't see who is to profit by the continued insistence that the deed was done from political motives. Such stubbornness would only have evil consequences. You yourself would remain in danger of arrest by the Boches and Saint-Martin would continue to be treated worse than any other city in Burgundy. Your friend, Xavier Bastide, will confirm that only this unfortunate affair is responsible for the restrictions."

Her face remained non-committal, inscrutable. He stepped close to her and put a hand on her shoulder. She smelled the odour of the Pernod from his mouth, and she saw his ear, pointed at the top, abnormally thick. Her shoulder shrugged the least bit, and he took his hand away.

"I admit," he began anew, "some of the people in the community, especially those who have nothing to lose, regard what you did as magnificent. But many are angry that they have to suffer so much on your account, and a few are furious. You haven't any idea what people are capable of when their pocket-books are in danger, and there are plenty who believe that they are paying the bill for your heroism. I'll tell you frankly, they won't hesitate to accuse you of having committed sabotage at a time when the Boches have already announced their penalties for it. There are many who don't like the Planchard family, and especially not the daughter of Pierre Planchard. There are many who believe that better relations with the Germans would not be too dearly bought if paid for by a little inconvenience on the part of Mademoiselle Simone Planchard. You are in greater danger than you think. We all know the Châtelain, and we know what to expect from men of his type. It seems wiser to me to bargain while there is still time."

Uncle Prosper poured himself another Pernod; he raised the glass with a hand that trembled slightly, and set it down without drinking. His large face that eloquently reflected his every mood became gloomy. "I won't speak of myself," he said sadly, more to himself than to her. "I won't even mention that I lost my business, the purpose and aim of my life, as a result of your rash action. Not only have the Boches stolen my firm, but I am also in the bad graces of the local people who are of any importance. They are playing what they call realistic politics; they believe that I was behind your action and they won't have anything to do with me. I'll tell you frankly, Mother preaches to me all the time that I should simply wait until the Boches grab you, and then everything would take care of itself; she just wants me to let matters take their course. It goes without saying that I won't do that. I won't think of sacrificing you to save my own skin. I will fight for you against the Châtelain and the whole gang. I will not leave the daughter of my Pierre in the lurch because she has committed an equally foolish and noble act. I will stand by you and protect you. But the only effective protection in this case is a trick. Be sensible. Sign the statement. It is an insignificant formality, and by doing it we disarm the Châtelain."

Simone was thinking so hard that her brows contracted. "What would be in such a statement?" she asked matter-of-factly. Uncle Prosper answered promptly and lightly: "Well, what I have already indicated. That you acted from personal motives, let's say, for instance, because you were angry over a scolding from Mother. The whole thing would have to be represented as a childish trick."

"But such a declaration would be criminal nonsense," Simone replied furiously. "Nobody on earth would believe it."

"Quite so," Uncle Prosper rejoined, "nobody in Saint-Martin would be fooled by it. But the Boches are set on their idea of collaboration. They believe in stamped papers, and they have expressly stated that they would be satisfied with such a declaration."

Simone thought for a couple of seconds. Then she said: "I won't sign anything like that."

Uncle Prosper breathed hard and turned red. But he succeeded once more in restraining himself. "You are pig-headed," he said. "What you did was intended as a noble act; I've never failed to recognize that, no matter how much I have suffered from it. But if you go on refusing to repair the consequent damage, you debase your action and ruin yourself and all the rest of us." He arose, stepped close to her once more, and looked urgingly into her eyes. She sat in her chair with an obstinate expression; she did not move; she did not answer.

He turned away from her. Heavy footed, his step less firm than usual, he walked back and forth.

And then something unexpected happened, something uncanny. He sank limply into an arm-chair. His big torso sagged forward. He covered his face with his hands. He began to weep. He wept loudly, without restraint.

Simone stared as the otherwise so virile, powerful man suddenly broke down and wept without inhibition. She was in a turmoil. It was unbearable. It was hard for her to remain in the room.

After a while Uncle Prosper composed himself. With a somewhat distorted smile he said: "Pardon me. It was too much. The excitement of these last few days was too much. They crowd in on me from all sides on your account and insist that I should disown you. I tremble for your life. They ruin my business to which my heart is attached, and I stand there helpless with bound hands and can't do a thing. Then I have an inspiration. I go to Francheville. I run from the prefect to the Boches, and from the Boches to the prefect. I consult all sorts of lawyers. I finally succeed in selling my idea to the Boches. I finally succeed in loosening the grip in which they hold you. You are as good as saved. And now this. The obstinate whim of an exaggerated heroism again smashes everything to bits, and we are right back where we were before."

He was standing at the window, staring out at the garden; she only saw his back which was heavy and round now. Very softly, so that she scarcely understood him, his back still towards her, he said: "And what's more, I was afraid that would happen. I've seen that before. Pierre persisted the same way. And now I see you racing towards the abyss. And here I stand again, eyes open, knowing it, and can't help. I can't help myself and I can't help you, simply because you won't listen to reason."

Simone asked drily: "And if I signed something like that, do you think the Boches and the Châtelain would then give you back your business?"

The directness of this question evidently shook his composure. He spun round and started to make some grandiloquent answer. But he swallowed it down and only said: "I think they would."

"And what would happen to me if I signed?" asked Simone.

"To you?" Uncle Prosper repeated in surprise. And at once he eagerly assured her: "Nothing at all. I'm telling you, the whole thing is a pure formality."

"They wouldn't bring any proceedings against me?" Simone asked dubiously. "They wouldn't lock me up?"

"In such cases," Uncle Prosper answered smoothly and with assurance, "in such cases the courts take action only if the injured person makes a complaint. Can you imagine that I would make a complaint of arson against you? The whole thing is a farce. The Boches want something in writing. As soon as they have it, they'll be satisfied."

"And nothing at all would happen to me?" Simone insisted suspiciously. "I wouldn't have to go to prison?"

"I have told you," Uncle Prosper replied a little impatiently, "that unless a complaint is lodged against you there can be no legal prosecution. Entirely aside from the fact that you are not of age. I don't understand your suspicion," he continued with some resentment. "Your life is at stake. The welfare of the whole Département is at stake. My business is at stake. And you hesitate to fulfil a trivial formality."

His big, helplessly angry, pleading face was very near to hers. The torrent of his words confused her. She felt tired, exhausted from this eternal bickering, by this eternal resisting and being dragged. With all her heart she longed to yield.

She collected herself. She did not want to make a second rash decision, she did not want to be bowled over by Uncle Prosper's words and looks. She did not want to make the decision in his presence. She wanted to weigh all the pros and cons, calmly, alone, twice, three times, ten times. She pressed her lips firmly together. She would say neither yes nor no at this time.

As if Uncle Prosper had read her thoughts he said very kindly: "I won't go on urging you. I want you to think of yourself, only of yourself."

She rose and started to leave. He stopped her. "I could not bring myself," he said, "to discuss with Mother in your presence the question whether we should make the sacrifices that are necessary for your deliverance. I've told you frankly that Mother objected at first. But now I have convinced her. There are no longer any secrets between the three of us. You know everything there is to know. You know how you can save yourself and that we are all ready to help you." He smiled. "From now on, of course, you will eat at the table with us again." He patted her. "It has gotten late. Go change your dress, Simone, and be sensible."

VII: The Recantation

ON THE following forenoon, while Simone was cleaning house, Madame, contrary to her habit, came into the Blue Room.

She sat down in the wing chair. She sat there stiffly, her head pressed down, so that her enormous double chin protruded even more. Silently she watched while Simone quietly and deftly did her work.

Finally she began to speak in her harsh, low voice.

From the very start, she said, she had not been in agreement with Monsieur Planchard's efforts to protect Simone from the Germans. If Madame had had her way, Simone would have been forced to bear the consequences of her impertinence. Monsieur Planchard, however, had been determined to save Simone regardless of the sacrifices and dangers that might ensue, and as he was the head of the family, she had finally given up her resistance. It was not easy for an old woman, she said, to participate in the disgusting comedy that they were concocting in order to dish up crooked and dangerous lies to the Boches. But the family was at stake, the unity of the family, and for that reason she had submitted.

Simone wiped dust and listened. Madame made no bones about anything. Madame said straight out that she had been willing to deliver her to the Boches. Simone remembered the moment when she had seen that flash of abysmal hatred in Madame's eyes.

Monsieur Planchard, Madame continued, had humbled himself for Simone's sake as he would never have done for his business or for himself. He had besieged the prefect in Francheville, he had humiliated himself before the Boches. "My son has aged by years," Madame concluded, "but he accomplished it, he saved you."

Simone was kneeling on the floor and rubbing with a cloth. "Maître Levautour is coming this afternoon," Madame informed her, "in order to notarize your declaration. Put on your black silk dress. This is a memorable day for you."

It was only natural that Maître Levautour should be called to notarize her statement. Yet a chill ran over Simone when she heard it.

All night long she had considered the question: shall I do it, shall I not do it? In the face of bare reason, Uncle Prosper was right. Now, after the armistice, only the harmful consequences of her action remained; viewed from the present day, the destruction of the trucks was foolish. But in her heart of hearts she knew that these rational arguments were only seeming truths. Her deed had been right; in spite of everything, it was still right today; and if she signed, then she recanted and betrayed her action.

Her inner voice cried: No, no, I will not sign, never. Aloud she said—and her own voice frightened her: "Yes, Madame."

The three ate their noon meal together. Uncle Prosper did not have much appetite but he was very loquacious. To be sure, he carefully avoided the subject that ceaselessly occupied them all. Not until they were in the Blue Room did he say to Simone while she was pouring his coffee: "Head up, Simone. By tonight it will be all over. Tonight everything will be finished, and it will be as though it had never happened."

"But it did happen," said Madame.

And: It did happen, Simone thought, proudly and bitterly.

Then, after she had washed the dishes, she went to her room and dressed herself, with calm, stiff, mechanical motions. She washed herself and fixed her hair and put on the black silk dress that had become rather small for her.

Half an hour later they were sitting in Uncle Prosper's study. Maître Levautour was sitting at the desk, in the swivel chair, with his back to the desk, and in a semicircle in front of him sat the three Planchards, Madame, Uncle Prosper, Simone.

It was a large desk. On it stood the antique set that Uncle
Prosper held in high esteem; it had a wooden background on
which a reproduction of the *Burial of Christ* from the Hospital
at Tonnerre had been carved with great skill. Beside it on the
desk lay the big letter opener of old ivory. Then there was
Maître Levautour's brief case.

Maître Levautour lounged in the swivel chair, turning gently
left and right; he had crossed his legs. He was a portly, little
gentleman; everything about him was fat, smooth, and clean;
he fitted tightly into his light grey suit; he spoke rapidly and
courteously; his black, cunning eyes slid quickly from one to the
other; his small, white, fat hands made friendly gestures; the
large bright stone in the ring which he wore on his index finger
flashed.

"May I get right down to business?" asked Maître Levautour.
He drew the brown brief case nearer and took a document from
it. He scanned it and then he read aloud: "In the presence of
Madame Cathérine Planchard and of Monsieur Prosper Planchard, both residents in the House Monrepos, in the City of
Saint-Martin, Quartier Sainte Trinide, Mademoiselle Simone
Planchard, resident at the same address, makes the following
deposition. I confess voluntarily and without compulsion that,
on the seventeenth day of June 1940, I set fire to the buildings
of the Transfer Establishment Prosper Planchard and Company.
I did it because I was deeply offended and regarded as unjust the
criticism of Madame Planchard that I did not satisfactorily perform the duties imposed upon me in the Villa Monrepos. I saw
no other means of venting my resentment, and I believed that
through this act I would grievously annoy and injure Madame
Planchard. Read and subscribed."

Maître Levautour read rapidly and smoothly. Simone watched
his round mouth, his small teeth, from between which these
monstrous words issued fluently and with elegant precision. Simone watched the man's little flat nose with its wide nostrils;
she watched the tiny pimple at the right-hand corner of the
mouth in the smooth, white face; she watched the beringed index

finger of the carefully manicured hand that held the document. This man filled her with such disgust that she had to pull herself together in order to grasp the sense of the words that came from his mouth. And yet her senses were particularly alert and sharp, just as they had been yesterday when the discussion with Uncle Prosper began. She saw with remarkable clarity the desk behind the notary and everything that was on it. She saw the carving on the background of the desk set so distinctly that she could have described every detail with her eyes closed. And she smelled the leather odour that emanated from the big, brown brief case so strongly that she knew she would never forget it.

Maître Levautour had finished. There was a little silence. Then Simone asked—and after the bright, rapid, urbane voice of the notary hers seemed even fuller and calmer than usual: "Do you believe that, Maître Levautour? Do you believe what you just read to me?"

Maître Levautour made no reply. He directed his black, cunning eyes at Simone, without expression, not even astonishment. In his stead Madame spoke. Without looking at Uncle Prosper, she said: "You see, she does not want us to help her. She prefers to let the Germans settle the affair." Maître Levautour, however, as if neither Simone nor Madame had spoken, pointed with his beringed index finger at a place in the document and said politely: "Here, if you please, Mademoiselle. Will you kindly sign here."

Simone stared at the beringed finger and at the white spot of the document to which it pointed. In her ears rang the words of Maître Levautour, rang the words that Uncle Prosper had said yesterday. She knew they wanted her to write her name there, now, and that was probably to the advantage of many people, perhaps even to her own. A part of her urgently wished to yield, to take the pen which lay before her, to put her name on this white spot, if only so that all this tugging and pulling would finally come to an end, that everything would be decided, and she could have peace and quiet. Another, a deeper part of her, resisted with all its strength. And it seemed to her as if she had experienced all this once before, the finger and the white spot in the document, and the proffered pen, and the wish to sign, and the wish not to sign.

It cost her an effort to collect herself. She tore herself out of the spell, tore herself away from the sight of the flashing ring. She moved her head very gently, as if to shake off something, and looked about the room as though just awaking. She saw Uncle Prosper, sitting in his chair, slumped down a bit, his head slightly inclined. Her eye clung to him; more and more life came into her eyes, more and more firmly her glance fastened upon him, and softly, but with deep intensity and pleading, she said to him: "Uncle Prosper, shall I sign that?"

Now Uncle Prosper had to look up. Indeed he raised his head and directed his large, blue-grey eyes at her, and looked at her. But he gazed sadly and with strange lifelessness through her and past her. Still more urgently she repeated: "Shall I sign that, Uncle Prosper?" She uttered only these few syllables, but in her heart she entreated him in meaningful words, and by the memory of her father, to advise her honestly, and she knew that he understood.

Maître Levautour looked straight ahead, unconcerned, with a polite expression; behind his smooth forehead he was probably surprised that they were still raising questions, and that the affair had not been more properly disposed of before they had troubled him to come to the Villa Monrepos. Madame, however, turned her big head with its well-arranged, mottled hair towards her son in a scarcely noticeable motion, and looked at him askance from the corners of her eyes; in these eyes lay encouragement, pity, and a little contempt.

Uncle Prosper drew up his shoulders, his face twitched, he writhed. A slight grunt came from him; it might have been an impatient refusal or helpless perplexity; it might have been anything that any one wished to hear. This little grunt was his only reply.

Whereupon Simone signed.

VIII: The Imperishable

THAT night, in her room, she repented.

She should never have signed. She had held out until then. One last effort, one last No was needed, and there she had failed.

Not Uncle Prosper, not all the sober business men put together, had been able to rob her action of its sense and value. Only she herself had been able to do that by her criminally stupid signature.

She had trampled, besmirched, erased the best thing in her life. Because she had not been able to bear the sight of Uncle Prosper's tormented, desperate face, because at the last moment she had grown weak, for that reason she had betrayed and bungled her action.

She had bungled everything. She had bungled her life. For how would she live on after that signature? She had not only disavowed herself, she had disavowed her father, too.

What should she do? There was no one to advise her. The only person who had been willing and able to help her, she had sent away, foolishly, senselessly, out of false gratitude to the Villa Monrepos.

She could not go on thinking the same thoughts over and over. She would lose her mind.

She tore herself out of her numbness and grief. She picked up her books.

And again the books mercifully covered her own confusion, and the events round Joan occupied her so that she forgot her own distress. She read what had happened to Joan's memory, and what had happened after her death to the people who, in one way or another, had touched her life. With gloomy satisfaction Simone took note that most of the friends who had deserted and betrayed Joan, and most of the enemies who had persecuted her, had little enjoyment from the fruits of their false friendship or of their merciless enmity.

While they were still in this world, so Simone read in her anecdote book, God's judgment struck down most of the judges who had condemned the poor, innocent Joan.

The priest, Nicolas Midy, who had preached the sermon of damnation to the Maid on the day of her fiery death, was afflicted with leprosy a week later and died.

A month after the martyrdom of the Maid another of her judges, Nicolas, Abbot of Jumièges, died.

The Canon Loisseleur, that priest who had passed himself off in Joan's cell as a prisoner of war of her own party and had wormed himself into her confidence in order to spy on her, died on a dung heap, obscurely and unexpectedly, without the dying sacraments.

Miserable, too, was the end of Joan's accuser, the Canon d'Estivet, who had shamefully abused the defenceless captive. He was found dead in a cesspool outside of the walls of Rouen.

The Bishop Cauchon himself, who had presided over the Tribunal, did not long enjoy the honours which the English heaped upon him as a reward for his role in the cruel trial. He died a sudden death while he was having his hair cut. Later on he was excommunicated by the Pope and his bones were thrown to the dogs.

And an evil fate overtook not only many of the judges but also Joan's other enemies, the golden anecdote book stated with grim satisfaction.

There was the King's General and favourite, La Trémoille, the man who used all means, no matter how foul, to destroy Joan. Simone read that after Joan's death his enemies pressed him harder and harder and that finally the King left him in the lurch, just as he had left Joan in the lurch. Once while he was apparently still in the King's highest favour, La Trémoille was staying with Charles in the latter's castle at Coudray. At night, enemies of the General entered the house; they were armed and they forced an entry into La Trémoille's bedroom, tore him from his bed, and wounded him. He received a sword thrust into his belly and only the fact that he was a very fat, fleshy man, saved him from death. The King, who was sleeping in a near-by room, awoke and asked what was the matter. He was assured that nothing had happened so he lay down and went back to sleep. The wounded La Trémoille was meanwhile bound and kidnapped. He was forced to acknowledge with his signature and seal that he had unlawfully taken possession of many landed properties and treasures and he had to return everything. He received neither help nor support from the King; he was banished from the court and he died in exile, embittered, and without having seen the King again.

The villain Guillaume de Flavy, the Commander of Compiègne, who had sold out the Maid to the Burgundians by raising the bridge and locking the city gate, he, too, found a cruel death. His wife, a lady of beautiful appearance named Blanche, with the help of a lackey, strangled him in bed, in his Castle Neel.

And in the same castle at Rouen where he had held the Maid chained to a miserable cot, the Duke of Bedford died not long after her. It is said, however, that he died from grief over the disgrace which the downfall of the English in France caused him. For from that day when the English raised the funeral pyre in Rouen, they experienced nothing but grief and defeat, and they were thrown out from all their French possessions in great disgrace and ignominy.

And the Cardinal of England died, poisoned by his rival, the Duke of Gloucester; and Henry the Sixth of England, in whose name Joan's verdict of death at the stake was pronounced, died a brutal death. He had been crowned King in Paris, it is true, but he, too, was murdered by his cousin, Richard Gloucester.

The haughty, wild Queen Isabeau, the fiercest enemy of Joan and King Charles, likewise outlived Joan by only a few years. She died in almost complete oblivion and was buried without pomp and without thanks by the English, whom she had helped.

And so it came about, said the anecdote book, that the majority of those who had played a part in the martyrdom of the Maid, did not come to a happy end.

Charles the Seventh himself, that wavering, irresolute man
whom Joan had crowned and who had left her in the lurch, did
not end happily. To be sure, at first he enjoyed many years of
success and of gratification. But later he received his just dues
for the wrongs he had committed against Joan and other friends.
His son rebelled against him, the King died in a state of feud
with his son and, as he believed, poisoned by him.

But before his death he had found time to rehabilitate Joan's
memory. Joan had confirmed his legitimacy in the name of God
before all the people; by the fact that the Church had convicted
her as a liar and false prophetess, this legitimacy had been made
questionable. After the English had been driven out of their
French possessions, Charles believed himself powerful enough to
force the Church to recognize Joan's divine mission and, along
with it, his own legitimacy.

Joan's mother and brothers therefore demanded a reopening
of the case, and the Church complied with their demand. And
there appeared before the court Joan's friends and playmates
from the time of her childhood, mature men and women now,
and there appeared generals and statesmen who had been near
her in the days of glory and who had witnessed her deeds. The
friends who had remained silent during the first trial now opened
their mouths and vied with each other in reverent praise of the
dead Joan. Her opponents, too, had changed. The eloquent
Thomas de Courcelles who, at one time, had proved with irrefu-
table logic that Joan was a liar and a witch, now proved her
divine mission with equally striking arguments. The clerical
judges unanimously decided that their predecessors in Rouen
had erred and that they had unjustly convicted Joan, and they
placed most of the blame upon the dead Bishop Cauchon. Unanimously they acknowledged Joan's divine mission and, along with
it, the legitimacy of King Charles, now victorious.

And Simone read that Joan's fame and the people's faith in her
became greater and greater through the centuries. The State
honoured her by commemorative speeches and monuments; the
Church honoured her by glorification, prayers, and finally canon-

ization. "The French Nation," Simone read, "has many great men and women of imperishable fame, soldiers and statesmen, scholars and scientists, artists and poets. But in the hearts of the French people, two dwell most deeply and most vividly: Napoleon Bonaparte and Joan of Arc."

Simone felt and knew that it was so.

She smiled. Joan had recanted, but this recantation of the harried, betrayed girl did not count. What counted, what remained, was her great deed. Her deed had been done, her deed lived, and no scribbling, no stamped paper, could undo it.

It was a good thing that she had sought refuge in her books. Her panic was gone; she realized that she had no reason to despair. Her action lived, even though she had signed Maître Levautour's document. Paper could not compete with fact. Maître Levautour and his document could not compete with fact.

She had permitted herself to be intimidated, to be led into doubt. She had almost been persuaded that her action had been wrong. Her action was right, even in the light of reason. Her action had had sense. At that time, they had still been fighting. There had been a reasonable chance that we would continue to fight, that we would win. If two thousand communities had done what she did here in Saint-Martin, if they had destroyed everything that could be of use to the enemy, France would not have fallen.

And France had not fallen yet. Not even today. The armistice, signed by traitors, did not count. The war was going on. Maurice was a man of good judgment; he would not have gone to Algiers unless he knew that there was still hope. Not all the generals were traitors; there were still some who went on fighting. The war was going on. And so her action had sense.

Her realization was not yet too late. She had made a tremendous mistake by rejecting Maurice's proposal. She had permitted Uncle Prosper to confuse her. She had permitted him to confuse her for all of ten years. But now she could see clearly.

Since she had not gone with Maurice she would have to go alone. She would have to find her way to the Unoccupied Territory and, if possible, to Algiers. And she would have to leave now, at once. She dared not wait until the others made use of that silly document.

She got up, very softly. She dressed, dressed as she had the other time. She picked up a change of clothes, took the same sturdy shoes. She had already reached the door when she turned and took from the chest the little, old-fashioned anecdote book with all the gilt and the many decorations. Then, on bare feet, just as the time before, she crept down the stairs. This time there would be no Maurice; she would have to look after herself. She groped her way into the dark kitchen and took the household money from the drawer. She counted it; it was not much. Then she sneaked through the hall and opened the front door; it creaked only very softly.

There was a pale moon this night; it was not very dark. She was not the least bit afraid. She raised herself over the wall. She did not think of that which she was leaving behind; she was thinking ahead. She went away.

IX: The Grey House

ON THE very next evening as she arrived by autobus in Nevers, she was arrested. She was brought back to Francheville in a prison vehicle.

At Francheville the gendarme, Grandlouis, took her in charge. He was taciturn; when she asked him who had reported her and of what she was accused, he was evasive. But he was very polite and tried to mitigate the rigours of the long trip.

In Saint-Martin the gendarme, Grandlouis, took her to the Deputy Prefecture. Simone's old friend, the concierge, distressed, received her cordially. Then the three, the concierge, the gendarme, and Simone, went into the record room. The gendarme hung round with an embarrassed air; the concierge asked Simone whether he could get her something to eat or to drink. The gendarme declared that they had eaten in Chatillon, and not badly at that; he went into details about the meal at Chatillon, pleased to bridge the clumsy situation in this way. The concierge said that one could always eat. Simone thanked him politely; she said that she wanted nothing more to eat and asked to be left alone. The gendarme looked at the concierge uncertainly. Then he made up his mind: "All right, Mademoiselle," he said. They both left. They did not lock the door.

There sat Simone in the record room. She knew it well. There stood a large table and a few comfortable, worn leather chairs. Round about on high shelves were piles of documents; behind the glass door of a bookcase stood many volumes of annual records, beautifully bound by Père Bastide with thick brown leather backs and red labels.

The air was cool and a little stuffy. A heavy door excluded all noise. Simone felt comfortable; she leaned back and closed her eyes.

She was calm. In her heart she had never believed that her flight would be successful. She was no *débrouillard* like Maurice; she had taken no clever precautions; she had had to expect that Madame would head her off by means of the telegraph and the telephone. But it had been her duty to make an attempt to escape

She had done her part; she had done the right thing. The others appeared to think so, too; they treated her with respect. Unruffled, quietly defiant, she awaited what was to come. The abortive flight had given Madame the upper hand; she would certainly try to get even and it looked bad for Simone. But she had firmly made up her mind not to give up. She would hold out, she would stay alive until those who were cleverer, Maurice and his lot, had scored.

She sat there for a while, pondering. Then Monsieur Xavier came in. He tried hard to act casually, but Simone saw that the birthmark on his right cheek was swollen and she realized what an effort it cost him to conceal his agitation. "Did I do something foolish, Monsieur Xavier?" she asked, happy to look at the face of a friend. Monsieur Xavier's lively brown eyes were sad; he hesitated and gulped before answering. "You did your part very well, Simone," he said. "All of us, the friends of Pierre Planchard, are proud of you. If things went badly it is our fault. We should have done more, and we should have done it sooner."

After a while Simone asked softly: "Is it going to be hard, what I have to go through?"

Monsieur Xavier gulped again. "It will not be easy," he said and then added resolutely, looking straight at her: "It will be hard."

Simone drew her shoulders a little higher. "Can you tell me what to do, Monsieur Xavier?" she asked.

Monsieur Xavier answered: "Don't try to be clever and diplomatic. Just speak out as your heart dictates. Whatever you have to say will not make your situation any better or any worse. Perhaps it will help if you make that point clear to yourself. It is up to us to help you. The way things are now, we can't do it. But the time will come when we can, that's sure." He spoke a little like his father; Simone almost smiled, but his words were a comfort.

His tone changed. "You really ought to eat something, Simone," he urged with forced cheerfulness. "I hear you refused. Be sensible. You have a couple of bad hours ahead of you." Without awaiting her answer he ordered food, and soon afterwards they brought her something to eat. While he walked up and down and spoke of indifferent things, she ate, obediently and without appetite.

Monsieur Cordelier came in. "Don't let me disturb you, my dear child," he said when Simone started to rise. "Just go right on eating. Yes, that's a bad business," he commented and dropped into an arm-chair. "These are bad times for all of us. At any rate, all our sympathies are with you. Go on and eat, eat," he urged her. He sighed a few times. "You are a brave, sensible girl," he said after a bit, "the true daughter of our Pierre Planchard. That's a comfort, at least." He paused and his tone changed. "But perhaps it is not entirely proper," he turned to Monsieur Xavier, "for us to be here with Mademoiselle Planchard today." He arose. "No, Monsieur le Sous-Préfet," said Monsieur Xavier, "it is not proper at all," and he remained seated while the deputy prefect withdrew.

A few minutes later the old bailiff, Jeannot, and the gendarme, Grandlouis, appeared. "You are being asked for, Monsieur Xavier," the bailiff reported, and the gendarme announced awkwardly: "And they want you, too, Mademoiselle." Simone got up quickly and obediently. But Monsieur Xavier said: "Just take another swallow, Simone, and don't be in a hurry. They can't start without you. We'll go together."

They walked through the familiar corridors to the deputy prefect's office, Monsieur Xavier with Simone, behind them the embarrassed bailiff and the gendarme. The officials in the anteroom fell silent when the little procession entered, and Monsieur Delarbre, the chief clerk in this room, arose, bowed his head, and said: "How do you do, Mademoiselle Planchard."

The shades in Monsieur Cordelier's office had been lowered so

that the large room was dusky and pleasantly cool. Several of
the fine old chairs had been moved up to the large desk which was
covered with green cloth; on it lay quantities of paper and pen-
cils; a jug of water and glasses stood ready, as for a conference.

The assembled group included Madame, Uncle Prosper, the
Marquis, and Maître Levautour. No one said a word when Simone entered with her little retinue. The bailiff, Jeannot, withdrew at once; the gendarme remained. Monsieur Cordelier said:
"I don't think we need you any more, Grandlouis."

"Pardon me, Monsieur le Sous-Préfet," replied the gendarme,
"but I have to have a receipt that I have handed over the pris—
I mean Mademoiselle."

"You'll get your receipt in my office, Grandlouis," said Monsieur Xavier, and the gendarme withdrew.

Simone stood there calmly, her head high; her deep-set eyes
under her broad forehead passed slowly from one to the other.

Madame sat in one of the heavy, faded, dark red arm-chairs;
she regarded Simone just as calmly as Simone regarded her; she
did not make use of her lorgnon. Monsieur Xavier did not sit
down; he had stepped behind a chair and held its back in a
firm, hard grip. Maître Levautour lounged comfortably with
professional indifference, his legs crossed, his brief case in front
of him on the green desk. The Marquis, lean and erect in an
arm-chair that was too large for him, looked Simone up and
down with a sneering expression of idle curiosity. Simone would
have liked to see Uncle Prosper's face, but he stood at the window with his back to the room.

The deputy prefect, at his accustomed place behind the huge
desk, was playing with a pencil and blinking his pale eyes.
Finally he said: "Sit down, my dear. Sit down, gentlemen." He
seemed to be nervous. They disposed themselves ceremoniously
and someone fussily pushed Madame's heavy arm-chair closer
to the table.

Then, at long last, after clearing his throat repeatedly, Monsieur Cordelier said: "Prosper, in your capacity as Simone Planchard's guardian, don't you—?" He left the sentence incomplete
and toyed with his pencil.

Uncle Prosper took a deep breath. "It isn't easy for me," he began, "it's damned hard." His eyes met the calm, searching look of Simone; he exhaled through his nose; he stopped speaking.

"Ladies and gentlemen," the Marquis intervened in his croaking voice, "you know I am here at Monsieur Cordelier's request and with the consent of the German authorities in order to give a report on what is to go on here. I understand that it may be painful to one or another of you, or perhaps to all of you, to explain things satisfactorily. But if the situation should not be clarified, then conditions here are going to become very unpleasant. In the interest of all of us I would be much obliged if you would speak out without any mistaken sense of consideration."

There was an embarrassed silence. All eyes looked at Monsieur Planchard.

Then, with her low, harsh voice, Madame took over. "Since my son cannot persuade himself to do it," she said, "I will speak. We all understand clearly that the various hard inconveniences which the Département has to suffer from the Germans are attributable to the deed which was performed by the daughter of my stepson. Our fellow citizens here in Saint-Martin, and the Boches along with them, have assumed that the incendiarism arose out of immature but well-meant patriotism. I must confess I suspected from the very beginning that the act was not intended solely for the defence of France. Nevertheless, I was still inclined to seek the girl's ultimate motives in a romantically overwrought patriotism, and we, my son and I, refrained as long as possible from attributing the incendiarism to other motives. But my secret suspicions remained. I know the daughter of my stepson. For ten years I have tried to tame her difficult, violent character. Unfortunately without success. And unfortunately also, in this case, certain utterances on Simone's part, as well as her general demeanour, proved beyond a doubt that the act, which was regarded as one of patriotic heroism, was nothing but a wicked deed of revenge of a depraved child."

Madame stopped. She had spoken softly, as always; it was an obvious effort for her to speak; she breathed heavily. Every one sat motionless. There was complete silence in the great, dusky room; there was no sound save Madame's breathing and the buzzing of a fly that flew round the Notary. Every one watched Maître Levautour warding off the fly with his fleshy, white hand.

"Then, when we perceived," Madame resumed, "that the enemy made the entire community suffer for Simone's unfortunate act, we, Monsieur Planchard and I, were faced with a difficult problem. We knew that the measures which the Germans inflicted upon us were based on a misunderstanding. Was it not our duty to clear up this misunderstanding? But if we did that, we would have to expose the grand-daughter of my husband; we would have to accuse her of a crime."

Again Madame stopped. She reached for the water pitcher. Politely Monsieur Cordelier poured water for her. Every one watched while she drank two small swallows.

"But then," she resumed her discourse, "my son had an idea. He went to Francheville and frankly explained the situation to the prefect; through the prefect's mediation he came in touch with the German Military Authorities. He succeeded in reaching an understanding with them. The German Authorities do not insist that the disgrace of the Planchard family be spread abroad in a public hearing. They do not demand that the Courts of Justice be called into the matter. They are satisfied to have us take statutory measures against the perpetrator. The German Authorities have agreed that they will withdraw the special restrictions against the community as soon as that has been done. My son," Madame continued even more softly but with emphasis on each word, "my son still hesitated to expose the daughter of his step-brother. I argued with him for several nights. He could not bring himself to the point of communicating our unhappy knowledge to the public."

There was complete silence in the room; the only sound was Madame's breathing and the buzzing of the fly, which had now left Maître Levautour and was bumping against one of the windows again and again.

"A new incident," Madame continued, "had to occur before Monsieur Planchard made up his mind to abandon his exaggerated consideration. For many years my son treated this child,

Simone, like his own daughter. He pampered her, he took her along to Paris, he satisfied her every whim; when she wanted dark green slacks, she got them. In return Simone had once before stolen the key to his private office out of a drawer in his bedroom. And now she did a thing like that for a second time. This is the second time that she stole something. She took the household money and ran off with it. Only now, when it was definitely proved that Simone is an habitual household thief, my son finally made up his mind to expose her. We cannot let the entire Département suffer in order to protect this hopelessly depraved girl. It is our sad duty to amputate the gangrenous member. You know, Philippe, what is to be done. We hand Simone over to you. If any other statements or signatures are necessary, we are at your disposal."

Madame had finished. She had presented her preposterous lies with such assurance that her hearers listened as attentively as though she were reporting something quite new, although they had known from the beginning the sort of farce that was being played. Having finished her accusation, she sat enthroned black and erect in the faded dark red arm-chair; her head pressed back so as to emphasize the great double chin, her body and thighs formed a shapeless bulge, her arms lay clumsily on the arms of the chair, the chair and the woman merged into an inseparable mass. Thus she sat enthroned, a massive hulk, breathing heavily yet motionless, a wicked idol; and round her lips was a tiny smile.

Simone arose. Wretched, dirty, her haggard face with the large, deep-set eyes quiet and collected, she stood there, defeated, condemned, before she had opened her mouth. Madame's feud with this child had been unequal from the start; Simone had never had the slightest chance. Whatever she might say would change nothing in her fate; she knew it, they all knew it. And yet the others watched this battle with burning interest and waited with bated breath for Simone's words.

She said: "I did it on account of the Boches. Everybody knows it. All of Saint-Martin knows it."

These were simple words; they added nothing new, they did

not refute Madame's accusations. But Madame's accusations were indeed refuted by Simone's face. It was a young, serious, severe, accusing face, and not one of the men assembled here in the office of the deputy prefect would ever be able to forget it.

At Simone's words Madame remained immovable as before; only her smile became a trifle evident. "Are you calling me a liar?" she asked. She did not raise her voice; she spoke with friendly, superior assurance, as though she were speaking to an insane person. "Are you calling me a liar?" she asked in a tone which made it impossible to say yes.

"Yes," said Simone.

It was a calm yes, not defiant but rather polite. And yet it was saturated with truth, so that Madame's magnificent accusation vanished before it.

This calm yes sounded so convincing, so annihilating, that it misled Madame, who up to this time had been devilishly clever, into making a mistake. "I think, gentlemen," she said, turning to each of them, "that the flight of this girl is confession enough. There she stands and pretends to be a patriot. And what did she really do? She set fire to the loading yard in order to cause my son and me grief. She ran away and took with her not only the household money, but also things that belonged to strangers." The men looked at her with close attention, Simone with astonishment, as she declared: "She took a book with her that she had borrowed."

At that Simone smiled and, almost with amusement, she turned to Monsieur Xavier and explained: "Madame means one of the books that Père Bastide gave me."

Monsieur Xavier could not contain himself. He leaped up, the little man, and turned violently to face Madame, but at once he regained control over himself. In a voice which trembled only a very little he said: "My father is very fond of Simone. Simone had a perfect right to regard the books as her property."

"Nevertheless," Madame replied, "Père Bastide came to the Villa Monrepos in order to claim his books."

"I may assure you, Madame," Monsieur Xavier answered, "my father will be pleased to hear that Simone took the book with

her. He regarded it as his duty to do his part in the education
of the daughter of his friend. You understand, gentlemen, we're
not talking about light reading; it's about a book on Joan of Arc.
Or am I wrong, Madame?"

Now, for the first time, Madame's rage broke into the open.
Now they all saw the hatred that Simone had once seen gleaming in her eyes for a brief moment. "It is well known," she said,
and her voice sounded a little louder than usual, "that the elder
Monsieur Bastide contributed, by means of dangerous talk and
extravagant advice, to the confusion of this child, and that he
helped to put her on the downward road. We do not hold a
grudge against him for that. Monsieur Bastide is very old."

Madame would have done better not to mention the matter of
the book, for now even the deputy prefect opened his mouth. "I
fail to see," he said, "that it is a point against Mademoiselle
Planchard if she took a patriotic book with her." And now for
the first time Uncle Prosper also said a word. "Let us drop the
subject," he requested in a subdued voice.

Maître Levautour leaned forward a little in his arm-chair.
"Pardon me for interrupting, ladies and gentlemen," he said.
"I believe this entire discussion is superfluous. There is on file
here a written declaration by Mademoiselle Planchard," and he
drew out of his large brown leather brief case the document which
Simone had signed.

The sound of the bright, courteous voice of the man irritated
Simone. The sight of his smooth face and of the flashing ring
on his white, rounded index finger, the odour of his brief case—
all of it angered her. Up to this point she had remained calm,
but now she replied violently: "But that was not the agreement.
The signature was to be a pure matter of form. The signature
was only for the Boches. These gentlemen know—"

The Notary interrupted her, politely but with authority: "Permit me, Mademoiselle, first to read this document." And he read
aloud: "In the presence of Madame Cathérine Planchard . . . I
confess voluntarily and without compulsion that . . . I set fire to
. . . I did it because I was deeply offended . . . the criticism
of Madame Planchard . . . I believed that through this act I

would grievously annoy and injure Madame Planchard. Read and
subscribed: Simone Planchard."

Maître Levautour read it evenly; he emphasized nothing and
omitted nothing. By this very manner of reading each word assumed a devilish meaning and stood in the room as a living
menace.

He had scarcely finished, however, when Simone began to
speak, and the first breath of her dark, resonant voice wiped
away the clear words of the Notary. "But Uncle Prosper expressly assured me—" she cried briskly. Madame interrupted her.
"Maître Levautour," she asked, "did Simone make this confession of her own free will?"

"The question is superfluous, Madame," the Notary replied in
a somewhat offended tone. "I witnessed by my signature and
seal that Mademoiselle Planchard made the confession voluntarily and without compulsion."

Simone, recognizing the hopelessness of the trap into which
she had fallen, turned to Monsieur Planchard. "Uncle Prosper,"
she pleaded with him, "you assured me that nothing would
happen to me, that it was purely a matter of form. You gave me
your word—" Uncle Prosper sat there slumped, the usually well
set-up man looked bloated, broken; with a mechanical gesture
he raised and lowered his hand from the table back to the table;
he avoided her eyes. Simone fell silent.

Monsieur Xavier explained in a nervous, hoarse voice: "Simone evidently is trying to say that she was induced by promises
and by misrepresentation to sign this statement."

Monsieur Cordelier, inspired and stimulated by the words of
his subordinate, remembered his legal training. "Mademoiselle
Planchard," he turned to Simone, "were you tricked into signing
this declaration?"

Before she could reply, Uncle Prosper intervened. For the first
time he looked straight at her; his large face was racked with
fear, torment, and inner struggle. "Simone," he pleaded, "I explained to you that I would never bring a charge against you.
I brought no charge. Neither did Mother. This is not a judicial
proceeding. It is something purely administrative." He had com-

posed himself; he had forced himself to resume his customary, pleasing cordiality, his old triumphant self-assurance. Now, however, he turned to Monsieur Cordelier in obvious distress and perplexity: "Will you please explain to her, Philippe, what it is about?" he implored. "Won't you help me, gentlemen?" he plaintively urged the others. "Please tell her that the fate of the whole Département is at stake here. Please tell her that every one has to make sacrifices."

Monsieur Cordelier meanwhile, fortified by Monsieur Xavier's attitude, had again become the complete official. "I asked you, Mademoiselle Planchard," he repeated with the air of a solemn judge, "whether you were tricked into signing this declaration. A great deal depends upon your answer. Consider it well."

"I fail to understand what you're driving at, Monsieur le Sous-Préfet," the Marquis suddenly croaked. "If you proceed this way, I think it may be better for me to absent myself from the rest of this discussion. Our German guests will properly be displeased with the senior official of the Arrondissement if he casts doubt upon a plain written declaration, properly attested, and if he suggests to the maker of the declaration that she ought to retract it. That can only be interpreted as an attempt to juggle a criminal act committed for a personal reason into a patriotic deed."

The deputy prefect turned a shade paler. "Monsieur le Marquis," he began to reprimand the Châtelain.

Meanwhile, however, Monsieur Xavier had stepped very near to Simone. He put his hand on her shoulder and spoke to her, kindly and persuasively. "Simone," he said, "did they induce you by all sorts of lies and trickery to sign that thing? Please answer me. I tell you frankly, it won't make things better or worse whether you say yes or no. But tell us."

Simone sat there in her dark green slacks and in her rumpled, somewhat dirty blouse; her tanned face with the obstinate forehead was composed. They had invited her to tell the truth, and they had pleaded with her to tell lies. What was the truth?

All at once she saw the truth. The mists with which feeling, wish, and desire had surrounded it all were gone. Abruptly reason illuminated past events so that their outlines and interlinkings were laid bare and cruelly clear. Young as Simone was, and imprudent as she had shown herself, at this moment she was wiser than all the others in the room.

With painful distinctness she saw and felt all the mendacity about her, the mendacity of the acts and deeds here in this room, the spuriousness of the fronts that had deceived not only her, but the entire French people.

Simone plunged into those depths where eternal truths prevail. There was neither day nor hour; she was beyond the confines of time. Her own life and the life of Joan of Arc flowed into each other. The net of lies, in which she had been trapped and in which Joan of Arc had been trapped five hundred years before, was one and the same, the eternal one.

And Simone accepted her fate; she knew that it was necessary and useful; she made up her mind to be tough, and to hold out. But she accepted this useful and necessary fate of hers with bitterness. There was so much painful knowledge in her face that it became distorted and much older than the sum of its years, and Monsieur Xavier could not suppress a little snarling sound of ache and of anger.

This sound brought Simone out of her spell. A moment ago she had been the wisest of humans; now she changed back into Simone Planchard, a girl of less than sixteen years. She looked at Uncle Prosper. His eyes clung to her, pleading, as the eyes of a dog; he was bewildered.

It would change nothing in her fate, Monsieur Xavier had explained, whether she said yes or no, whether she lied or told the truth. But it did change something in Uncle Prosper's fate, she understood that clearly. Only a minute ago, before the moment of realization, she might perhaps have spared him. Now she had no mercy on this contemptible man.

"Did they induce you by trickery to sign the document?" she had been asked. "Yes," she answered resolutely. And: "He told me," she accused Uncle Prosper, "that it was a mere formality. He gave me his word that nothing would happen to me."

Uncle Prosper, driven into a corner, sought refuge in impatience. "I told you again and again," he said angrily, "that this is no trial. You're not being accused. It's a matter of administrative procedure."

"But they can't proceed against me," Simone cried. "There isn't a word of truth in that paper. Everybody knows that. You, Monsieur le Sous-Préfet, ordered Uncle Prosper to destroy the loading yard, and Uncle Prosper consented to do it at the right time. But when the right time had come and nothing had happened, then, at the very last moment, I did it, because otherwise it could not have been done at all. You all know that it was so. All Saint-Martin knows it."

Maître Levautour pointed at the document: "Your written confession, Mademoiselle," he declared quietly and kindly, "puts it another way."

The Marquis turned to Monsieur Cordelier with icy irony. "Your most admirable quality, Monsieur le Sous-Préfet," he commented, "is your patience."

The deputy prefect, so warned, straightened up, was about to say something decisive, failed to do it, sagged down again, looked absently from one to the other, drummed mechanically with his big pencil on the green, sound-absorbing table covering. This helplessness of his revealed to Simone that the fate which had been prepared for her would be something terrible. "Will you please put an end to it?" she demanded grimly. "Go on and tell me what you are going to do with me." And: "What are they going to do with me, Uncle Prosper?" she turned to him.

There was a brief silence. Then Monsieur Xavier said: "They are going to put you into the Grey House, Simone."

At these words there rose before all their eyes, darkly and dismally, the picture of the Grey House, the reformatory at Francheville. Some time ago, and again two years ago, there had been a scandal concerning this Grey House. Horrible stories about the beating and torturing of the inmates had appeared in the papers and had provoked a violent debate in the Chamber of Deputies. Pictures of the House had been published, and pictures of the mistreated adolescents, as they slunk about the dormitories, the corridors, and the desolate yard, with evil, dull, frightened faces. At the words "the Grey House" there now arose in all of them an image of tormented, humiliated young people.

In the next moment, however, they were torn back from those dismal pictures into the present and into the room in which they were sitting. It was a scream that tore them away. It was Simone who screamed. It was a loud, piercing, childlike scream.

When she had heard Monsieur Xavier's dire news, Simone, for the first fraction of a second, had caught only the sounds of the words. She had seen the faces of all those present turned towards her, embarrassed, rigid, evil. She had sought Uncle Prosper's face, but it had been lowered so that she could see only his hair-crowned forehead. In the next fraction of this second she had fully understood the meaning of Monsieur Xavier's information and, since she had the gift of imagination, she had transplanted herself into the midst of the evil things she had heard about the Grey House in Francheville. She had seen herself, slinking about with the inmates of the Grey House in its yard and corridors. She had seen her own face as one of those evil, dull, frightened, dead faces. Fear had closed over her, fear of immurement and of the black years before her; fear had swept away all her self-control and so it came about that she screamed that piercing, childlike, terrible scream.

"Oh, oh, oh," she screamed. And: "Never, never. That can't be. It isn't true that the people of Saint-Martin want that. Not the Grey House! That's treachery. Not the Grey House!"

But her scream had penetrated through the door, out into the ante-room, and into the corridor, and someone outside, startled by it, had opened the door, and people had come running into the ante-room and into the corridor of the old building because of the scream that she had uttered.

Simone saw the people, familiar people and strange people. "They want to lock me up," she cried to them. "They want to lock me up in the Grey House. Because I destroyed the gasoline and the trucks, because I did not let the Boches get their hands on them, they want to lock me up. This bad man," and she pointed at Uncle Prosper, "this bad man promised me that, if I signed something, it would be good for all of you and nothing would happen to me. And now they twist it round and want to lock me up in the Grey House. Don't allow it, don't let them do it." She breathed hard and sobbed.

Madame, with her cold, low voice, called upon Monsieur Cordelier: "Put an end to it, Philippe." The deputy prefect, extremely nervous, fingering his rosette, called: "Will you please at least close the door," and one of the attendants outside closed the door.

Simone dropped into her chair. She sobbed. But not for long. She remembered her resolution. She would not permit her act to be robbed of its meaning. She would survive the Grey House. She would survive the evil. With this resolution her strength grew at a tremendous pace. She felt it. In a motion picture she had once seen a plant growing from a tiny seed into a mighty, broad-boughed tree, in the course of a single minute. Just so Simone's strength now grew with her resolution.

She wiped off her face with her soiled handkerchief. Much more calmly, with a controlled voice, she said: "I did it on account of the Boches. You are going to lock me up only because I am against the Boches. You don't want anybody to know that it was done against the Boches. But everybody knows it. And I will not be quiet. And they won't permit you to kill me. The people of Saint-Martin will not permit it. The people of France will not permit it. I will say it again and again. It is not true. I did not do it on account of Madame; I did it on account of the Boches."

Meanwhile, however, as she was saying all this, prudent Monsieur Xavier had committed the most imprudent act of his life. With carefully restrained, measured steps, with his bright red lips tightly pressed, the birthmark on his cheek swollen, his vivacious eyes dark with anger, the little man had walked to the door which had just been closed and opened it again. Outside the people were still standing and waiting. Their number had increased; the ante-room was crowded; there was a mass of faces.

No one stopped Simone as she walked nearer to the door. Those outside stood in silence. And she said to them: "Let them all know that I only did it on account of the Boches."

The Marquis, with a little, mildly amused shake of his head, said to Monsieur Xavier: "I should never have thought, Monsieur, that a grown man would throw away his office for the sake of a childish gesture."

Monsieur Xavier did not look at him and made no reply.

The deputy prefect, however, winced. Vaguely, in the general direction of the gendarme, Grandlouis, whom he espied outside, he said: "I think we should finish now." And to Simone he said apologetically: "You understand, I am only an instrument in this matter."

Slowly, uncertainly, the gendarme pushed through the crowd and stepped towards Simone. She said to him: "In a moment, Monsieur." She looked at the assembly, one after another; with eloquent eye she said farewell to Monsieur Xavier; she impressed upon her memory the Châtelain's haughty, cold face, the smooth, wicked one of Maître Levautour, the bulky one of Madame; she held fast the pale, evasive eye of the deputy prefect. Monsieur Cordelier raised his shoulders uneasily under her glance; Maître Levautour looked indifferent; Madame, however, stared straight back at her, and on her face there appeared again that scarcely visible smile. Last of all Simone's eye sought Uncle Prosper. But she did not find his eye; he kept his large head lowered. She said to him: "You are a bad man, Uncle Prosper." Then she quietly followed the gendarme, Grandlouis.

Once more, for the last time, she walked through the familiar corridors of the Palais Noiret. "I think, Mademoiselle," said the gendarme, "we had better go out by the back door. There are so many people out in front." But the concierge said gruffly: "There are just as many at the side entrance. You might as well go the front way. The car is waiting out in front."

He accompanied them to the main entrance. The great, beautiful portal ordinarily remained closed; usually people went in and out through a small door in one of its wings. Countless times Simone had slipped through this small door. Today, however, ceremoniously and grimly, the concierge opened wide both wings of the great portal.

Simone blinked as the light of the sunny square flooded the dusky hall. The square was completely filled with people, a sea of white and brown faces extended before her. There was whispering as she appeared in the doorway with the gendarme. Then there was complete silence.

In order to reach the place where the cars were parked, Simone and the gendarme had to cross a part of the square. Over there stood the conveyance that was obviously intended for her, tall, black, closed. The people cleared a lane to let her through. They all stood still as she passed. Most of them were bare-headed; those who wore hats or caps took them off.

So she walked towards the car; the gendarme carried the little bundle of her belongings after her.

An old man pushed through the crowd and stopped her, Père Bastide. The ruddy face under the gleaming white hair quivered. He stepped very close to her. With an awkward motion he handed her something, evidently a book; it was well wrapped and tied. "There, there," he said; the usually so eloquent man found no words. "Good-bye, my dear," he said. And: "Good-bye, Père Bastide," she answered.

She had reached the car. In its interior she saw indistinctly the uncouth outline of a woman.

She turned round. With a long look, for the last time, she embraced the sunny square, the noble façade of the Palais Noiret, the people whose faces were all turned towards her. So she stood; the door of the car had been opened for her, the gendarme had handed her belongings up, the interior of the car awaited her.

Suddenly the crowd, which had remained silent and motionless, stirred into motion. Arms were raised waving to her, women and girls wept, the gendarme had come to attention, shouts sounded in her direction: "Good-bye, Simone—good-bye, Simone Planchard—take care of yourself, Simone—so long, Simone—we won't forget you, Simone Planchard—we'll come and get you, Simone."

"Adieu," Simone said, with her fine, resonant voice; she had it under perfect control. "Adieu, my friends. Au revoir." She recognized how many were on her side. She thought: "I will have to stand the test; I must be the daughter of Pierre Planchard." She was not afraid. Determination, born of realization, had given her strength.

Amid a storm of shouts she stepped into the old vehicle in which the uncouth woman was waiting for her. With a creaking, groaning sound the car started. Simone rode away into the black years of waiting, the salutes of solidarity in her ear, in her heart confidence that she would survive the Grey House.